THE FABLE
OF MYTHRIAN:
CONJURER OF THE
ZODIAC

Ross Baker

Published by

MELROSE BOOKS

An Imprint of Melrose Press Limited
St Thomas Place, Ely
Cambridgeshire
CB7 4GG, UK
www.melrosebooks.com

FIRST EDITION

Copyright © Ross Baker 2008

The Author asserts his moral right to
be identified as the author of this work

Cover designed by Catherine McIntyre

ISBN 978-1-906050-92-4

Printed and bound in Great Britain by:
CPI Antony Rowe, Chippenham, Wiltshire

With special thanks to:
Melrose Books
My family and friends
Most notably my older brother Guy
For their support and encouragement
With an extra special thanks to Tom Ray
For helping me understand the world of writing

Dedicated to:

Andrew Bell

- 'If you never give up, you will never fail'

Thank you.

✝ ABOUT THE AUTHOR

I WAS BORN IN Kettering on March 31st 1988. I grew up in the town of Wellingborough before moving to Oakham in Rutland at the age of 11. When I acquired my first instrument, an acoustic guitar at 13, I developed a love for music and writing. After leaving school I went on to Rutland College to study music for a year, before going to Brooksby College to learn Countryside Management. It was during this course that I was inspired by the world and our need to preserve it and began writing my first novel, the fable of Mythrian. Now, hoping to become a full time writer, when I have finished this series, I would like to move onto many of my other ideas....

 # FOREWORD

DEEP IN THE heart of every human is the potential of good or evil; the continuous battle that rages within ourselves and that which we give out to the rest of the world. When the scales of life are tipped in one direction, then the other has to re-gain its ground. A time comes when those unknown are called to fulfil their destiny. They do not always accept the call nor do they see themselves as heroes. But through these troubled minds, one will make a stand. That one is Mythrian and in his hands, he must decide the fate of those on both sides, between good and evil. It was not his choice, it was his destiny. And now it must be fulfilled.

† PART ONE †

CHAPTER 1 † THE BEGINNING

So, HERE IT is. In your very hands you hold the tale of Mythrian.

A tale of a young boy with an incredible gift; of how he grew from a simple apprentice to Saviour of the Zodiac. Of his battle with the forces of evil: to retain the magic of the Enchantment.

This is his adventure and these are the characters he met along the way.

The genesis of Mythrian's adventure begins a long time before his birth. It lies at the very beginning of the Zodiac – the name given to the Earth by its early settlers to describe its correlation to the suns and moons above.

In the beginning, the Zodiac was a landscape covered in dark marshes, barren plains and impenetrable mountains. No form of creature had ever inhabited or set foot on the terrain.

But that was all about to change.

For, in the centre of the world, at the very heart of its unearthly domain, lay a forest of simple tranquillity and peace. This place was latterly referred to by the first settlers as The Enchantment.

It was a realm of great beauty, where life sprang from every leaf and knowledge from every branch. A shining light brought energy and life to this uninhabitable world.

Many myths of the great Enchantment have been recounted over the years but some well-known facts, passed down over the generations, remain. One of those facts is that it isn't actually a forest.

Inside every tree that grows in the Enchantment lies a spirit.

1

These Spirits are the Gods who created this world. But while they all may be Gods, they themselves stand down to the One who resides in the tallest and largest tree in the Enchantment.

He is known to all as Ajia.

No action is permitted by any of the Gods without Ajia's assent. With his power and knowledge he controls the world and all beyond it from this great tree.

Early on in the genesis of the Zodiac, Ajia told the other spirits that it was time to send forth the first form of creature to build a civilisation.

They chose the form of a human man and a human woman to start their civilisation in the West.

To form the landscape into a more habitable place, where generations could grow food and other much-needed resources, Ajia told the couple that when a creature of their form dies, their body must be taken to a place known as the Triad.

The Triad is a monument, a circle made of stone that lies cemented into the ground. It was given the name because, around the stone circle, stand three statues in human form, watching over the site. Their linked hands form a triangle, hence the Triad.

When Ajia activated the stone circle, it crumbled into fine dust, releasing a bright blue beam of light from under the earth, rising up into the sky. The Triad had been opened and as it came to life, gaining in power and strength, so did the three statues around the circle. They were ordered by Ajia to guard and watch over everything that came into the light.

Ajia told them that to replenish the landscape and to build the land into a haven for future generations, they must send the spirits of the dead down into the very heart of the Triad.

The man and woman did as Ajia told them. As the generations passed and as more and more spirits were placed into the Triad, the land was populated, the meadows became lush and fertile, the forests vibrant and the waterfalls breathtaking.

Standing on the hills of their homeland, gazing at their new paradise, the settlers gave themselves the title of Ajia's People.

They quietly sat back and watched the world float by. Life in the Zodiac was peaceful; in time new areas of land were discovered, new settlements were built and the community grew dynamically.

But not everything brought joy and prosperity. The good souls of the deceased creatures that were interred in the Triad gave life to the kingdom, but there is no such thing as an entirely good soul. Darkness beats inside every living heart and the bad deeds of the deceased – their crimes, their hate, their betrayal – poured into the Triad.

This cauldron of evil was channelled away from the Enchantment to the other side of the Zodiac, away to the East.

There, nestled deep within the undiscovered darkness, stands a monumental volcano, forever spilling more splintered rock and ash around its core. The evil of the dead from the Enchantment all end up here, sucked and siphoned through the underground network of labyrinths and caverns, below the molten lava of the volcano.

Bad spirits rose up through the lava flow and they began to take form.

The first creatures of evil were born. Hearts dark, hearts black.

As they grew in number, the creatures became stronger. Soon there were creatures of unspeakable proportions, waiting patiently in the shadows until the right moment came to spread evil into Ajia's land.

Caught by surprise, Ajia's people quickly had to establish defences and organise troops to repel the invasion of this vermin. With the Enchantment helpless in their powers to attack the creatures or help defend their land, the people of Ajia were forced to teach the young and old to fight for the freedom of their lands.

Fortunately, they were able to repel the creatures and over time, people began taking apprenticeships in various forms of fighting. Whether it was with the sword as a foot-soldier, the bow as an archer, or on horseback in the cavalry, the people of Ajia became better equipped and stronger as a unit.

The only weakness in their enemy was the lack of a leader. Any evil creature, no matter how big or strong, needs a leader to guide it, to make strategic decisions. Otherwise, they can only attack with brute force. But with a strong leader at their helm, they can be turned into an army of unnatural might and power.

To the north-east of the Enchantment lay the volcano of Siren's Gore. In the fiery molten lava, where all bad spirits arrived to create their spawn, a new creature of great evil was born. This creature was to bring a plague, an infection, which was to bring an end to a once densely-populated civilisation.

Rising from the fires of Siren's Gore, this evil creature was born physically stronger than any other being known to man.

It was an evolutionary miracle.

So dark was his complexion, so evil his heart, not even the foulest creatures ever spawned dared to look into his fiery, vanquishing eyes.

His real form was hidden behind a giant sheath of protective white armour, in the form of a barbaric skeleton. Horns extending from the skull that he bore as his helmet, hid any expression, grim or unsightly; his inflamed eyes cast visions of fire across its helm. His chest was simply a rib-cage, thick enough to hide his evil heart like a prisoner in a cell. Perpetual screams tortured his mind, speaking to him only in the words of pain and suffering.

In his merciless grasp rested his mighty sword. "Like a pendulum of fate" was how one onlooker described it, running from the carnage when his village was under attack. He wanted dominance and that's exactly what he epitomised.

His death-defying image was to be feared and remembered forever in the dynasty of Ajia's People.

Those people gave him a name. A name that would send fear into the heart of men, yet give them a reason to fight.

They called him Draigorn.

With his new army of unmatchable might, Draigorn led them underground through their long network of caverns, where the creatures re-emerged, crawling out of hidden patches all over Ajia's land.

Without warning, in the dead of night, Draigorn's creatures were about to lay down their first assault and commence the beginning of a long and endless war.

It was a flawless victory and the first of many in their evil campaign.

Attack after attack, Draigorn's army pushed Ajia's People further and further back. Settlements fell, burning under the blazes left by his minions.

Unsafe and afraid, the people turned to their God for help, but help could not be found, for one simple reason. None of the spirits of the Enchantment were allowed to leave the forest, or they would face imprisonment in exile and would never be able to return to the forest – unless found and brought back by one of their people.

The constant losses were pushing Ajia's People back so heavily that many died simply because the remaining settlements were over-populated and there was no more room or enough food to share out. The north of their land had been taken in its entirety and now Draigorn's forces were furthering the assault to the south.

It was only months before Ajia's People were all hiding away from the ever-approaching evil, in what was to be the last settlement of their era.

But this particular settlement was in fact a fort, built during the first attacks to act as a sanctuary for the recuperating troops and homeless villagers. They were low on their units and low on resources, yet this fort was to mark a new chapter in their war.

Its walls were built like mountains, too tall to scale. Indestructible.

For the first time in their long and hard fought war, Ajia's People claimed their first victory.

As thousands of minions charged up to the walls of the fort, they instantly met death with a blaze of arrows. Some attempted climbing the walls, only to be met with boiling oils or stones thrown from above. Battering rams did little to crack the dense walls or bend the iron gates. On the open battlefield, nothing could stop their relentless drive, but with solid bricks and mortar, Draigorn's creatures were suddenly brought to a halt.

They had little understanding of siege weapons, nor had they learnt the use of ranged artillery. Their main form of attack had been with the sword and shield.

It seemed as though Draigorn had been outwitted.

But their triumph had done little to console the People of Ajia. With the enemy at their gates, the people were prevented from gathering food and other vital resources and their current stock was dropping heavily.

They had no other choice but to take the battle to their opponents, in one final confrontation.

Further to the south, along the mountains of Morbian, the troops squared up for battle against their evil counterparts in a desperate hope that perhaps, acting as one full, solid unit, they could defeat Draigorn's evil swarm of creatures. The odds were too great and they were outnumbered heavily, but there was no other option left but to combat the issue.

Against such a mighty force, the People of Ajia needed a brave warrior who would lead them against Draigorn in the fight for the freedom of the Enchantment and the Zodiac. One man stepped up to the challenge. A strong, courageous knight called Aedorn.

A well respected knight, regarded by many as perhaps the best foot-soldier ever to be born into Ajia's People, Aedorn had an unbreakable aura of bravery and honour that had set him on a different scale to the other high-ranking Generals. He was a legend of his time. If there was anyone who could inspire courage in these fearful troops, it was Aedorn.

Leading the biggest force ever deployed by Ajia's People in recorded history into their final battle, Aedorn commanded the first attack, ordering his whole army forward as one giant unit. As the march turned to a sprint, the Draigornian army began their growling calls, filling their minds with anger and rage, before charging at full pace towards their destiny.

As battle commenced, the screams of pain and glory ran riot through the air.

As Aedorn's foot-soldiers tried to gain the upper hand in the heart of the battle, archers and artillery threw all they had at the minions, hoping to dent the advantage held by the Draigornian army.

With both sides engaged in warfare, it was time for the two leaders to meet, to battle to the death.

Above the battle, on a ridge cut into the mountains of Morbian,

Aedorn and Draigorn drew their swords and began their duel.

Whoever won would claim the right to rule the Zodiac. The future of the world rested entirely on their shoulders.

As the two leaders crossed swords, they began what became a long and gruelling duel, fighting for all they owned and for the whole of the Zodiac.

Long they had fought, but the end of their battle was nigh. Aedorn had duelled well and the People of Ajia had chosen a great leader in him, but he couldn't match the immense might of Draigorn, and in front of the millions of troops, good and evil, he fell, mortally wounded with Draigorn's blade resting in his heart.

Draigorn had won the war and it seemed as though the Zodiac was his for the taking.

For the People of Ajia, it was as if time had stopped completely.

Their once peaceful world was almost a forgotten memory, as the darkness drew a tighter grip around its new land.

The age of Man was over, had it not been for an unsuspecting arrival from afar.

For while Draigorn was revelling in his triumphant glory, to the astonishment of the crowd below, Ajia, God of the Zodiac, had left the Enchantment and then re-appeared as a blinding ray of light behind him.

Casting a sword of solid white crystal out of thin air, he slowly crept up behind the unsuspecting target and thrust his blade deep into the back of Draigorn. As the giant brute crashed to his knees, he saw his dreams of domination flicker away into the darkness.

His reign had come to an abrupt end and as his body disintegrated into dust, it drifted calmly away in the wind, leaving behind only his hardened outer shell.

With their great leader fallen, the creatures of evil ran back into the holes from whence they came in disarray, the dust of their great leader in their fists.

As for the People of Ajia, their lives had been saved by their God and their lands were theirs to roam once again.

But Ajia's intervention had brought forth a new problem.

In leaving the Enchantment, Ajia faced exile, to be imprisoned away in an unknown location, never to be found. Without Ajia, the Triad would close and the world would fall back into the uninhabitable chaos it experienced once before.

Greatly in fear of their grim future, the People of Ajia asked if there was any hope and they were greeted with a reassuring answer.

Ajia told them that he would place his power into a mystical tablet, which would be secretly hidden somewhere within the Zodiac. Whoever found the tablet would grow under its power and would one day find his destiny, rescuing Ajia from his exile, restoring peace across the Zodiac.

But the great God also warned them that evil would remain in the shadows and that they must always beware the threat from the East. If they were going to survive after Ajia's imprisonment, they needed to quickly adapt to the ever-changing world around them. They needed to build a Kingdom that could withstand the ravages of time, without the powers of their Gods.

It was time for the race of Man to write his own destiny, not to have it written for him.

With nothing more to offer in help, Ajia told them not to give up hope. He said the other Gods of the Enchantment would do all they could to keep their land prosperous and help would one day arrive, but until then, their fortune was in their hands. As he finished his statement, he vanished from sight, to his imprisonment far away.

His crushed people wondered whether he would ever be seen again.

Moving back north to begin the construction of their new kingdom, they had mixed feelings about Ajia's disappearance. Some rejected the idea of this hidden mystical tablet and of the powers within it. Some people wondered whether, without Ajia, the other Gods would be powerless or would be able to keep their lands alive.

But while there were those who turned their backs on their recently-exiled God, many remained loyal, still believing that the civilisation of Man could only keep on growing and that their new kingdom would flourish just as Ajia assured them.

It seemed that Man was not the only creature in the new era recovering from Draigorn's evil reign.

In the midst of their lands, villagers spoke of seeing strangely mutated creatures; half man, half otherwise. But the People of Ajia were never provoked by any of these newly-bred species and the attacks from the East were of little consequence. They were easily dealt with.

With the world rapidly changing around them, the People of Ajia began to make use of its deteriorating land.

Before, Ajia and the Gods had helped in gathering crops and other resources. Now, the people had begun to work on new ways of planting, gathering crops and sustaining their grassland or other forms of habitat. The land was now beginning to renew and replenish, and it was all because the people had learned to grow their own food and feed themselves without the help of their Gods.

With thousands of square acres of evergreen fields reappearing, the People of Ajia could suddenly see their beautiful haven re-emerging from the ashes. It gave them hope of a bright future, but they could not forget how close they came to losing everything. The creatures that were responsible for their downfall were still out there, possibly growing in their numbers and they needed to fortify their lands against another attack.

New settlements began to emerge all over their kingdom, each one being more defensively hardened than the last. The People of Ajia began to dig deep into the mountains and hills, mining tonnes of raw material.

They began construction with a vast, great wall, thirty feet high, five feet dense, stretching from the Atlian Mountains of the North to Ynyr's Range towards the South. With giant towers marking every mile of the wall, no army of evil, no matter how great in number, was going to cross their lands without being immobilised by this strong, protective barrier. It also gave the People of Ajia a sense of security while they began to build forts and defensive posts around several settlements. These were now housing thousands of villagers each, and were still growing in number.

With their people now prospering in safety, in new and well established homes, the leaders of Ajia's People decided it was time to formalise government in the community. As local majesties and mayors were appointed for the various settlements, the leaders felt that they needed a domain of their own. A Citadel that would show the great achievements of Ajia's People in this new world, a capital at the heart of their kingdom, to signify dominance and permanence to the rest of the world.

And so Hagenherde was built. The kingdom's fortifications were a mile squared, defying all notion of attack.

But while it was strong defensively, their army was low and Ajia's People realised that if another attack was to come from the West, they needed to strengthen their force. Many brave souls from across the kingdom enlisted in the infantry and the forces. Others studied in schools of healing and spirituality. Guilds were established to teach these topics, and as years passed, hundreds of gifted students graduated as heroic apprentices.

In time, there was no need for an army or a large military force as hundreds of these heroes, skilled in various arts, began to clear the kingdom of any threats from the East. Their enemies were pushed back into the shadows.

The People stood on the hills of their land, gazing across the miles of green before them. They knew that they had begun a new era in their civilisation. They had built themselves a kingdom that could withstand the face of time. They had all the food and resources to feed the generations, they had an endless supply of troops and heroes guarding their lands and had a community that watched over everyone's shoulder, no matter how far apart they sat.

They called their new land the Kingdom of Aedorn, after the great General who had led them into their final battle against the evil from the Kingdom of Draigorn, in the East, remembering the evil leader whose reign had so nearly driven the Zodiac into eternal darkness.

Nearly two decades have passed since the creation of the Kingdom of Aedorn and it is here where our story begins.

With something found.

CHAPTER 2 ✝ THE BABY HAS BEEN MARKED

RUNNING BY THE brook, the scout kept to a syncopated speed, eyes wary of the slightest movement or sound.

The night was dark and cold.

A mist that had covered the plain was now clawing its way up the Cronian Valley, which rose to the left of the scout, towering and majestic. The last few nights had brought heavy rain and thunderstorms across the northern part of the kingdom, yet it did little to slow the runner down. Tightly holding his sword in one hand, with his other guiding him on his assigned scouting track, he was poised for any ambushes that might be thrown by any creature, lurking in the dark.

Coming to the end of the brook, the scout made his way into a small unnamed woodland, to the north of the village of Hamlynstone. Inside the woodland, the mist made it almost impossible for the scout to see the path or a way out, but this, for the moment, was not what concerned him. His attention had been caught instead by some peculiar noises coming from the forest.

Stopping, he listened carefully to the sound and began to hear the high-pitched squeal of a wounded animal.

Unsure as to why such a sound would be heard from out here, the scout carefully and quietly drew his sword, turning his body into an attacking stance, positioning himself to where he judged the sound to be coming from. He crept slowly over towards a scrabble of bushes, each step taken shorter than the last, edging ever closer to the strange sound. Moving his hand over to the bush, he hastily brushed the leaves aside and lifted his sword high into the air, only to find a young baby lying in a crib, on top of some dried-out leaves on the muddy terrain.

The scout quickly checked the site for traps, and then looked back down at the baby. There was something unusual about its features. But this place wasn't safe for anyone; there wasn't time enough for an examination. Picking up the baby, he ran back in the direction of the nearby village of Hamlynstone.

The gates burst open as the scout crashed through like a bolt of lightning. He ran directly through the market, heading straight for the biggest building in the village, the Guild for Gifted Apprentices.

Ascending the stairs he ran through a series of anterooms before he entered the main chamber, where three attending Guild Masters sat in their chairs, meditating. The shadowy coloured light from the giant stained glass windows on all four walls made it impossible to see their faces clearly.

As the scout slowed his run down to a walk, careful not to rudely awaken them, he stopped in front of the one who sat in the middle chair. This, he knew, was Brennius, Master of the Guild.

The Master opened his eyes, fixing his gaze on the young child cradled in the scout's arms. Lifting himself from his meditation, he rose to his feet and walked over to the tired, drained scout.

Removing the child from his arms, Master Brennius lifted the baby into the light. He was instantly shocked to see strange, artistic markings scarring the child's body. Dark, violet-blue in colour, the uncoordinated spirals swept over the child's body, gleaming ever brightly under the light that poured in at the windows.

The old man cradled the baby in his arms and stared into the child's eyes.

"What are these markings that tattoo this feeble child? A blessing, perhaps, from Ajia ..."

"I found the poor thing in some woods, in the Cronian Valley." The scout seemed pleased with his find.

"I see good omens in this child. He will achieve great things. I will raise him myself, teach him the art of everything I know," Brennius announced.

As he looked up into the light, repeating the name Mythrian in his mind, he gazed back down at the child and gently whispered,

"Yes, good omens."

Brennius was right to say that the child would one day achieve great things. For as the boy grew up, his profound ability was to shine like a star on his Master and guardian, who treated the young boy like a son. He showed him how to read and how to write, how to use spells and how to apply his powers. There was much to teach and much to learn. One skill after the other was quickly passed from the old Master to his protégé.

The years passed quickly.

At the age of twelve, Brennius placed him in one of his specially selected classes, where the boy learned a wide range of skills and subjects. The boy learnt all skills well, but the Guild Master spotted a rare gift in the boy. It seemed that he had a rare talent in the art of conjuring and summoning. Brennius borrowed all the books he could from all over the Guild and even some from other villages, and was startled at the pace of the boy's progress.

The boy would work through each book quickly, and then look back at Brennius with eager eyes, waiting for him to find yet more material.

Brennius was pleased to have found the boy's great talent, but there eventually came an end to what the Guild Master could teach about summoning. So, through day and night, Mythrian worked long and hard, writing fresh and interesting spells and developing new techniques in harnessing his special skill. Book after book was written and shown to his Master, who began to whisper his name around the Guild and village, telling people of his special student and his incredible gift.

The boy was now in his mid-teens and his appearance had become far more pronounced and recognisable. Short, slight and slim, Mythrian had a seemingly fragile frame. But inside his heart, behind his level stare, lurked an immense, intuitive, latent power, waiting to be unleashed.

His piercing eyes shone like crystals, reflecting light through every shade of darkness. As for his nose, so thin and straight, it seemed to draw his face inwards somehow, greatly intensifying his sharp, audacious image. A pencil-lined mouth, making his expression sometimes inscrutable, his cheekbones flush and well-pronounced, his jaw straight as the blade from a sword.

Mythrian looked wild and tenacious.

But there was more. Something beyond this, that made him magnetic. Ever since he was a child, Mythrian had been covered from head to toe in mysterious, unfathomable tattoo-like markings. A network of deep purple spirals cascaded down his body like streams, mythic and indelible. People were puzzled by the boy's markings. They gave Mythrian a very distinctive appearance that made him recognisable to everyone he met.

Those who greeted the boy proclaimed that it was a godsend and that he was surely blessed by Ajia, sending his love from far away. Others were unsure and stated that it was purely witchcraft. At the time, there were rumours that witches were lodging in the nearby wild woods of Anthelstone and anybody with a slightly unusual and original appearance like Mythrian was considered to be under their spell. But Mythrian never came to any harm from anyone. Most people chose rather to ignore his markings and treated him no differently to any other person.

As for his character, Mythrian was a very quiet and timid boy. Every night, he would sit on his bed, by the window, and gaze out into the distant lands, dreaming of one day exploring them. While he presented a wild and eye-catching image, Mythrian was sometimes shy to take up a challenge. He was often too nervous to speak with a lot of the other students and spent most of his time nestled deep within his books.

His nervousness was, however, overcome by the presence of his guardian, Master Brennius. Their affinity was natural, easy and unshakeable. After all, it was Brennius who had elevated him into the Guild. While in each other's presence they communicated like tutor and pupil, but deep inside both their hearts, between them was a father–son relationship that grew stronger with every passing day.

The old Master approached him. Mythrian was dreaming by his window. He opened his mouth to speak, but Brennius, raising a forefinger, silenced him:

"Destinies are found in dreams and only you can make those dreams reality. Some day, when the time is right, your destiny will find you and every dream you have wished for from this window will be answered. But until then, be careful what you wish for. Keep your dreams close to your heart."

The truth, Brennius knew, was that the adventure that lay ahead of Mythrian was wilder, more fearful and more amazing than anything he could possibly dream.

Chapter 3 † The Tree that Yields the Stone

I<small>T WAS A</small> beautiful day in Hamlynstone. The third sun, the brightest of seven that orbit the Zodiac, was beaming rays of fresh, warming sunshine to the delight of the people below.

The villagers began their daily routine, gathering food from the bustling markets. It seemed like everyone had come out to make the most of the good weather. There was a spring in everybody's step. Even up at the Guild at the far end of the village, apprentices were allowed out to enjoy the freedom away from their work, to do whatever pleased them in the basking sun.

Inside the quietness of the Guild, Brennius was checking all the rooms, tidying away books and furniture. The apprentices could be careless with their spell books and equipment. There never seemed to be enough storage. Therefore, Master Brennius and the other tutors had from time to time to go round each room, checking that there were no hazards.

All seemed to be in reasonable order. Finally, Brennius came to the last room, the highest one on the highest tower, home to his most special student.

Entering the room, he found Mythrian quietly sitting at his desk. He was staring with intense concentration into the book open before him. Light fell in bright pools from the arched window behind him.

Unlike most of the other rooms occupied by apprentices in the Guild, Mythrian's room was always meticulously tidy. All of his books were arranged alphabetically on the shelves. Other pamphlets and papers were stacked neatly on his work desk. His bed lay next to the window along the right hand wall and was carefully made, not a crease in sight. There was a chair and the work desk. They looked old and well used, but overall the rest of the room was immaculate.

Brennius stepped into the small, rounded room, carefully shutting the door behind him. Mythrian had his back turned to him, and didn't move. He seemed completely oblivious to his presence. Brennius watched and waited.

After a minute, Brennius raised his hand, cast a quick flying spell and closed Mythrian's book with a click of his fingers. It snapped tightly closed, causing the young boy to jump back with surprise.

"Sorry, but sometimes that's the only way I ever get you away from those books." Brennius grinned at his young pupil.

Brennius was a great teacher with lots of wisdom and intellect and always able to answer any questions. He was, in fact, quite a jolly character, and though disciplined, he was a very loyal companion, who could always be trusted by those who served under him.

He was dressed from head to toe in a night-sky purple robe and cape, and on his head he occasionally wore his hat to hold his long, wispy hair back. His face was very soft; his beard was long and white. Always, he had the ability to make other people smile.

They felt at ease in each other's company. Mythrian realised he was very lucky to have such a well-respected teacher and guardian as Brennius; in turn, the kind old soul always knew that his young apprentice acknowledged his support.

The young boy, still startled by the unexpected surprise, turned to his tutor and pulled a short, half-hearted smile in return to his Master's giant beam of a grin.

"It's a lovely day outside. I thought you would have been out in the sun like the other students," he chuckled at the young boy. "Why, I've never felt such a gentle breeze swift through my beard in many long years."

Brennius continued to laugh.

Mythrian rose from his chair, stretching a little. "I'm sorry,

Master; I just got a bit carried away with the book."

"What is it you're reading?"

"It's called 'The Architect'. It's basically about developing your own techniques of casting magic," the boy said.

Mythrian handed the book to Brennius.

"Oh yes, by Clerwyn Cowan. I taught him a few tricks myself, you know."

Mythrian watched his tutor scan the book. "Brennius, did you … want to ask me something?"

"Yes. I need you to leave."

"I'm sorry?" Mythrian felt a sudden rush of blood, and his heart was suddenly pumping. Had he committed some foul misdemeanour?

Brennius quickly explained, "Did you not receive the note I sent to everyone? All students were supposed to make themselves absent from the Guild this day, directly after breakfast. That includes you. I am convening the tutors. We must have no disturbances, no intrusions."

Brennius removed his spectacles, continuing in a quieter tone.

"Besides, I think you could do with a bit of time away from all these heavy books. Why don't you go and have a look round the market? Such a beautiful day …"

Nodding, Mythrian slowly rose. Shaking the creases from his dark brown suit, he made his way towards the door. Watching his apprentice leaving the room, Brennius called after him, "Come back into the Guild when the third moon appears. By then, our work will be done."

With that comment, Mythrian shut the door and headed down the vast array of steps to the ground floor.

As Mythrian walked out of the Guild doors, he paused to smell the fresh air, lifting his head up into the clear blue sky. Raising an arm to his face in an attempt to block the blinding light from the sun, he scanned the horizon. There was neither a cloud nor a shimmer of disturbance to taint this pleasant day.

A minute later, in the market, he was suddenly immersed in the sound of hagglers, bargaining for a deal, and joyous villagers buying exquisite items to add to their household. The cacophony of their calls was deafening.

The daily market was the heart of Hamlynstone. The stalls ran from the gates of the Guild through to the centre of the village. The market was packed, heaving with people.

Mythrian was instantly greeted by owners of market stalls attempting to lure him to buy their wondrous products. The aromas from food stands were overwhelming, the sunlight glinting off the shiny silverware made him blink and close his eyes. The whole thing was simply irresistible.

Bravely ignoring the first few stands, the apprentice was making his way deeper into the heart of the market, when one of the stallholders spotted him. He was intrigued by the boy's enigmatic appearance and walked over to introduce himself.

Mythrian had his nose buried in one of the plants on a stand. He was captivated by its complex perfume.

"Wild Marmora. You don't find much of them around here these days. May I introduce myself?" The man held out his hand to Mythrian, still completely baffled by the boy's unusual appearance. "My name is Gwyn. I am the chief stallholder of this market."

Mythrian smiled. Before him was a neat man, dressed in a clean, white linen shirt, coated with an embroidered, gold jacket that finished around the knees. He wore silky white, loose and baggy trousers, which were covered in gold patterns of entwined leaves and plants, running up towards the knees from his ankles. The stallholder had a very plain, simple face, that didn't quite seem to go with his very extravagant attire. But he seemed very nice, and easygoing, and Mythrian was quick to his reply.

"It certainly has a powerful fragrance." He bent forward to take in the scent of the flowers once more.

"May I ask your name?"

The boy raised his head from the rose, looking directly into the man's eyes. "My name is Mythrian. I come from the Guild of Apprentices, at the far end of the village."

"Ah ... Mythrian. I remember Master Brennius talking about you."

Gwyn threw a hand in the direction of the other stalls. "Like me to show you around?"

They began to walk, feasting their eyes on all the goods on each and every table. Gwyn stopped at a table spread with gemstones, picked up a heavy piece of crystal, and brought it up close to his eyes.

"Yes," he said, "I know your tutor, Master Brennius. In my position you tend to meet a lot of interesting people. He talks about you a lot, how quickly you learn new things, how well you are progressing. It's hard not to be impressed."

"Thankyou, sir."

Mythrian glowed with pleasure. Gwyn could sense this. He quickly cut to the chase:

"Actually, I've been looking for you all day. Your Master told me that all the apprentices would be out of the Guild today and that I would most probably find you wandering around the market."

"Why would you want to speak with me?"

"Oh, I've been looking for you for a long time." Gwyn lowered his voice, and stole a sideways glance, as if to check they were not being watched, or overheard. "You see, I have an item that belongs to you. A very special item. I've been keeping it safe for many years, for I never knew its rightful owner. However, I recently received a letter from an anonymous sender, which landed upon my work desk in my caravan. Upon reading the note, it informed me of the rightful owner of the item – you, Mythrian – and that you were living in the Guild of Hamlynstone. I spoke with Master Brennius and after his description, I have been looking out for you in the market. But now that I've found you, I can finally hand it over to its rightful owner. Come on, follow me."

Mythrian was astounded. He had absolutely no idea what the item might be, but nonetheless was enthralled and intrigued by the idea. He followed Gwyn to his market stall, then around the back, to where his caravan lay. This was where he safely kept his goods and items for the market.

The caravan was almost new. It was covered in beautiful painted flower motifs, all around the door, and even up on top of the roof. As Gwyn unlocked the padlock on the door handle, they entered the caravan and Mythrian was instantly stunned by what confronted him inside.

The place was a treasure trove. All sorts of goods, materials and relics were strewn around the room. There were expensive items on every shelf, table and even scattered across the floor. Gold, silver and bronze flashed from every nook and cranny. There was no denying that Gwyn must be a very rich, wealthy man, and yet, seen like this, the overall effect was quite unsettling. The entire room was a tip. Some of the items in the caravan were worth enough to feed an average family for a week, but they sat nestled amongst other items of no worth, as if discarded, as if neglected. It made no sense.

While Mythrian continued to survey the room, Gwyn walked over to the far end of the caravan where on his work desk was an item hidden in layers of a thick fabric cloth. He carefully removed it, revealing a rough, darkened tablet, scarred by luminous sky-blue markings spreading like veins all over its coarse texture.

Mythrian edged his way closer to the item, eyes widening and jaw dropping. As he did so, the markings on the stone began to flash with more vigour on every pulse. It was as if the writing was somehow alive.

Slowly, the boy began to raise his hand up to the tablet. His hand felt as if it were being pulled, as though he was being guided closer.

Just as he was about to touch it, Gwyn covered it with the cloth, stepping quickly between the tablet and the boy, for he could not let its beauty blind him. Fools can be made from desire. This tablet had a powerful air of mystery about it which could enthral any onlooker.

"We mustn't tarry," Gwyn whispered. "It would be foolish to look too long."

Mythrian rubbed his eyes, regaining his thoughts from his hypnotic state. Gwyn continued:

"As I said, this item belongs to you. I am handing it on, but at the same time, I must warn you. This is no ordinary stone. It is hiding something."

"Hiding … what?"

"I cannot say. But I can tell you, Mythrian; that it once belonged to your father."

Mythrian's heart skipped a beat.

"Yes, to your father, Aiden. Before his untimely death, he told me that if any circumstances were to arise … well, that if he was not to return, this stone was to be handed down to his son. That is you, Mythrian."

Mythrian had never known his real father. The only person who Mythrian ever thought of in that way was Master Brennius. But he listened intently, as Gwyn continued:

"Yes, I knew your father very well. I used to sell timber to local villages. Your father was one of the lumberjacks. He worked hard at his job, cutting all the trees down so I could sell them on."

Gwyn cleared his throat. Beads of perspiration were appearing on his brow. In his mind's eye, he withdrew to the vision of the past.

"It was a fresh, still morning. We were working just outside the village of Thyreian, cutting logs from the woodland …"

"Go on."

Mythrian was eager to hear the story. His companion appeared subdued. Mythrian feared Gwyn would stop.

Gwyn took a deep breath, as if resolving to continue.

"Your father cracked a log open to find that very tablet nestled inside it. I remember him calling me over. I remember how startled we both were. Such a magnificent stone, well … we had never seen anything like it. It was unbelievable, unfathomable – to find something of that kind, placed within a tree."

"I can hardly imagine."

The truth was, though, that Mythrian could imagine this scene; he could picture it, vividly, fearfully.

"Well," said Gwyn, "… at that moment, there was nothing to be done. Your father entrusted it to me. He was being assigned to a different post over at the Forest of Hollman's Hollow; it was only supposed to be temporary."

There was a short silence. Both Gwyn and Mythrian were trying not to think the same thought.

"This was before anyone knew that bandits had occupied that forest. Your father and the other workers were treated with hostility on their arrival."

Mythrian said nothing. It was difficult to picture the face of a man he had never known.

Gwyn's face grew grey and sad as he recollected the last days with one of his best friends.

"Your father was a good, good man. He was a fine person to work with and a fine trustworthy friend. That tablet was his prize possession and I vowed that I would keep my promise to my friend and hand it over to its rightful owner. That is you, Mythrian."

The boy knew not what to say.

"I'm just so thankful that he did give it to me. Just think of what might have happened if it was found by the bandits."

"Did he suffer?"

"Yes."

Mythrian looked devastated. Gwyn hadn't wanted to ever see the boy this way, but he knew that the truth needed to be told. It was better coming from him, a friend of his father, than anyone else.

Gwyn placed his hand gently on Mythrian's shoulder.

"Take good care of it, won't you?"

Mythrian tucked the tablet safely under his shirt, thankful to have a piece of his true family back with him.

No further words were spoken, nor needed. Mythrian left the caravan and headed towards the Guild.

It was impossible to concentrate. He was paying little attention to the activity of the market around him. As he walked back on the main path leading up to the Guild, Mythrian began to rub his tummy, where the stone was placed under his shirt.

So warm was the tablet. He could feel its powerful draw itching his skin through the thick fabric cloth. While he tried to restrain himself, the temptation was just too strong. He needed another look at it, but he needed to have complete privacy, in some place where there was no danger of interruption. There were too many people around because of the market.

The third moon was clearly visible in the sky.

Suddenly, Mythrian thought of Brennius. He remembered that his Master had mentioned that the Guild would be ready for all the apprentices at this time.

✝ ✝ ✝

There was activity in The Enchantment. From their vantage point, the Gods were watching. They were talking between one another. They were nervous.

"He has the tablet. The boy has the tablet! But I thought ..."

"Silence," the elder God ordered, "... let us not jump to conclusions. True, he holds the tablet, but does he have the power to unlock its secret?"

"But he has the markings. He is the key," another God quarrelled.

"Tell me! Why have we have never been able to locate this tablet? Sixteen years have passed and not one of us has been able to locate it," the elder remarked. "Why?"

The Gods remained silent. None were willing to take the blame. The elder God grew aggravated with their silence:

"This man, who has now passed the tablet on. He appears to be a simple man. For one, he has no immediate powers. In fact he is just a trader. That tablet has been in the hands of a trader and you couldn't find it!"

"Elder, our efforts had been blanked," a God insisted. "The tablet had been wrapped in a dark material of sorts. Its sheath must have been so dense, our powers couldn't connect with the energy of the tablet ..."

"But we are Gods!"

The elder's voice was sharp and sudden.

"We have created everything from the highest mountains to the lowest lands. Do you expect me to believe, that we couldn't locate an artefact because it was wrapped in a dense cloth? Where was the tablet originally found?"

"Inside the bark of a tree," a God returned.

"Where?"

"In a region known to Ajia's People as Amblyn Downs. It parts with Hollman's Hollow to the north," the God continued.

The elder God made a disgruntled growl. It seemed the Gods had been after the tablet. By why did they need the tablet? Did they not want anybody to find the tablet? After all, with Ajia gone, they were in charge now.

"Elder, what should we do?"

"Now we know the boy has the tablet, we will follow him and watch him closely. There might be a way in which we could part the boy from the tablet."

"How?"

The elder God paused. "An event is taking place in his home village. Perhaps we could make contact with him there. Let us not scare the boy but simply warn him of the inevitable truth. If he wants the power of the tablet, we will tell him of the evil he must face."

"But there will be others there with him. How are we just going to contact him?"

"Through an illusion," the elder remarked.

The Gods were interested.

"What sort of illusion?" one of the Gods asked.

"You'll see ..."

CHAPTER 4 † OF DRAGONS AND LIGHTNING

PON ENTERING THE Guild, Mythrian instantly froze at the foot of the doors. He spotted Master Brennius speaking to two other Guild tutors, in the main entrance. They were deep in conversation.

Mythrian slowly crept over to the staircase, hoping that the old man would miss him, so he could get to his room to look at his tablet. But just as he thought he had got away, he heard Brennius calling:

"Did you have a nice day at the market?"

Brennius was laughing at Mythrian's attempt to sneak past.

Coming to a halt, he turned round to face his Master. Mythrian pretended surprise. Brennius approached:

"You want to head off to your room, I know, but there is something taking place in the main chamber which I would like to show you. Come."

Brennius put his arm around the boy's shoulder, leading him. "You must trust me."

The main chamber was a place where young apprentices would perform tricks and spells in front of other students and Guild tutors. It also served as a common room for the Masters of the Guild.

The chamber was calm, silent and beautiful. There were tall, powerful columns posted like gallant knights against its high walls. Between each of them, stretching from the floor to the ceiling, was a stained glass window. The different colours of daylight – blue, red, yellow, ochre and green – fell in soft and subtle shades, from all sides. The floor was made out of pure, blue-black coloured marble: it glistened like grass under morning dew.

The audience was arranged in a ring around a large open area in the centre of the chamber. Seniors and Masters stood waiting patiently behind them.

Brennius and Mythrian sat down on some spare chairs towards the back. They had a clear view of the open space. Brennius whispered:

"An apprentice is putting on a little show. Light spells, tricks and so on. I thought it might give you a few ideas."

Brennius looked straight ahead, calm and relaxed, waiting patiently for the show to begin. Mythrian looked up at his Master, who sat to his left, with a growing sense of frustration, as his thoughts remained on the tablet, hidden under his shirt.

The silence was finally broken as the audience began to applaud. An apprentice had walked into the centre of the hall.

"His name is Riener," Master Brennius whispered, "and that's his teacher over there, to the left. I hear great things about him. They say he is one of the Guild's best students."

"Best in the Guild?" Mythrian sarcastically replied. "Well, at least I'll know where I stand when I see his performance."

Jokingly punching Mythrian on the arm for his cheeky comment, Brennius replied:

"Let's just see what he does before we pass judgement."

As Riener made his way on to the centre of the stage, the audience greeted him with more applause, all eagerly anticipating his show.

With his right hand, he reached down to a stool which stood before him at waist height. On top of the stool was a green velvet bag.

Putting his hands into the bag, he drew out a shiny, fiery red crystal.

Brennius leant over, whispering into Mythrian's ear.

"He's using the crystal to cast his spell. It's a simple matter of intense concentration. The moment that the crystal has gathered in the caster's thoughts, the crystal must be destroyed. As it shatters, it releases dust, and as this rises – if the spell is successful – it mimics the shape and form of the spell that the caster had conjured in his mind's eye."

"What if it is not successful?" Mythrian whispered back.

Brennius said nothing. He put his finger to his lips, commanding Mythrian's silence.

Taking a few steps back from the stool, the apprentice raised his head upwards into the light, taking deep breaths as he paused to conjure the image of the trick in his head. Tightly clenching the crystal in his fist, with the image of his spell showing strongly in his mind, he threw the gem sharply down on to the jet-black marbled floor.

The sound was ear-splitting. The collision of crystal upon stone released a cloud of scarlet smoke upwards into the air. The apprentice Riener began to wave his arms back and forth, cutting patterns in the air. The dust from the crystal began to wrap around the patterns he was making. An incredible shape began to materialise. Mythrian was astounded. It was as much as he could articulate, as he gabbled:

"Why it's a … it's a …!"

Brennius whispered back: "Yes, it's a dragon! Beautiful, wouldn't you say?"

The dragon hovered above its creator, spreading its wings, stretching out to its full size. The audience held its breath, captivated by the incredible spectacle. Mythrian was speechless.

Brennius smiled. "I told you it would be a good show!"

Then Riener began waving his arms frantically, giving direct orders to the dragon, which began to mirror the shapes the apprentice was making. Tucking its wings to its sides, spinning closely around Riener's head, the dragon looped, circled and performed its tricks. It flew down and right in between his legs, before jetting off, high up to the chamber ceiling. Not only did the dragon do this with blinding pace and incredible precision, but it seemed to be under the total command of its Master, looking down every so often at Riener to read his instructions.

Gliding around the top of the chamber pillars, the dragon lined itself up and Riener parted his legs again. He commanded the dragon to shoot through the gap. It looked dangerous; the space didn't seem wide enough for a creature of that size. Some of the younger apprentices were too frightened to watch.

The dragon began its descent, flying down towards Riener at a frightening speed. The creature tucked in its wings, calmly bracing itself, before accelerating through the gap. The beast was like lightning out of the skies above, and about as dangerous. It was incredible. The dragon rose back into the air. The crowd was awe-inspired; the applause was deafening.

Turning to face the assembled audience, Riener pointed as if to command the dragon to a particular member in the front row. Immediately, the dragon came hurtling over his shoulder, heading straight for Riener's designated target. But mercifully, at the very instant of collision, the flying beast suddenly swerved downwards, shooting through and underneath the chair. Indeed, the dragon weaved through the gaps under the chairs of the entire front row, before flying out the other side, and back over to its Master.

The audience stood to applaud the performance, truly dazzled. Mythrian shook his head in disbelief.

Master Brennius smiled down upon his apprentice. Mythrian sat silent and still. His eyes were fixed on the dragon as it continued to mesmerise the crowd. It was as if everyone in the room had been hypnotised.

Gliding back round its caster's head, the dragon finished off its show with some slow, graceful spins, dropping sprinkles of scarlet dust from its wings, drenching the floor in a sea of red. Bowing to his audience, Riener thanked them all for coming, while the dragon ceased its tricks and simply hovered in the air behind its Master.

There was a mighty, roaring ovation. However, Mythrian, staring up at the dragon from his chair, couldn't help but feel an uncomfortable vibration from the cast creature. He froze, just as the dragon dropped its head, then lifted it again very slowly, and this time with a very different expression. The beast was looking straight ahead at the audience.

Its eyes were still, as if it was under some form of hypnosis. And as Mythrian gazed deeper into them, he saw bright flames spontaneously appear from within these eyes, burning wildly as they grew brighter with every flicker of the flame.

Mythrian was falling into a trance.

Someone or something had cast a spell over the dragon. Mythrian was falling into its deathly grasp. Nobody in the crowd realised.

As the dragon flapped its wings, the scarlet dust that it had scattered on to the floor began to rise. A cloud of it swooped around the audience, absorbing everything in a violent whirlwind, and within seconds these members of the crowd were merely a million different fragments, disappearing and drifting out of sight.

Snapping out of his trance, Mythrian looked around frantically, trying to find help. But the boy was suddenly alone. Brennius and the rest of the crowd had vanished. Everyone was gone.

He was alone with the dragon.

There was a sudden clash of heavy sounds, like great buildings were falling, but the noise was coming from beneath his feet.

As Mythrian looked down, he saw that thin cracks had started to appear in the marbled floor. They were increasing in number, and fast. As they opened wider, the cracks began to flash an orange-yellow colour, burning like the sun. Intense shafts of light began shooting up into the chamber, just as huge sections of the floor began to crack.

A river of living molten lava was swelling up from under the earth.

Mythrian lifted his legs up on to the seat of his chair. He was terrified. The floor split and sunk into the fires beneath him. He turned on the chair when he heard the booming voice of the dragon:

"A new dawn is beckoning! The heart of Siren's Gore is burning brighter than ever before! Can you see it, boy?"

Mythrian, summoning up the courage to speak, simply said:

"Who are you? What do you want from me?"

"It will only be a matter of time before the Beast is released and then all shall burn under its wrath."

"The Beast …?" Mythrian was struggling to make sense of the dragon's proclamation.

"I speak of Draigorn ... and his resurrection! He has a new

body, a new form. Stronger than ever before, he knows that time is short and while his army is massing in numbers never seen before, his power grows in the heart of Siren's Gore, from where he shall rise, to bring destruction to all who refuse to bend to his will."

Still hunched up on his chair, Mythrian began to feel a cold, disturbing chill shooting in all directions within the frail frame of his body. It sent shivers of fear down his spine, to the very core of his soul.

"Why me? What have I got to do with any of this?"

"You hold the key. You hold the power to stop this menace. Quick, before it begins."

"Please ... I don't understand?"

"You will know soon enough. Beware all that you hear from the East. For when the time is right, the armies of Draigorn will rise out of the darkness. And in the darkness, they will strike you dead. Yes, you boy; you and all your kind."

As the dragon spoke these words, Mythrian felt a sharp jab. It was as if he was being stabbed with a dagger, it was going into his back, and he fell forwards off his chair, on to the marbled floor.

Just in time came a pair of strong arms to save him. Brennius caught him just before he hit the ground. And just as quickly, the dragon, the whole terrifying vision and violence of the Chamber, was gone. It had all vanished into thin air.

Brennius cradled the frail boy in his arms. He was aware only that something had taken place beyond his control.

† † †

Opening the door to his room, Mythrian stumbled in. He put the back of his hand to his forehead, felt the sweat there. He found his way to a chair.

He pulled out the heavy stone that lay still under his shirt. Clumsily, it slipped out of his hand on to the desk.

Mythrian sank backwards into his chair, covering his face with his hands. He wanted to drown out any more thought. His head ached, the strain on him felt almost unbearable.

Mythrian pondered for a moment, trying to recall some of the dragon's words. And then just as he did, he quickly tried to forget them. Best to try to get some rest, he thought.

He placed his head between his crossed arms on the desk. His tired eyes closed and he drifted off to sleep.

He didn't wake till midnight. As he lifted himself from his slumber, stretching his arms out as far as they possibly could be pushed, his sleepy eyes caught sight of an envelope on his desk.

He hadn't noticed it before when he'd come back to his room. The boy curiously looked around to check if anyone had been in, to place it there while he had been sleeping. Mythrian picked the letter up and hastily tore open the envelope. It was from the Counsel of Aldremayne:

'Congratulations, Mythrian. You have been entered into the Avalin Tournament of Apprentices, and if you win your contest, you will be given the chance to compete further at the great arena fort of Aldremayne. You will be aware of the significance of such an opportunity. Success at Aldremayne would elevate you to the rank of Hero. The finest scouts will be watching your progress. But there will be no pressure on you here at Avalin. Our goal is that you will enjoy your time with us. The tournament will take place in exactly three days. Do not disappoint us. We look forward to your arrival, Mythrian.

Yours faithfully, the Board of Aldremayne.'

Dropping the note back on the desk, the boy slumped back in his chair, wiping some of the sweat off his face. As the words of the note ran around Mythrian's head, his eyes caught sight of the tablet on his desk. He grabbed it, feverishly, and began to unwrap the cloth. The next thing that happened took his breath away.

A bright blue beam of light ejected through a gap in the fabric, rising up towards the ceiling. Mythrian looked on in awe. The light was mesmerising. It rose high above his head.

Quickly, he pulled the rest of the cloth away to reveal the full light of the tablet.

Mythrian was stunned by what lay before him. The stone was immensely beautiful. It entranced him. Its luminous markings began to flash vigorously, as if the light was about to leap right out of the tablet.

Leaning over it, Mythrian shook with delight. He calmly placed his hand on its surface. He stroked the rough texture of the tablet. As he did so, a warm tingling sensation ran up his arm, and the markings on the tablet became brighter. The blue light from it flashed quicker and quicker.

Gwyn had warned him to handle his treasure with care and caution, but without thinking, Mythrian picked the tablet up off the desk, held it firmly in his hand, and brought it up close to his eyes.

The tablet suddenly began to throb and pulse in the boy's hand. It seemed to have an energy all of its own. Mythrian tightened his grip on it, but just as he did so, something extraordinary happened.

Mythrian suddenly felt a vibrant sensation moving up his arm.

He pulled his sleeve back up to his shoulder and leapt up from his chair.

He screamed.

Before his very eyes, the markings on his arms were transforming in colour and intensity. The script from the tablet was bleeding into his very skin, igniting the markings that covered his body. It was unbelievable. His body was changing, second by second. The cryptic markings began to illuminate, flashing just like the pulse from the tablet. It brightened, from an indigo-blue to a fluorescent, mesmerizing violet.

The light from the tablet was intensifying the markings on his torso, running up his arm, crossing into his chest, before spreading out to his limbs.

Mythrian began to feel a strong current of energy running through the markings. It was as though the tablet was like a key and it was unlocking a hidden power nestled deep within his body.

The boy was frozen still, yet his heart was on fire. He couldn't understand what was happening to him. He sobbed. He screamed. Gwyn had been right to warn him.

Mythrian tried to let go of the tablet but he absolutely couldn't relinquish his grip. With the boy transfixed under its awesome might, the tablet simply threw him back into his chair with a supernatural force.

It glued him to the seat.

By now, the script from the tablet had performed a full body tattoo over Mythrian. It even crept up to his face. The boy's body and the tablet were entwined as one.

There was no way out. Mythrian was under the tablet's spell. Only his mind remained free. Transfixed in his chair, Mythrian began to feel a pulse, ticking through his body with a consistent beat like a clock, as if some form of outside energy was being carefully infused and fed into him.

His right arm shook from the power of this energy, while his left fell limp from loss of control, resting faintly on the side of the chair. Then suddenly, as if the power from the tablet had overfilled in the boy, a stream of liquid blue light trickled out of his hand. It coiled its way around the chair, leaving an imprint of its snake-tailed energy. The light spiralled down towards the floor.

The light was alive. It was moving. It crawled across the floor, embroidering Mythrian's markings into every item of furniture that came into its path. The light from the tablet reached the window, and as it flew out into the sky, the sound of heavy thunder began to roar across the village.

The energy from the tablet was being pulled through the window, as if it were a puppet, attached by strings, controlled by some higher force. It shot upwards to the rooftop where there was a weather-vein, rattling violently in the growing gale.

The weather-vein turned from the colour of rust to fluorescent blue and formed the perfect conductor. Lightning lashed across the skies bringing heavy rain and thunder that shook the cottages all around with immense force. Suddenly, a bolt caught the weather-vein, whipping down the line of energy, straight through Mythrian's window, towards the unsuspecting boy. The current of lightning raced along the energy line, hurtling across the floor.

It screamed up through the chair and entered the body of the boy that sat there:

"AAARRRGGGHHH!!"

Mythrian screamed in agonising pain as high levels of current shot through his unprotected body, shaking him uncontrollably in his chair.

Mythrian couldn't even call for help with the amount of immense powerful force was shaking him. Every second his body weakened unto its grasp.

As his mind fell deeper into darkness, his eyesight dimming, his body numb and his consciousness fading, Mythrian was without any strength to fight on.

As the tablet loosened its hold on the boy, its task complete, Mythrian fell hard on to the wooden floor.

The current had broken, but the force still shook his lifeless body.

While Mythrian lay cold on the floor, the markings that were displayed around the room began to coil back into his body, reabsorbing the powerful energy.

At last it was over.

Mythrian would remain unconscious until the morning and his memory faded of the event.

If only he knew what was to become of him.

While the boy lay unconscious in his room, eyes were looking down on him. Eyes from afar had been watching his actions closely.

"Foolish boy. He has absorbed the tablet's energy. Does he not know of the power within," a voice cried.

"The tablet is no more. Its power is drained. What should we do?" another voice panicked, sensing defeat.

"Nothing. His time will come, but his actions have not safeguarded his people from the East. He has now mounted an immense task on his shoulders. One I doubt he will overcome," the elder remarked.

"But he has the power. There will be no other one," a voice argued.

"No!" the elder corrected, "there may yet be another one ..."

CHAPTER 5 ✝ LEAVING HOME

YTHRIAN OPENED HIS eyes and was instantly blinded by the sunlight that streaked through his window. He scratched his aching head and tried to recollect what had happened the previous night.

The first thing he saw was the tablet. It was lying on the floor, just a simple piece of common stone. It was lifeless now, not mesmerising. Mythrian no longer felt drawn.

The bright markings had disappeared. He picked up the tablet, and rose to his feet. Mythrian gently laid it on the table, quietly resting it underneath the warming rays of morning light.

Mythrian felt incredibly strong this morning. His legs were like pillars of stone, his arms felt like wings. He moved quickly and easily through the air. He felt revitalised and eager to test himself.

He was on the stairs, running towards the open door and the fields beyond, when he suddenly thought of Brennius. His Master would be worried after what happened in the Chamber. He felt he should let him know that he was OK.

He stopped at the foot of the stairs. Two apprentices were passing, approaching the entrance to the Guild Hall.

"What do you think then?"

"About …?"

"About the noise, last night. I mean, what was that?"

"Well, I heard a roar …"

"Thunder and lightning?"

But no rain ... strange? Come on, we're late! We'd better hurry!"

Their footsteps, leather slapped on stone, disappeared across the hall as they ran to their first lesson.

Something clicked in Mythrian's mind. It was because of those words – "thunder and lightning". Something in that tablet he had held last night had in some way changed him. For better or worse? He was unsure. Although his body felt strong, his mind was still shaken from the night before. He had a mighty headache.

Mythrian turned his head slightly, and suddenly, in the entrance to the library, saw the tall figure of Master Brennius standing directly opposite.

Mythrian rubbed his face with his hands, and approached.

"Ah, my boy. One assumes you are feeling much better?" There was a look of genuine concern on his tired old face.

"I'm OK."

Mythrian lifted his head then, looking Brennius directly in the face.

Brennius was instantly stunned by the boy's markings.

"Why …!"

The markings covering his face and upper body had grown brighter. Something had reacted with the boy's markings and they had been intensified.

For a few moments, Brennius was speechless. His brow furrowed and his eyes narrowed as they took in the transformation in the boy's appearance.

"Mythrian, I ... I ..."

"Yes, Master? What is it?"

"I take it you read the letter that was left on your work table, in your room."

"About the tournament. I can't wait. In three days' time."

"Two days' time," Brennius quickly asserted. "We must begin the journey there tomorrow morning. I have gathered all the apprentices who are going to the tournament at the garden gates. They have been waiting patiently for you to wake."

Brennius saw a moment of hesitation in the young boy's eyes.

"But you are unnerved. What is wrong, my boy?"

"Oh … nothing."

Mythrian wanted to tell Master Brennius about everything that had happened in the Chamber, but he simply couldn't find the words to describe it.

"Are you sure?"

"Yes. It's nothing. As you say, we'd better go."

The Guild Master cast his eyes over the chosen group of apprentices, waiting patiently in the garden.

"My, to look at you all now. Why, I remember the first time you all arrived at the Guild. So eager and imaginative, all with a burning desire to excel at any given task. How quickly those years have passed by and here you all are, all grown up and ready to explore the world and share your gifts with it. Now, you've all proved your abilities to me over the years and I'm sure you will prove them to others. I'm referring of course to the Tournament of Apprentices at Avalin."

Brennius could see pride and excitement burning in the young eyes of the apprentices assembled before him. For a moment, he paused. It occurred to him that he was growing older, that he too had once had that look in his eyes. That eagerness and willingness to achieve, to strive for success.

"Be confident. This is what you have been trained for. You possess incredible gifts, but the competition will be fierce. All I ask is that you do not let me down.

"On your way to Avalin, you will pause at the village fort of Helianthe. A chance for a break and for you to calm any nerves. You leave tomorrow, six and a half hours after sunrise. Don't be late! And be sure to remember, that no matter how far you travel, you will always be remembered in the Guild and always welcomed. Good luck, good luck to each and every one of you!"

Brennius received a standing ovation. One by one, the apprentices approached their teacher, to show their respect for him. To them, he was their inspiration. Then they turned to make their way back to their quarters, to prepare for one of the biggest days of their lives.

The next day, Hamlynstone was bustling. People were running about, a long line of transport wagons came through the gates. As they trundled through, a man jumped down off one of the carriages and began calling out from a register of names.

Inside the Guild, apprentices were madly dashing around quarters, making sure they had all their luggage – food, books, spare clothes and weaponry, before hurrying out of the Guild doors.

"Alright, my boy. Got everything you need?"

Brennius beamed at Mythrian. He realised the boy had so many questions to ask, but there was no time now.

"Everything I need," replied the boy, watching the other apprentices running like mad dogs around him. Wrapped in his arms was a bag containing eighty gold coins, a book to read on his way and a spare blanket for extra warmth during the night.

"Good luck, and don't be intimidated by any of the other competitors. I am sure you will do fine. Now, I cannot talk to you or any of the other apprentices on the journey, but ... if you need to talk with me, you know how and when to contact me."

"Name?"

"Mythrian," the boy said instantly.

"Carriage 48, three from the back," the man spoke without looking up at him. He merely gestured over his shoulder, pointing with his thumb in the direction of the assembled carriages, and put a tick against the boy's name on his register.

"Next!"

When Mythrian found it, carriage 48 hardly seemed strong enough to get them as far as the tournament. There were two enormous Shire horses chained to the front of it, waiting, heads down and forlorn, but in truth it was really nothing more than a box-shaped carriage made out of a dry, dull oak. Its wheels were rough, uneven, and split-rimmed. The whole vehicle looked just about good enough to be thrown on a fire.

Inside the carriage, there was only room for four apprentices.

Jumping on to the last remaining bed on a top bunk, Mythrian checked it for comfort. It was as hard as a board. He tried to put a brave face on it, turned, and forced a smile. The crowds outside the window were cheering enthusiastically.

Above the din, Mythrian heard the guard bellowing:

"All aboard, what's coming aboard!"

There was a series of terrific bangs as the doors of the carriages clattered shut. And then the thump of the guard's fist as he passed Carriage 48.

"Ready to go!" he shouted, before moving on and away up the line.

The village gates were hauled open. A heavy, churning sound echoed from the line as iron scraped against stone. The cavalcade of carriages started their journey slowly and reluctantly.

Soon they would reach Anthelstone, to pick up the next line of apprentices, before slowly trekking on to Helianthe.

Old Brennius stood under the Guild doors, surveying the spectacle of departure.

"Ah, the young! So much energy, so little time …" he muttered to himself, turning away the moment they were gone.

CHAPTER 6 † DAYDREAMING

B Y MIDDAY, THEY had been travelling for four hours. The fifth sun was high in the sky, throwing maroon light in all directions. The road down to Anthelstone was very bumpy, the wagons were moving slowly.

Mythrian was restless. He tried to distract himself with the passing scenery, counting fields and meadows, but his mind was racing.

Salen was lying flat out on his bunk, arms resting behind his head. He was staring up at the cracks in the roof. He had been chattering incessantly for more than an hour:

"… I mean; I can hardly believe it."

"Hardly believe what?" Rinen was on the bunk below.

"You wait all these years for something like this to happen and when it comes around, you're so full of excitement and joy that you just lose your senses."

"Salen, you lost your senses years ago," Rinen was mocking him, "… along with every game of cards you ever played."

"No, no," Salen was insistent. "It's as if this is where we change from childhood to manhood."

"Give me a break!"

"I'm serious, Rinen. You know, I don't care about winning or losing at this tournament. From this point forward, we're no longer apprentices – we're men. We'll be allowed to do whatever we want, whenever we want. For me, this is where my life truly begins."

Salen was a kind, disciplined apprentice, who always worked hard and showed high levels of trust and honour in his work. He had shoulder-length blond hair; his face was soft and gentle, the kind that girls fall easily for. He'd been packed off to the Guild at Hamlynstone by his parents, to gain an apprenticeship in one of their specially selected classes. He had a natural gift for the arts; the young apprentice worked hard and had distinguished himself as one of the leading apprentices in the Guild.

With Rinen, it was different. He had close-cut, raven black hair and a hard face that always hid his feelings. He was already a giant, taller even than Salen, who himself stood head and shoulders above most in the guild. Rinen liked to play the joker, he was full of pranks and tricks, and they often got him into trouble. Nevertheless, he too had natural talent and when he applied himself, his ability shone.

Both students were eager to impress at the tournament. Rinen leant on the window frame of the carriage, breathing in lungfuls of fresh, country air. Over his shoulder, he said:

"I expect your family will be throwing a party when you get back."

"Maybe."

"Speaking for myself, when I'm done with this tournament, I don't want a big celebration. I'll just go down the tavern and ask for a nice, cold pint of beer." Rinen's mouth drooled at the very thought.

"For the love of Ajia, Rinen, you're going to need to stop thinking about drinking all the time. We're apprentices; we've got to keep a sharp eye out at all times."

Mythrian, on the other side of the cart, was sitting quietly on his bed, just staring out of the window and watching the scenery pass. On the bunk below him lay another apprentice, Bodel.

"I see Dozy's lively today," Salen said, nodding in Bodel's direction.

Mythrian leaned over the side of his bed, hanging down.

Rinen was feeling mischievous: "Go on, Mythrian. Clap your hands, cast a spell, it won't wake him, I bet!"

"Oh, yeah?"

"Yeah, I'll bet you anything you like, he'll sleep through it. He's unbelievable."

"No. I can't do it," Mythrian said, "… it's just wrong."

"Alright then, I will."

As Salen and Mythrian looked on, Rinen crept over to Bodel, fast asleep on his back. He pulled a crystal out of his pocket and slowly raised it up above the sleeping boy's head. There was an audible intake of breath from Salen.

"Where did you get that from? You could get expelled for that!"

But Rinen was not to be dissuaded. He was determined to perform his trick.

He crept up to Bodel slowly, every step slower and softer than the last. When he was just inches from the bed, he carefully raised his hands with the crystal tight in his palm above Bodel's head.

He followed the system in his mind, exactly as he had been taught.

Image, concentrate hard. Eyes closed.

Then, throwing it to the floor, he suddenly smashed the crystal and jumped out of the way, as fireworks began shooting off in all directions around the bed that Bodel slept on.

There was an explosion, like fireworks, inside the carriage. Noise ricocheting around: whistling; fizzing; hissing. It was a deafening cacophony of sound.

But incredibly, Bodel slept on. As Rinen, Mythrian and Salen jumped for cover, and then peeped out over their beds, they found him still fast asleep.

Falling backwards on to the floor, arms wrapped around his chest, Rinen laughed so much his sides ached and he could hardly take a breath.

As for Bodel, he was still snoozing away, to the astonishment of Mythrian and Salen, who both unfortunately did not find the joke quite as humorous as Rinen did.

"Oh, cheer up you two," Rinen giggled, clambering up to his feet, resting his arm on Salen's bed. "There's nothing wrong with having a bit of fun, is there, hey?"

Noticing Salen's rather unamused look, he pointed at Bodel and returned, "Look, he's not even awake".

"Yeah and what would you have done if he had woken up? I

call that pushing your luck," Salen replied.

Sometimes Salen would find Rinen's humour hilarious, although there were times when Salen wished the trouble making would abruptly stop.

"Oh, you worry too much," the apprentice whinged, falling flat on to his bed, causing a loud bang on the wooden floor, as the bed jumped slightly from the impact.

Once the apprentices had calmed down from their little charade of excitement and had become more used to the uncomfortable journey on the road, the time had quickly passed by as the fifth sun began to set along the horizon, drawing the peaceful sky at night behind it.

By now the transport wagons had approached the village of Anthelstone.

A long line of carriages was stationed, waiting to join the back of the already very long queue.

By the time the carriages had joined the back of the line and were all set to begin the next leg of the journey, it was getting close to midnight and the moon sat bold and clear in the sky, acting as a lighthouse for those travelling in the dark below.

Inside Mythrian's carriage, the four apprentices were bracing themselves for a very long and uncomfortable night.

While Bodel remained fast asleep, not the slightest bit bothered about the bad effects from the journey, Mythrian above him sat tirelessly on his bed. In his hand was a book which he had brought on the journey with him, to take his mind away from any feelings of anxiety.

By now, all the apprentices were asleep.

Dropping his book on to the bed, Mythrian gathered his sheets and wrapped himself up, nice and warm.

Despite the heavy grind of the wheels churning loudly through the carriage windows and the rough feeling of the poorly-made bed beneath him, it wasn't long before Mythrian drifted off into sleep.

But it wasn't to last long ...

Mythrian, opening his eyes, found himself standing on top of a cliff.

The ground, far below, was covered by a dense fog. It was creeping its way up the mountainside, as if it were alive. The air around was thick, Mythrian could barely see his hand in front of his face.

He dropped to his feet and reached for a handful of dust.

Morbian dust. Incredibly, he found himself suddenly in the Mountains of Morbian.

Footsteps drew near. Giant footsteps and they grew louder, approaching. Whatever it was that was coming towards him, it was of a giant stature. Its progress was regular, as though it was mechanical, and after each step came the chiming sound of metal clashing. Whoever – whatever – this was, it was wearing armour.

Mythrian swallowed. The footsteps came to an abrupt halt. There was complete silence. Mythrian stood frozen to the spot, staring ahead down the valley, hearing only the eerie whistle of the wind sliding past his ear.

There was something behind him.

He could sense it.

He could feel it. It was breathing down the back of his neck with its cold, sickening breath.

Mythrian froze solid. At the same time, he knew he was in a position of great danger and that he needed to do something.

Slowly, he turned around. His eyes were closed shut. He stood, taut, hunched over as if he was waiting to be struck.

Very slowly, he opened his left eye to look at what stood before him.

"DRAIGORN!"

Mythrian screamed. He instinctively placed his hands to his head in disbelief. He stumbled back, his eyes wide open.

His heart stopped inside him.

Mythrian cowered into a ball on the ground, begging the creature of hate to have mercy on his soul. He babbled, like an infant:

"Don't hurt me, please. Leave me … alone."

Draigorn just stood menacingly still, moving not a fragment of his body. His eyes were on fire. He moved closer, very close now, bearing down on the feeble frame of the boy, his sadistic smile spread wide across his shining, bony white skull.

Reaching down to his left side, jerking his crimson cloak out of his way, Draigorn reached for his sword.

He drew it slowly. It seemed as if there was no end to its blade.

Mythrian's eyes rained tears. He heard the spine-tingling scrape of the sword grating against its sheath. He cried out:

"What do you want from me?"

The beast Draigorn gripped his great sword tightly with both hands, pointing its very tip towards the boy. He advanced to within a metre of him, and raised his sword above his head.

"I WANT YOUR SOUL!"

Draigorn's dark, droning voice boomed, echoing loudly around the mountains, as he dropped his sword down on to the boy, plunging it deep into his chest.

Shooting forward into an upright position on the bed, Mythrian wrapped his arms around his chest, covering the area where contact was made.

He found no mark or any sign of a wound. He checked again.

Mythrian suddenly came to, back in the carriage, with his fellow apprentices.

But if this was just a nightmare, why could he still feel a sharp pain where Draigorn had stabbed him with his blade? Why could he still hear the evil creature's loud, disturbing laugh, echoing through his head?

Mythrian took in deep breaths to calm himself down. He wiped the sweat from his brow. Salen woke and saw him trembling in his bed.

"Bad dreams?"

Mythrian nodded slowly.

The two boys stared at each other across the darkness.

CHAPTER 7 ✝ IN THE WARM
GLOW OF HELIANTHE

MORNING BROKE. MYTHRIAN awoke in the carriage; it was still moving, still travelling on. He opened and then straightaway closed his tired eyes. The sunlight blinded him. But even so, and despite the fatigue, he felt anxious and excited. He knew he would soon be at Helianthe.

About a half-mile away from their next stop-off point, they entered a small, nameless woodland. The tall trees there were so tightly packed together that absolutely no light broke through. The progress of the wagons slowed to a crawl, the drivers looked out for the lights that had been laid down to guide them. As darkness filled the carriages, a cold, chilling wind swept through.

The road began to narrow. Mythrian sat motionless on his bed. He listened nervously to the sound of their cartwheels, grating against the bark of trees, laid either side of the cobbled road. The squawk of nesting birds in the woods unsettled the apprentices.

A thousand trees in the forest cast a million dark-winged shadows. The perfect hiding place for creatures dark of heart.

But then light appeared at the edge of the woodland. A few splinters of it scattered their way into this secret grove, breaking silently into Mythrian's carriage. As the boy and his fellow apprentices sat eagerly on the bed, Rinen quietly muttered to his companions:

"Brace yourselves."

Suddenly, they emerged from the wood and there, high up on the hill in front of them, looking over a wide flat plain, stood the village fort of Helianthe. The apprentices shifted to their windows to gaze at it.

There were four high towers, one at each corner of the fort. The scale of it was monumental. It rose from the very centre of the village, symmetrical, defensively impregnable and visually awe-inspiring. The village clustered around the ramparts of the fort. It was dwarfed by it; it looked intimidated and dominated.

Helianthe. A place of rest for wounded heroes. They sat in the gardens around the fort, in peace, in tranquillity or drinking outside the tavern.

The wagons turned on to the path leading down to the gates of the fort. From there, they entered the village orchard. Looking out of the window, Mythrian and the apprentices surveyed the endless rows of apple trees. The sight was mouthwatering.

"So much scrumpy ... I think I've found my new home," dribbled Rinen. His eyes were practically glazing over. "I hope they've got some inside."

The apprentices entered the fort. The many vivid colours of the flowers there practically blinded them.

Their wagons drew up in a wide, open courtyard. It was to be their base for the night. Guards approached each carriage, unlocked the doors, and ordered the apprentices inside to show themselves.

Mythrian, Rinen, Salen and Bodel stepped out of the wagon. They stretched their cramped, aching limbs.

The exquisite perfumes of the flowers in the surrounding gardens were overwhelming. It was as if the scent was laid on as some kind of greeting. The chief of the guards, who had a huge, vicious looking dog on a lead, addressed them:

"Good morning, and welcome to Helianthe. I expect you've heard a lot about this place, however there are a few things I would like to point out to you. Behind me you'll see the fort; it is where you will be sleeping for the night. Though we are pleased to have you staying here with us, don't forget that we have rules. Helianthe is a quiet and peaceful place, so anyone what causes a stir or any trouble will be severely punished. I hope this does not apply to any of you."

The guard paused as he inspected the line of apprentices who nervously smiled back at him. At least both parties agreed that the rules were clear and were not to be broken.

"You can roam where you like, by way of leisure, in these here gardens. For those of you what is partial to a drink, there be the garden tavern, but woe betide you if I catch you staggering. Nobody, and I mean nobody, carries weapons around the village. You'll hand in any knives, bows, arrows and such at the stool by the fort gates before you go to your rooms, as I will now assign you."

The guard's voice was slow and deliberate. He seemed annoyed about something.

Pointing at Mythrian's group, who were standing towards the front, he gave them directions to their rooms:

"You four. I'll start with you. Your rooms are all on the third floor. Take the second from left staircase as you enter the fort, go up to the third floor, march past the first row of doors, round to the left and it's the third door on the right: door number 148."

He looked up, smirked a little, almost laughing.

"Enjoy your stay."

The four apprentices walked up to a stool outside the fort entrance, handed over their weapons and headed into the fort.

The interior was stunning. The walls and ceilings inside were covered in exquisite murals depicting soldiers in combat.

The craftsmanship that had gone into the construction and decoration of the fort was considerable. Marble columns framed every doorway; their carvings were delicate, classical and superb. The walls were built out of giant squares of polished stone. The ceilings in every room, hall and passage were decorated in a mesmerising swirl of gold spirals.

"Stunning ..." said Bodel, looking up.

"Inspiring ..." Rinen said. He too had his head tilted towards the golden ceiling.

"... Yeah ..." was the only word Salen could manage. He was dumbstruck.

Mythrian remained silent. His eyes too were fixed on the decorative ceiling above. Salen and Bodel each had to take him by the hand to lead him on. It was as if he had been hypnotised.

The four boys made their way up the stairs to their room, just as the Guard had told them.

"Room 148, here it is." Mythrian, leading the others, opened the door and stepped inside.

Their room was warm. Every item of furniture was clean and well cared for. The beds were soft and comfortable, a relief for the apprentices who had spent the previous night sleeping on those rough bunks in the transport wagons. A fireplace, hearth and chimney held pride of place at the centre of the room, with plenty of firewood by its side.

Mythrian stood before the window, looking far out across the plains. The view was wide, expansive and seemingly endless.

Rinen quickly made himself at home. While Mythrian made himself comfortable on the bed by the window, Rinen chose the neighbouring bed, jumping onto its covers and checking its softness.

"We should have a rest," Salen said. "A few hours here, then we could take a walk round the gardens."

"Sounds good to me," Bodel replied. He jumped on to his bed and within seconds had dropped into a deep sleep.

From his position, Salen could see Mythrian, who stood stationary by the window, head flicking from side to side scanning the wide, open view.

"You'd best get some kip, Mythrian," he called out to him.

"Not just yet," replied Mythrian. The sixth sun shone brightly in the sky. His full attention was cast on the vibrant setting.

"Well, don't be too long. You really need some sleep to boost your energy levels for the tournament tomorrow."

Noticing that both Rinen and Bodel were now asleep; Salen moved himself into a more comfortable position and drifted off into a peaceful and much needed rest.

As he watched Mythrian gazing out into the far distance, the tired apprentice slowly began to close his eyes, drifting into a peaceful and much needed rest.

CHAPTER 8 † OF FRIENDS AND MOONLIGHT

TWO HOURS HAD passed before Salen woke up. It was now late afternoon. Bodel remained asleep, but Rinen had left. As his eyes opened, he was presented with the same image of Mythrian, who was still in front of the window. Only now, he was in a deep state of meditation.

There was a candle burning on the window sill. Salen woke from his slumber, his senses becoming reacquainted with their surroundings.

He realised that Mythrian was whispering quietly out of the window.

Mythrian was communicating with Master Brennius back in the Guild of Hamlynstone, telling him about the journey, and about his first impressions of Helianthe.

Salen watched the boy's lips moving silently, watched him casting his wishes out of the window. They floated away with the wind, in the smoke from the flame of the candle. He was in awe of Mythrian's quiet devotion.

After a few moments, his distant conversation ended and Mythrian rose to blow the candle out. He walked over to sit on his bed, calmly collecting his thoughts.

"I thought you said you were going to sleep." Salen spoke quietly, so as not to wake Bodel, next to him.

"I know I should be resting, but ... I just don't feel tired. In fact, I don't feel like sleeping at all. I feel like I could walk from here to Hamlynstone and back again and still feel as energetic as when I first started."

Salen sat up. The cryptic markings on Mythrian's face had become brighter and more striking than he had ever seen before.

The violet arcs and arrowing, the intricate, maze-like patterning across his arms, shoulders and back, had seemed to spread. He looked mystical, coloured and wild in front of that window.

"What's up with those …?"

"With what?" Mythrian mumbled, hardly taking notice of Salen.

"Your markings. Looks like they're … moving on your skin. Like they're alive."

Mythrian was uncomfortable with Salen's comment, though he knew the apprentice was only showing concern. He ended the conversation, standing up and heading for the door.

"I'm going out, to see the village."

Salen was taken aback. "You haven't had much rest, do you really want to go now?"

"I don't see a good reason for hesitating," Mythrian returned, already halfway through the door.

"Alright, hold your horses. Let me put my shoes on and I'll come with you," Salen replied before the two walked down into the village.

Entering the village, the sixth sun was still cascading its full light across the skies, enlightening the atmosphere and scenery. Even with the evening drawing on, the flowers in blossom shone with extravagant colours and the scent was strong too. The flowers were delicate, subtle and intoxicating. Their petals danced in a gentle breeze.

"You know, Mythrian, we were in the same class …" Salen said, as they walked out into the sunlit garden, "… yet, I never spoke that much to you. You always seemed to have your head stuck in a book."

Salen paused for a moment, raising his head up to the clear sky, captivated by its ocean shade, before continuing.

"You seem different to everyone else, Myth. I mean ... well, how can I say this? Rinen and that lot are good fun, a good laugh, I suppose, but they can sometimes act a bit young for their age, whereas you tend to be the opposite."

As he turned to look back at Mythrian, he found the boy had moved away. He had his head buried in the flowers, of all things. Salen caught up with him.

"Don't tell me you're going to do that all the way round the garden."

Mythrian began wiping his nose, furiously.

"Salen, my friend, this place is wonderful. I often dreamt, looking out of my window, that there were gardens like this out here ..." Mythrian softly touched the petal of the nearest flower, holding one delicately like a leaf of gold between his thumb and forefinger.

"Yes. It is quite spectacular," Salen replied, smiling. "The colours, even at night, do seem strong. Quite spectacular indeed."

The night sky was drawing in. The sun was setting and the sixth moon was coming into clear gaze. The fort was an awe-inspiring spectacle at night, especially as the blue lights from the garden ignited every pillar and post in a calm, turquoise shade. From far away, it must have looked like a beacon, like a lighthouse.

Salen asked his friend: "So what will you do after the tournament is over?"

Quick to answer, Mythrian replied: "There is nothing for me after the tournament. By which I mean; this is everything to me. Who could think of anything else?"

"One thing's for sure," Salen said, "whatever the outcome, we won't be apprentices anymore. We'll have proper assignments, proper tasks to complete. We will be guarding some of the biggest forts in our kingdom or keeping areas of our land safe from intruders. But ..."

"But what, Salen?"

"I don't know if that's what I really want to do. I mean, I love my land and I would die a happy man fighting for it – don't get me wrong. But I don't want to spend my whole life fighting. I don't want to spend my whole life with a sword in my hand."

"Well said, my friend," Mythrian agreed.

"I just want to live a happy life. I don't want all these troubles.

I'd just like a nice cottage, where I sit in my garden and just watch the world float by."

"But we have to fight, Salen."

"Why? Why must we always fight?"

"There is hate in this world. The scale of it is … well, we know that we can never disregard the threat from the East. We must fight."

It was obvious to Mythrian that Salen was uncomfortable with this conversation, with reality. He was from a rich background; he hadn't had to fight his way forward into an honourable life, like Mythrian.

"You'll soon get your wish, Salen. Ajia's spirit may be exiled away, but his presence remains strong. Nobody wants this war, but even if it takes a hundred battles, a thousand battles to win this fight, I for one would fight everyone if it meant gaining my freedom."

Salen smiled, and slapped Mythrian on the shoulder. He felt reassured.

"Myth, you will be a great hero one day. Many will look up to your achievements. But whatever paths we both take, just remember that you will always have somebody watching over your shoulder."

He raised his hand, and Mythrian's met it. They understood one another.

With the evening drawing ever on, the two apprentices were starting to feel the effects of the long day. Their legs began to tire beneath them.

Looking for somewhere to rest, Salen noticed a tavern not too far away.

"Come on Myth. Let's go grab a pint."

CHAPTER 9 ✝ A DARKNESS
AMONG THE LIGHT

SILVER AND GLASS slammed down on wood.

Beer mugs, thundering down on barrels and on tables in the tavern. The sound of drunken soldiers letting off steam. Some of them were already the worse for the experience, laid out in the hay on the stone floor.

A place of calm. A welcoming atmosphere, despite the huge row being made by some of the heavy drinkers.

Light, warmth and comfort came from the fire in the hearth to the right hand side. Every seat near the fireplace was taken and was not easily given away. Goose fat candles burned brightly in the tavern's great chandelier. Rising fumes from the beer barrels had stained the wooden beams above smoke black. The stone floor was cracked and worn; an indication of just how popular and busy the place was.

"Go and find a table if you can," Salen shouted to Mythrian. They had just appeared in the great doorway to the tavern and Salen had to shout above the din. "I'll go and get us some drinks."

Rinen was at the bar, sitting on one of the stools, slumped over his beer. He looked desolate. Salen put his hand on Rinen's shoulder and was about to speak, but Rinen interrupted him:

"Whatever it is you're going to say, don't."

But Salen had no chance to protest. A tall, rugged, beast of a man suddenly appeared before him, too close, too drunk and too angry. This was Ghabrian. To most, an arrogant bully with no care except for himself.

Both Salen and Rinen had come into confrontation with Ghabrian in the past. Even as a child, Ghabrian was a giant compared to the rest, but had always seen Rinen, with his tall stature, as competition. Ghabrian's voice boomed:

"So ... you brought a friend with you. Is he your bodyguard? Your guardian spirit?"

Salen sensed trouble. He grabbed Rinen by the elbow; he was all for leaving straightaway:

"Let's go. I've had enough."

But the giant drunk's big mouth stopped them in their tracks. The rowdy tavern suddenly became silent.

"Wimps! Pathetic, puny wimps!" The big man shouted, laying a massive, gloved hand on Rinen's shoulder, turning him. He was heavily armoured, more than a little unsteady, and, in the heat from the fire, sweating like a pig. Something the boys had said or done had enraged him.

This was trouble.

Rinen, refusing to let even a man of Ghabrian's stature bully him out of the tavern, fronted up to the giant warrior. He held his ground, stood up to him, staring into his eyes.

The giant brute laughed. "What do you think you are doing? Standing up to me like that. Do you want me to kick you out or something?"

"I would be pleased to do the same to you."

"Have you never learned, Rinen? Or do I have to discipline that childish brain of yours?"

As Ghabrian rolled back his sleeves, the thugs surrounding him sprang to their feet, squaring up for a fight.

But Rinen was in no mood to back down.

"You know what they say: big guy, small mind. All noise, no action ..."

Mythrian, aware of the commotion, had by now stopped looking for a table and was trying to find a gap in between the crowd of people circled around Rinen and Ghabrian. He'd heard tell of Ghabrian, knew of his reputation as a bully, a troublemaker and as a ruthless swordsman. He was certainly not to be trifled with.

Ghabrian's face swelled a bright red. His blood was up. His hair stood static and on end. He reached back behind him, took up a mug and downed a huge gulp of beer. Wiping his mouth with the back of his sleeve, he began to scream and seethe:

"Boy, I'll make you squeal like a little girl if you dare cross that line!" Ghabrian pointed to a crack in the floor that separated the two arguers.

"Oh yeah? Like to see you try," Rinen replied, placing half his foot over the line.

His teeth gnawing, his mouth foaming, Ghabrian bellowed once more at Rinen:

"… Behind bars, like rabid dogs, is where you and your kind belong. You cruise in here, thinking you can take over …"

Rinen had had enough. Reaching into his pocket, he pulled out a shiny red crystal. Enclosed in his fist, Rinen was just about to release the crystal when Salen stopped him, seizing him by the hand.

The crowd in the tavern were transfixed. Crystal spells are a capital crime in Helianthe, ever since the discovery of what can happen when the spell goes wrong.

Through clenched teeth, Salen whispered:

"What are you doing? I thought you said that crystal on our journey was your only one?"

There was a long pause. Everyone but everyone in the tavern seemed to be holding their breath.

Then, ashamed of himself, at his loss of control, Rinen slowly lowered his hand. Ghabrian took full advantage:

"You disappoint me, child warrior …" he hissed. "You haven't the courage of a man. You haven't the strength to throw your crystal. You're way out of your league. Go on, boy! Throw it!"

Salen, desperate, called out: "Rinen … don't!"

"Come on Rinen. Now, before the guards get here. Throw the crystal. Don't waste your chance."

"Rinen, I am ordering you. Don't do it!"

Slamming his hand down hard on the nearby table, Ghabrian goaded, "Throw the crystal now!"

Fist clenched, arm taut and stretched backwards, before returning in a violent arc. Energy, released, violent, deadly, aimed: Rinen's arm shot through, his hand released the crystal, which soared across the room towards Ghabrian.

For those brief seconds, with the magic crystal in flight, time literally seemed to stand still, as everybody waited for the impact.

To see what spell the young boy had cast against the foul-mouthed warrior.

The gemstone smashed on the floor, releasing a dust cloud. Everyone in the tavern watched intently, waiting for the air to clear.

But when it did … there was nothing. Laughter began to ring round the tavern. Ghabrian, all his cohorts and hangers on, were mocking the boy apprentice. They were practically in hysterics.

"I might have known," Ghabrian spoke victoriously, "You don't have the guts to stand up against me. You'll never have the guts to stand up to your enemy. You're an embarrassment!"

Turning round to face his crowd, Ghabrian took in the applause from his followers. But Rinen had not finished his fight.

Catching the attention of everyone in the tavern, one of the villagers in the crowd pointed to where the crystal had smashed.

"Look, something is appearing from the crystal. It's coming from under the floorboards."

The laughter ceased abruptly. Ghabrian watched over his shoulder as a dark, shadowing mass rose up from under the floor. As the mass began to take shape, a figure inside the cloud emerged and then opened its eyes.

It was a Valun.

Like a giant dog but with fangs the size of a grown man's fist, Valuns are quick and agile. They can kill with a single bite.

Ghabrian stared at the creature, looking deep into its orange eyes, which burned like the fires of Siren's Gore. The fur on its back, a deep midnight black, stood on end as it glared angrily back at the warrior.

The beast licked its lips. Stringy saliva sapped from between its giant teeth, leaking out across the floor. It bubbled as it swept outwards to all four corners of the room.

The Valun's breathing became heavier, its behaviour became more agitated with every second that passed and it began to scratch its long, razor-like claws across the floor.

It was going to make a move.

Ghabrian had slain creatures far more grotesque than this. Out of reflex, he calmly reached for his sword, but suddenly remembered, under Helianthe's strict rules, his sword was in the hands of the guards.

The giant man panicked. A wave of fear ran through him.

The blackened beast took its chance. With its hind legs it pounced on the defenceless man, opening its fangs the closer it came.

Ghabrian turned away instinctively, shielding his face, waiting for the inevitable.

But nothing happened.

Ghabrian opened his eyes, and blinked several times. What he saw was unbelievable. The beast lay dead on the floor, a knife lay wedged into its spine.

He wiped the hot sweat from his brow, looked up, and saw Mythrian.

Mythrian pulled the dagger from the beast's back, wiped the blood from the blade and quickly tucked the weapon back under his shirt.

But it was already too late.

The barkeeper had fetched the Guards. They stormed in, grabbed Rinen, and put him in chains. The one in charge pointed to Mythrian, who was still breathing heavily from the exertion:

"You too, boy."

Ghabrian was enraged. He set upon the body of the slain beast, grabbing it by the neck and lifting its limp frame up to close view. The body disintegrated in his hands not long after.

He had shown weakness in the presence of a Valun. It would take much to redeem himself in the eyes of the crowd.

CHAPTER 10 † A HARD RAIN

CRACK OF THUNDER. A storm. Rain, falling in sheets, inundating.

It unsettled and unnerved the apprentices. On the eve of the tournament, they needed all the rest they could get.

Rinen and Mythrian were punished for their brawl in the tavern. They were cast out of the village fort for the night.

They set up camp as best they could on the sodden, muddy ground by the main gates of the village. They were soaked; drenched by the heavy rain.

Rinen was bitterly cold. He sat with his arms around his knees, hunched over, his cloak wrapped round him like a blanket. His teeth chattered in the icy wind. He tried to distract himself with thoughts of home.

Mythrian, on the other hand, sat calm and still, mind and body somehow completely sealed against the weather. Perhaps it was the warm blood in his veins, burning with anger. He was not in the mood for apologies.

"I've said I was sorry," Rinen mumbled.

Mythrian remained silent. The cold wind blew through them both; they gritted their teeth. After a minute, Mythrian said:

"It's not me you should be apologising to. You lied to your best friend. Who can Salen choose to trust when his best friend lies to him?"

Rinen began to sob. He knew Mythrian was right. His hands covered his cold, wet face, attempting to hide his shame.

"Will he forgive me, Mythrian?"

"In time," the boy told him, "… in time."

From his pocket, Rinen dug out three more crystals. Denial and guilt flooded his mind, as he stared at his reflection in the gems. He was angry with himself, ashamed that he had lied to Salen.

Looking ahead towards the orchard fields just a few hundred metres away, he picked up the crystals and threw them; they lay just under the apple trees.

Mythrian looked on, speechless. Rinen was aware he had done wrong. There was nothing more to say.

A wet, cold and lonely midnight. The only lights they could see were from the flaring torches on the village wall. Mythrian thought about the creature Rinen had cast in his spell, in the tavern. He couldn't get it out of his mind. What puzzled him was how the imagination of a boy like Rinen could have summoned a spirit of such prodigious anger – a creature so dark, so evil.

"Rinen ... can I ask you something?"

The cold apprentice showed his attention.

Mythrian continued, "What was that creature you summoned, in the tavern?"

Rinen understood Mythrian's curiosity. He told him:

"The Valun is a dog of evil from the deepest pit of Draigorn's lair. They attack from the shadows, silently, invisible to the naked eye. They take their prey by surprise. One bite from their fangs is enough to completely paralyse a fully grown man. They rarely miss an opportunity to kill and to feed ..."

Mythrian laid his hand on Rinen's shoulder, interrupting:

"But you're a good apprentice. It is not right for a boy like you to cast a creature of pure evil. I understand why you had to stand up to Ghabrian, but to bring out such evil – it's just plain wrong. You know our creed. We conjure only peace."

Rinen looked forlornly down towards the ground, watching raindrops sink into thick layers of mud. A few moments passed before he spoke.

His tone was bitter, sore. His voice was low:

"See, that's your problem, Mythrian. You always go by the rules. So what. So what if I cast a creature of evil soul. That foul mouthed grunt deserved it. Everybody always thinks they know me inside out. And now you're doing it, telling me what I've done wrong. You give me one good reason why I should listen to you. You know nothing about me."

"Then tell me what I should know."

Rinen tried to make himself more comfortable on his patch of uneven ground. Drenched from the heavy rain, he was irritated with everything, even with himself. As he recounted his story, he stared solemnly into the fields ahead.

"I was five. It was a bright, clear day. The trees were reaching the end of their season, dusty leaves covered the ground. My sister, Lyana, was helping my father clear the leaves from the village track, I joined in. Everything was fine and normal, until, out of nowhere …"

"What was it? Tell me."

"I saw a figure … something running down the road, towards us. I couldn't work out what it was. It wasn't human in shape and I'd never seen an animal like it."

"A Valun?"

Rinen only nodded. It was clear that the memory disturbed him intensely. Rising to his feet, he paraded in front of Mythrian, stamping his feet into the thick mud.

"I grabbed Lyana, pulled her back. We managed to get to the other side of the gate and I managed to lock it."

Mythrian asked: "What about your father?"

"He didn't stand a chance. He tried to fight it. But my father was no fighter."

"I see."

"He was dead within an instant. It only took one bite. The Valun looked at us, through the bars of the garden gate. With its fixed, bloodshot eyes, it looked deep into ours. I'll never forget … the way it made me feel."

"You got away?"

"The Valun turned and headed for the woods. I wanted to rush out to my father, to hold him. But I couldn't. My sister and I, we were rooted to the spot. Transfixed with fear. We thought the Valun might return to take us."

"Where was your mother in this?"

"Divorced. Left not long after we were born. Lyana and I …

from then on, we were on our own. But we were just children."

"Well, how did you escape? Did somebody find and rescue you?"

"No. Bravely, I went into the house and took the bow my father and I had made together. I stepped out into the open, locking the gate behind me. There I stood, waiting for the beast to return. I didn't have to wait long. As I caught its dark void shifting through the trees, it suddenly rushed towards me at full speed. Closing in on its prey. But I didn't flinch. The beast fell down before me, my arrow in its chest."

Rinen paused. The event was still very clear to him. He continued:

"After that I sent a letter to the nearby Guild of Hamlynstone. They agreed to take me on. On that same day another young boy joined – Salen. We quickly became best friends."

The rain fell. It was cold, steady, unrelenting.

"What happened to your sister?"

Rinen was crying. Tears fell steadily from his eyes. "She disappeared. I don't know what village they took her to. They never said."

"You miss her." Mythrian said this quietly, looking away, far into the distance. It was a statement, not a question. Rinen didn't respond.

Rinen was mentally, a very strong individual. He'd stood up to Ghabrian, he'd even slain a Valun. He gave way to no one and learned to master his emotions. It was the kind of strength that Mythrian needed for tomorrow's tournament.

The night seemed never-ending. The rain continued to bombard the two apprentices.

"Wake up!" a strong voice bellowed.

It was a guard. He towered above Mythrian. "Come on, get up. We're all waiting for you."

Mythrian lifted himself off the hard ground. He stretched as he made his way over to the main gate. Rinen was there already. He looked glum.

Mythrian didn't say anything, he just smiled at him. Rinen, still embarrassed about the night before, was somehow grateful for his silence.

They had to walk to the village to board the wagons.

Salen appeared alongside them. He had brought Rinen's belongings. Rinen took them without meeting Salen's eyes. He merely looked down at the ground at his feet.

"Lighten up, boys," Salen said. "This is our big day."

Salen had never seen Rinen so depressed. He'd been in deeper trouble the year before, punished by the Guild Masters for his wayward behaviour. Even then, he hadn't looked as low as this. But today represented a huge opportunity and Salen was determined not to let Rinen waste his chance.

"What happened in the tavern is history," Salen told him. "But we've been planning for this day for years. This is the tournament!"

Rinen didn't respond. He just fixed his eyes ahead, looking into the distance. Salen grabbed him firmly by the shoulders, stared deep into his eyes.

"Brother, I need you to be sound today. Sound and solid. I need you to be strong."

"Brother." Something stirred inside Rinen when Salen said the word. He smiled back at his friend, nodding slowly.

Ghabrian appeared, surrounded by guards. He'd been ordered to leave the village, they were escorting him out. He looked crestfallen.

Stopping in front of Rinen, Ghabrian leaned up to him.

"Enjoy your moments of happiness, Rinen, because they won't last long."

Brushing Rinen's shoulder as he passed, by a fateful coincidence a little further ahead, he walked straight into Mythrian. The two glared at each other, and then the guards pushed Ghabrian on. He quickly passed.

Worried about his friend's depressed state, not wanting it to get in the way of their tournament, Salen asked the guard:

"Do you have a spare wagon? I would like to talk to Rinen. Alone."

"Certainly sir. We'll load it on to the back," the guard replied.

Turning to face Mythrian, Salen said, "See you soon, Mythrian. We might catch you at Avalin. If not, good luck."

As the two apprentices walked to their awaiting carriage, a guard took Mythrian to his.

✝ ✝ ✝

Bodel was inside his carriage, making his bed, when Mythrian appeared in the doorway.

Bodel was an interesting character. He had long hair; it fell down over his shoulders, jet-black, like Rinen's. He had very thick eyebrows that loomed over dark brown eyes, which were enigmatic. He had a well trimmed, black goatee beard and spoke softly with a traditional, northern accent. At times, in competition with the other apprentices, he seemed shy; he appeared to struggle but he was nonetheless a bright young pupil and was enthusiastic about the tournament.

He lowered himself on to the bed, and took off his tattered boots. Mythrian sighed heavily, relieved the long night was over.

"That bad?"

Sitting down opposite the boy, Bodel continued:

"I heard about the incident in the tavern. You did the right thing. Here ..." he grabbed a sweet from his collection of items and handed it to Mythrian. "Have a sweet. You deserve it."

"Thanks," Mythrian gratefully replied, before he hastily tucked into the sweet.

Yawning heavily, Bodel said, "Well, I better get some rest, I guess. See you in a few hours, Mythrian."

"Alright."

Through the tiny window in the side of the wagon, he watched the seventh sun rising. It was luminous, a perfect circle underneath a veil of orange cloud. His day had finally come.

Lying flat on the bed, Mythrian began to dream away as the wagons were ordered out of the village of Helianthe and on to Avalin, the final point in their journey.

As the wagons made their way back through the orchard, the very brisk wind was picking up the scent from the apples and was sending it through all the wagons, giving the apprentices one final taste of Helianthe.

Exiting the orchard, they turned right and followed the road which took them around the village walls, before flowing into a straight road on the way to Avalin.

Like the Lochrian plain, Pacian's Roam was open and well-grazed, holding lots of prosperous crops and cattle-grazed grassland.

The seventh sun did little to bring the surrounding to its true beauty, weaving in and out of the darkening clouds, but it still captivated the apprentices on their journey.

Nearing within two miles of the village of Avalin, the roads started to become very bumpy. The road was littered with pot-holes and cracks and nothing had been done to help the cause.

"What is going on," screamed Bodel, angry and shocked by his rude awakening.

"It seems the path has been left in poor management," answered Mythrian, who was sitting with his legs crossed on the bed, face up against the window, eyes staring at the precarious road.

"Well I can't sleep through this," Bodel uttered, placing his hands across his face, shaking his head in frustration. "I was having the nicest of dreams as well."

"What, about reigning victoriously at the tournament?" joked Mythrian, giggling at his friend.

"Yeah, it was actually. Whoa ..." Bodel answered before nearly being thrown off his bed, as the wheel of their wagon fell into a deep pot-hole. "This really isn't safe, is it?"

"Just try to hang on to something. Anything. We must be getting close to the village by now."

Shortly after his word, the road began to calm down and as it sloped down the hill, straight ahead of them were the brightly coloured tents of the village of Avalin.

CHAPTER 11 ✝ THE TIME IS NOW

T HE VILLAGE HAD no defensive wall or ramparts. The caravan stopped in a field on the outskirts, behind ranks of other wagons bringing hundreds of apprentices from afar. The sight of so many vehicles, massed there, silenced the group of young boys.

Their wagon was marshalled to its designated parking bay. A guard appeared. He threw open the doors and called the boys down.

The town speaker approached, "Welcome to the village of Avalin, home to the tournament of apprentices."

He had a chubby, round face. His clothes dropped over his belly like a mushroom. It was hard not to laugh at his pomposity.

"Now listen carefully, what I say, I say once only and no repetitions. Afore you all go in to the village, you will be given a number. This number will be determining what field and where you will be performing in this here contest. There will be maps and such inside the village and helpful guards on hand, so on no account, don't worry your little heads about nothing. The first contests are in order and will start at exactly three hours past midday, ok?"

Everyone nodded.

"A speaker will go round calling which contests are 'bout to begin ten minutes afore their start time. That's ten minutes …"

He held up both hands, spread his fingers.

"So once you hear your contest number called out, you're to make your way – quickly mind, and with no diversions – over to your assigned place of combat. Your competition will be watched over by one of our chief scouts, who will be in charge of scoring and determining how well you have performed. I wish you the very best and good luck. Right, now let's begin."

Mythrian's number was called within the first minute.

"Contestants assigned to field thirty-two are Renard ... Cyra ... Gorvain ... and finally ... Mythrian. Those that I have read out may go through into the village. Good luck."

Mythrian quickly looked behind him to see if he could see Rinen or Salen, but there were too many heads blocking his view.

Just as he had been directed, the young apprentice made his way past the village entrance and followed the dusty path up to where the tents were stationed.

The wind was picking up strongly. There were rows and rows of tents, seemingly never-ending, radiating from the centre. Some stored apparatus or equipment used for the various contests, others were shops selling combat suits, weapons, books and crystals for spells.

There were also tents for the repair of apparel; taverns; even a whole row of tattooists.

The seventh sun shone brightly. The flags flying from the roofs of the tents whipped and flapped in the strong wind.

Mythrian found himself in front of a large clock, standing on a beautifully sculptured white stone pillar, at least twenty feet high. Apprentices sat on benches around the four sides of the pillar, waiting to be called to compete. They were nervous, excited and loud.

There was a lot of activity in every corner of the village, yet there was a calm, relaxing atmosphere around the open area and it swiftly captured the young boy.

Examining several of the tents, Mythrian peered inside, gazing intently at the goods. In one he found racks of smart, colourful suits and he decided to spend some money. The clothes were all tailored to perfection and Mythrian began to try them on, admiring himself in giant mirrors. But the prices were outlandish.

The merchant tailor peeped out at him from behind a rack of cloaks.

His face was lined and wrinkled. His back was hunched and he shuffled as much as walked. He wore a smart green shirt and baggy emerald trousers, covered by a white tailor's apron. Coins bulged in his pockets.

"Lookin' for a suit are you, young man?"

Mythrian nodded. Straightaway, he felt the tailor's clammy hand on his shoulder, drawing him towards a rack of newly pressed waistcoats and breeches.

"Best quality in all of Avalin, you'll find here, young sir."

The hunched tailor quickly flicked through the rack, pulling out a neat set of clothes in exactly Mythrian's size.

Maroon in colour with scarlet red trimmings, the suit was made from a tough linen fabric. When he tried it on, it felt comfortable and snug.

Mythrian knew that he did not have enough money to buy a suit like this.

"The thing is …" the boy explained to the tailor, "this is all I have."

He scratched his hairless head, his eyes darting around the racks of clothes arranged haphazardly in the tent. Rubbing his beard, he said:

"Thirty gold pieces! Well, I'm not sure we have any outfits that low in price … unless…"

As his eyes pondered around the shop, looking for a clue to help him, he suddenly snapped his fingers in the air, as the idea clicked in his head.

"Of course, I may just have the thing for you!"

Mythrian watched the tailor scuttle across the floor and take the lid off a bin that was rammed with rather tatty clothes. The young boy felt rather offended, but chose to allow the tailor to continue.

"Oh, yes – silly me, why didn't I think of it before?"

From a bin, which he dragged from a corner of the tent, he pulled suit after suit, dropping jackets, trousers and gloves on to the floor with little care or attention. The bin was mostly filled with odds and ends in a muddy brown and mossy green.

But at the very bottom, he came across a dark blue suit, with light blue trimmings. He pulled it out with a flourish.

"Ah, here it is. I knew I would find a purchaser for this one day!"

Holding the suit up by its shoulders, the garment unravelled itself in front of the young apprentice.

"Eighty pieces of gold. Certainly! There!" The tailor beamed at the boy, shuffling towards him. "What does my young man think of that?"

The shirt had short sleeves, but was fashioned in a lush blue fabric. The colouring exactly matched Mythrian's tattooed markings. He had never seen anything like it before. There were matching leggings. Underneath the shirt was chain mail, strong enough to be protective, but not heavy so as to impede sudden movement. The mail continued around the top half of the legs and ran down the arms, ending at Mythrian's wrists. Brown and black leather belts, like straps, cut across waist and chest. The overall effect was awe-inspiring.

The tailor shuffled up behind Mythrian, who was admiring himself in the mirror. "Handsome, that is. Go on," he said, "tell me that you like it?"

The boy, mesmerised by the suit, answered, "It's beautiful."

Getting rather enthralled by his finding, the shop owner beamed, "Yes, it's brilliant isn't it? Goes rather well with your tattoo's. Where did you get that done anyway?"

The boy quietly laughed to himself; amused by the tailor's question, who could not have imagined that he had been born with the markings, he decided to play on with the theme.

"Oh ... I got it done a while back. Can't remember fully when and where I got it from. But the tattooist was a good friend of mine."

"Huh, he must have been some artist," the tailor proclaimed, mystified by its original and daring design.

"Yeah," the boy followed, hoping to finish on the subject before the conversation started to get a bit deeper and moved back on to the suit.

"Thank you for the suit, I'll take it," he said.

"Wonderful! Ajia be praised! We'll call that thirty gold pieces then."

Buying some matching ocean-blue coloured boots, Mythrian left the shop in his new suit, extremely enthralled with his purchase.

Looking up at the marble clock outside, to his disappointment it was only two hours past midday. He still had at least another half hour to kill before he needed to make his way to the contest.

The young boy studied the area, hoping to see if either Rinen or Salen were close by, or perhaps anyone else he might be able to recognise. But he didn't recognise anybody.

It was an odd feeling for Mythrian. He had never been in a situation where everybody around him was a complete stranger. It made him feel uneasy and lonely. He felt very small with a large crowd around him.

Using his sharp, far-seeing eyes, the boy studied each shop from a distance, trying to find somewhere where he might be able to relax and calm his nerves while he waited until his contest began.

He nearly gave up hope until, by the entrance where he had walked in, there was a refreshment tent which looked reasonably empty.

The young boy quickly scampered over to the tent and once inside, looked for any free table.

Sitting down by the entrance, Mythrian was at first a bit twitchy and jittery. But as he became more at ease with his surroundings, sinking back into the chair, he slowly began to unwind from the unwanted tension that was building up inside him.

One of the barmaids, watching him from afar, walked over to his table and poured a cold, non-alcoholic drink from a jug into a pint-sized mug and placed it before the boy.

"There you go, young sir," she kindly offered, staring softly at the boy, waiting for a pleasant reply.

"Thanks," the boy replied, picking up the mug with his long, slender fingers and was about to take a mouth-watering slurp when ...

BANG! Came a noise from close by.

Shocked by the thundering boom, the boy, who lurched tensely on the edge of his seat, looked for a sign around the refreshments tent. His head was flickering from left to right faster than he could blink, as he tried to distinguish where that hurtling sound had come from.

It sounded like an earthquake, like a giant stamping his feet harshly down on the terrain below. But as he looked around at the expressions on every nearby face, to his shock, nobody else had paid any attention to it.

All around the refreshment tent people were sipping their drinks and chatting in wild and lively conversations. The apprentices outside were still walking in and out of every shop they passed, buying anything catching their gullible eyes.

Turning his head back to his drink in front of him, he looked up at the barmaid, who stared profoundly at the boy, totally confused as to why he was in such a jittery state.

"Are you alright there?" the young lady asked, placing the palms of her hands on the table and leaning over to listen to the boy's problem.

"What was that?"

"What was what?" the barmaid replied, lost in the boy's confusing conversation.

"What was that sound? That loud sound, a few seconds ago? It sounded like an earthquake or something," the boy muttered, staring at the barmaid, whose baffled look wasn't particularly helping his confidence level.

"What? Oh ..." she began to realise what it was the boy may have heard. "They've started the siege weapon contest in field fourteen. That noise you heard might have been coming from there.

"Blimey," she joked, "you must have good ears. I didn't hear a thing," before she began to lightly shake from the giggling that overcame her.

"Oh ... right," Mythrian breathed a sigh of relief, while he still sat on the edge of his seat.

His eyes were still flickering from side to side, suspiciously watching everyone who passed by.

As he slowly raised the mug to his mouth again, he just managed to take a gulp before another loud bang made him jump forward, almost spilling the drink on to his brand new clothes.

As the barmaid walked away to tend to others, Mythrian slowly began to hunch over the table, hiding himself from the curious onlookers inside the tent.

It was difficult for someone with such a striking appearance as Mythrian to remain quiet and tucked out of the way. While the strangers looking at him were not trying to make the boy uneasy in any way, it made the apprentice feel very nervous.

He watched the clock tick forward, waiting for the remaining half hour to disappear. Nevertheless, when his turn was called, he was excited and scared, all at the same time. A voice called out:

"Apprentices for contests in fields thirty-two and forty-five, YOUR TIME IS NOW! Please make your way now to your assigned competition!"

Mythrian jumped from his seat so quickly that it nearly fell over.

Chapter 12 † Let the Contest Begin

JUST LIKE MYTHRIAN, the apprentices on the path down to field thirty-two were shaking with nervous energy. After a short distance they came to a gate which opened and released them into a lush, well-cut field, a vast expanse of grass; green from corner to corner.

They pulled straws from the outstretched hand of the gatekeeper to determine who was to go first. Mythrian, mortified, drew the shortest straw. He would have to wait his turn.

Ahead of him, there was a rope, held up on posts running the entire breadth of the field. The nine apprentices were directed to their given positions, an equal distance apart from each other along the length of the rope line.

There were no spectators, for this contest was dangerous. To lose control over a casted creature, in a crowd, was unthinkable. The results could be devastating.

The apprentices waited patiently along the rope line. But soon their wait was over, as suddenly, from the right, a tall man on horseback sprang out of a gate. His horse's coat was chequered in red and blue, while he bore heavy, yet neatly fitted, armour. A gallant and noble man.

The scout approached his apprentices, inspecting each of them closely, greeting them one by one as he trotted his way down the line.

Having greeted them personally, he returned to his post from where he was to watch his competitors. It seemed he was just as anxious to begin as the competitors.

All the apprentices were in awe of the scout. He stood motionless on the plain, with pride flaring from his high stature.

His armour glared crystal white in the sun, which had peaked at its highest in the sky, making him appear like a bright spirit.

Ready to begin, he spoke, loud and clear:

"Welcome, young apprentices from across the kingdom of Aedorn. My name is Rocloar; I am to be your judge. You are here today to compete in the contest for the Art of Summoning. You may summon anything of your choice, but you must also demonstrate control. The winner of the contest will gain the title of Summoner to their name and will forever bear that title, to be remembered for their victory here in Avalin."

While he looked down on to the apprentices, he spoke in a calm, almost delicate voice, not in the least overpowering. The apprentices all found it easy to communicate with him and gently calmed down any unwanted nerves.

"But I'm sure you're all eager to begin and so we will. Lynne, bring out the crystals for our first competitor," he ordered.

A young girl in a yellow robe appeared. This was Lynne. She had a tray of nine magnificent coloured crystals. Judge Rocloar looked down on the apprentices, speaking calmly and openly. Reading from a scroll, he announced the name of the first contestant:

"Gorvain. You must select your crystal and be first to cast. Good luck."

Gorvain was an apprentice from Mythrian's Guild; dark hair, dark eyes and a very quiet, hidden personality. Gorvain was not somebody who communicated a lot with other students. Some said his ignorance didn't pass particularly well with Master Brennius either. He was not a hugely gifted student, but was very capable at many things.

Without hesitation, he chose the orange crystal. He steadied himself as the girl with the tray moved quickly out of the way.

When he was ready, the apprentice threw the crystal high into the air. As it dispersed, a Firebird screamed out of the dust circling in its inferno. A sudden whirlwind of fire erupted from its tail, flaring in its slipstream. As it casually drifted its way around the grounds, it blew balls of fire that filled the skies, hanging like suns over the onlookers.

Waving his arms frantically, Gorvain made the bird perform the most incredible aerobatic tricks, twists, turns, loops. It was a spectacle that was at the same time beautiful and perplexing.

The sheer speed of the bird was mesmerising as it climbed high into the air and then shot down to the ground in the blink of an eye, before turning and darting back into the air, just as the tips of its feathers had brushed the earth.

Despite its uncontrollable excitement and energy, the bird appeared to be well tamed and copied every instruction Gorvain commanded. So far, Rocloar was impressed.

As the bird continued to circle, almost tangling up with its high number of twists and bends, it suddenly, almost without warning, began to separate.

The apprentices looked on stunned as another Firebird appeared out of the fiery blur of the spinning bird. It was beyond belief.

While the first Firebird continued to spin and loop around, the other bird twisted and turned around its partner, igniting a ring of flames, a tunnel through which both birds could fly, faster than imagination itself.

Under Gorvain's orders, the two birds came to rest, hovering in the air, facing each other. Through flared nostrils they began to blow fireballs, each in turn trying to outdo the other.

They huffed. And they puffed. Every ounce of their energy was put into their balls of shooting fire.

But the Firebirds lost concentration. Suddenly, they both decided to ignore Gorvain's commands and began chasing each other around the field, playing tag, creating a chaotic tangle of fires. The young apprentice began desperately calling the birds back and looking over to Rocloar for help.

Gorvain's face was swelling deep red with embarrassment. Even in magic, a casted creature can have a mind of its own and these Firebirds were having too much fun to be given orders.

"Try to pull them back, Gorvain," Rocloar said, with a tone of urgency. "I'll give you another minute to do so. I can't give you any longer than that."

Seconds later, to everyone's relief, the Firebirds grew tired of their games and hurried back to their caster.

Gorvain tried to round off the performance with a couple more twists and turns but the magic had gone.

Clapping his hands, the birds turned to ashes. These slowly drifted to the ground, before disappearing with the wind.

"Well done, Gorvain. That was a very good performance. It's never easy going first, but I think that performance has set a very high standard. I'm very impressed. A round of applause for Gorvain everyone."

As the apprentices gave sporting applause for the boy, Gorvain knew that the slip-up with the Firebirds' unhelpful games may have cost him his chance of winning.

But nevertheless, he still felt proud to have put on such a great show at the tournament, which he would be sure to remember for the rest of his life.

"Well competitors," Rocloar continued, "Looks like you have a high standard to beat. Can any of you do better? What about our next competitor, Renard? Step forward and show us what you can do."

Renard was next. Like Gorvain and Mythrian, Renard was a student at the Guild of apprentices in Hamlynstone. The tallest of the nine, Renard had an innate sense of arrogance and boastfulness. Round headed, with shaven, blond hair he had a tough, hardened look and a no-nonsense character.

Picking the purple crystal from Lynne's tray, Renard began to play with the item in his hands, throwing it from one to the other. He conjured his cast creature in his mind, readied himself, and rubbed his fingers across the rough surface before unleashing it into the distance.

His crystal smashed into a thousand purple pieces and out of the dust, out of the violent air, sprang one of the many forms of a Halfling – This creature was half human, half horse.

The Halfling pranced and stamped around the grounds, bearing a bow and arrow in an attacking stance, before slowing to a composed, slow trot. It looked towards its Master, patiently waiting for its orders.

The sight of the Halfling was truly impressive, although in reality, Halflings are not treated equally to humans. In fact they are considered mutations and are forbidden to walk among humans. There are those who disagree; however, it is kingdom orders that you do not mingle with Halflings.

However realistic this one looked, he was not a real Halfling and the apprentices thought nothing bad about his appearance. In fact they were all mesmerised by his appearance.

Renard began casting an array of targets around the eager creature, setting the stage for his show. For his part, the Halfling looked around the field, memorising each target's position and distance. Then the targets sank into the ground, disappearing.

Renard cast more obstacles to test the Halfling; high hedges and hidden spring traps injected added danger to the display. What followed was going to be quite a performance.

Quickly assessing the field, the Halfling looked towards his Master. Renard gave the signal as several of the targets popped back up from underneath the ground and the Halfling began its test.

Clearing a hedgerow, it shot an arrow through the heart of a target. The sound of fast, sharp arrowheads hitting their targets at speed pleased both Renard and the spectators. The Halfling galloped at full pace, cutting and jumping through the traps.

Then two more traps rose up before the beast. But the Halfling was too good; it cleared them easily, before shooting another couple of arrows sideways on towards the centre of their target.

The Halfling looked incredibly confident. His eyes showed complete concentration.

Renard decided to up the stakes.

Slowing its rhythm, the Halfling creature noticed that all the targets were now moving. This required greater, subtler skill. Quickly and cleverly working out a new approach, the beast began its second wave of attack.

The Halfling found every target precisely, neither halting nor slowing down its speed of attack.

With moving targets falling easily to the Halfling's capabilities, Renard waited until the Halfling was to fire another arrow at its chosen target. Then, just as the creature released another arrow, the caster caused the board to shoot back into the ground, missing the oncoming arrow completely.

Renard sank the moving targets below the surface of the field in one quick movement. But this didn't stop the Halfling from continuing its task.

The Halfling began firing directly into the ground, across the field, and as he did so, the targets popped up, with all arrows in their bull's-eyes. The sight of this, repeated again and again in sequence all over the field of contest, was magical, truly breathtaking.

The pair continued to try to catch each other out, but the Halfling was winning the battle. The performance was going well and the casted creature looked faultless.

Or so he would have been, but Renard was getting far too over-confident with his show and was continuing to make it even harder for the Halfling.

It was only a matter of time before it would become too difficult for the casted creature.

As the creature dodged several spring traps, managing to hit a target in the process, it only narrowly missed a high spring trap, ducking under the apparatus which was aimed high around the neck height.

Looking back at what was a close call from a nasty exit, the Halfling failed to spot the other spring trap embedded on the floor in front of it.

It flipped up and caught the beast; the impact was hard, the iron trap; sharp and unyielding.

Renard held his head in his hands. His cast creature lay stricken on the ground, unmoving. He knew he had taken his performance too far. His arrogance had cost him dearly.

But Rocloar tried to emphasise that he would still fare well in the competition, despite the costly mistake.

"That was a great attempt, Renard. Perhaps you just took it a little too far. Nevertheless, I was very pleased with that. You followed Gorvain's performance very well. I'm very impressed."

Acknowledging the scout's support, Renard cast his injured creature away, freeing it of its pain, before looking mournfully at the ground, the consensus being that he had possibly thrown his chance away.

However, his performance was to fare well compared to the next few competitors.

Gorvain and Renard had both set a very high standard. The next five apprentices, all from the nearby village of Anthelstone, proved reasonable competition but lacked the intensity that their predecessors had shown in their performances.

One of the apprentices, Gladstone, lost his casted creature. It ran off despite his orders and had to be recaptured by village guards over two miles away. Rocloar laughed heartily at that.

It was clear that only Mythrian and the next contestant, Cyra, had a chance of beating the strongest competitors, Gorvain and Renard.

Lynne offered Cyra the choice of two crystals: light green, or rose. The young girl chose the latter, much to the relief of Mythrian, who was itching for his turn to begin. He really had drawn the short straw. The wait felt like an eternity.

Cyra released her crystal and, catching a sudden fierce gust of wind, it dispersed to release a beautiful, bright spirit, with golden wings and a soft face, beaming with elements of peace and calm.

The spirit hovered in front of the apprentices, its glow lighting up the grounds around.

Cyra signalled to the spirit to begin the show.

Lifting its arms up into the air, a bright cloud formed over the head of the spirit. The cloud grew in size and density, until it entirely covered the line of watching apprentices. Cyra began to command it.

As the apprentices and Rocloar watched, the shape of a tree appeared at the centre of the cloud. More trees sprang up around it, and as they grew into a dense forest, slowly the picture became clear to the apprentices.

Cyra had conjured the Enchantment itself. Rocloar was intrigued.

As the trees of the Enchantment disappeared, the cloud flattened to form the shape of green pastures and fields.

Two figures suddenly appeared, holding hands as they walked across the fields. Then, to the right in the cloud, a child came running towards them. The group embraced in a hug.

The figures changed. Suddenly, they were a large group of men, drinking and singing to the sounds of joy and prosperity. Then came a team of blacksmiths and other tradesmen, with their heads down, busy with their work.

Cyra's conjured images portrayed the happiness that the People of Ajia shared, during the first years of their kingdom.

But then came the rise of evil from the East, the giant smoking volcano of Siren's Gore and out of the ground around it, evil creatures wielding torches and swords. They screamed messages of hate into the air, running like wild dogs around the barren lands.

Next came an inferno, the exodus of people fleeing their land as their houses burned. This was cleverly done by the spirit, who created different shades of grey and black to emphasise the fire.

The spirit then showed Aedorn fighting Draigorn on the Mountains of Morbian. Draigorn's victory cry echoed around the grounds, his image burned triumphantly in the clouds.

Ajia appeared. Cyra's cast spirit created a bright light, which looked like a sun, rising through the clouds, as it hovered behind Draigorn's image. The light was so bright that the apprentices had to shield their eyes.

As Ajia killed the beast, the light from the God ripped through Draigorn's image, driving the vision away. The image of the tablet containing the God's powers rose up into the air, as if suspended.

As Mythrian watched this image appear, his mind recollected the item that he had received from Gwyn.

"That tablet. I have seen it before!"

He began to remember shades of what had happened, the night when he had held treasure in his hand. Holding out his hands, he gazed at his markings. They were illuminating and he could feel a strong force building up inside him.

"Could it be the same one?" Mythrian thought to himself.

His thoughts were soon answered, as thin strings of light travelled across the image of the tablet, like vines around a tree. It was the same tablet.

Mythrian was speechless and confused. There was no way of denying it. The tablet he had held … was the same tablet handed down by Ajia after his exile.

But what about the powers within?

Did he really hold the powers of Ajia within him?

What had truly happened to him that night when he had held the tablet?

There was only one way to find out ...

Ending her spell, the spirit casted by Cyra closed the cloud, before disappearing in a nova of silver light.

Rocloar applauded with great enthusiasm.

"Brilliant, Cyra! Well done! Not only was it very original, but it was very creative and you made good use of your imagination. I was very impressed with that."

There was resounding applause. Though her idea wasn't physically challenging like the Firebird or the Halfling, the level of skills displayed and control was unsurpassed.

Rocloar was delighted with Cyra's performance. Like the apprentices, he had enjoyed the spectacle displayed by his kingdom's finest. But there was now only one more apprentice to go.

He looked beyond Cyra, and saw Mythrian. The boy was staring at the moving spiral markings on the palms of his hands, still deep in thought.

"Mythrian my boy," the scout called from afar, "… it's your turn!"

CHAPTER 13 ✟ A BEAST FROM THE MIND OF A BOY

"THIS IS IT," Mythrian thought to himself, "This is the moment I have been waiting for all my life. Time to prove to everyone that I truly have a gift."

Lynne approached Mythrian and offered him the last crystal. She smiled nervously as he took it from the tray and gripped it tightly in his hand.

In his mind's eye, he conjured the image. Not even the strong wind stroking his skin was noticeable to him as he focused hard on the crystal.

His heart, his mind, his soul awoke with a new vision. With his eyes squeezed tight shut, he sent fragments of pictures into the crystal.

Drawing his arm back, he took a step forward and was about to cast his vision. But he stopped.

Underneath his foot, he noticed a small rock. It was tiny, thin, not even the thickness of his palm. His knowledge of rocks and minerals was not resourceful, but there was something about its shape and image that lured him.

He stepped back and took a closer look at it.

When he touched it, Mythrian felt an energy transferring through the stone into his marked skin. It felt like something was trying to call him.

Something from within the stone.

The crowd around were impatient with the delay. Mythrian saw Rocloar's puzzled face hurrying him from afar.

Tucking the crystal into his trouser pocket, Mythrian gripped the new-found stone tightly in his hand. He closed his eyes, searching for secret energy.

"If the power of Ajia flows through my veins, then let its power be shone through this stone."

The power released into his veins. It flowed. Mythrian knew the time had finally come. He held the rock close to his face and suddenly he heard a timid voice, coming from within. At first it was just a whisper, but it became louder. It emanated from the rock itself, calling out to the young conjurer:

"Release me," the rock said, "and what you wish for, you will see."

Mythrian paused, flexed back, tightened his grip for a second, and released the stone.

The stone flew. Mythrian cast it long, high and straight. It landed a hundred yards from the crowd, with an unnatural thump, uncanny for something of its size.

Nothing happened. There was a long silence, a collective intake of breath, and then a murmuring of discontent. They couldn't understand whether it was a joke or whether he was trying to be serious with his performance. Magic won't change a rock's appearance or structure.

Yet, as they looked over towards Mythrian, he remained focused on the rock. Confident that any minute something was going to pop out of its structure. Stun them all when they were going to least suspect it.

It remained highly unlikely. A few of the apprentices began gesturing towards Rocloar, persuading him to stand in and stop this foolishness.

But just as Rocloar was about to stop Mythrian, they paused to hold their breath.

A sudden tremor shook the ground beneath the gathering. A pulse, quickening, growing louder. All the apprentices looked to their feet, in confusion, in horror, in fear.

The pace quickened and now everyone in the field was observant of the rock. They watched it from afar. Waiting for a sign.

"Look, the rock, it's moving!" an apprentice shouted out above the noise.

He pointed, open mouthed, to Mythrian's cast stone. Flickering from side to side, the rock was only narrowly jumping off the floor.

But it was making substantial progress.

Watching with great intensity, they jumped back as the small rock suddenly cracked in two.

It echoed like the sound of a boulder crumbling away from its cliff.

As the rock continued to split, it began to jump and twist, as if it was a cage being shaken by the beast within, trying to escape.

To their disbelief the rock suddenly started to grow.

It was rising, from the earth, up, up, up into the air.

By now, the rock, once barely the size of the young apprentice's palm, was now taller than Rocloar on horseback. It was of a monstrous proportion.

More than capable of holding something of great size within it.

Mythrian moved forward, calling out to the rock, commanding:

"Show yourself!" His voice was harsh, impatient.

An invisible hand drew a line across the stone with an ear-splitting crack. As it did so, it began to jump and twist, as if it were being vigorously shaken.

Suddenly, they noticed something within the rock. Something was trying to break out of its shell.

The rock grew massively in size before the eyes of the stunned apprentices, so much so that it was suddenly as big as a two-storey cottage, and with this thing, this struggling shape, trying to break out of it.

Everyone halted. A face emerged from the stone, pushing itself outwards. Its face looked almost human and was nearly the same size as the giant rock itself as it began to move. The head twitched from side to side, and eyes began to form.

Eyes: open.

The apprentices screamed. Hearts, all around the stand, skipped beats. This enormous creature was a vision from a dream or a nightmare.

The beast made of stone slowly forced its mouth open, groaning loudly.

"Show us your true form!"

Mythrian's voice boomed around the tournament field. Straight away, the beast from the rock began to wriggle and squirm. A set of long, broad fingers appeared around the circumference of its head.

The beast grabbed the edge of the giant rock and with one enormous push it began to release itself, rising higher in the air with the effort.

Arms stretched out of its shell, a hand placed itself on the ground and the living thing pushed itself up into the sky. A broad chest broke through and expanded. Air was taken in.

The beast was now standing higher than any feature in the village and yet it had still to rise on its legs.

Everything suddenly became clear. Mythrian had cast a Giant Rock Troll.

A Troll is a creature born of the Earth, from rock, sediment or foliage. This one, though emerging from stone, had assumed a human shape. It reached up to the sky, its massive spindle legs raising high, towards the clouds above.

Higher and higher it rose; there was seemingly no end to its growth.

The cast creature from the stone was finally free. At first the creature was unclear and unsure of its surroundings. But as its senses developed, its movements and emotions grew stronger.

It cried out in one continuous, agonising roar, heard for miles around.

Everybody present was deafened by the sound. Rocloar's horse reared on its hind legs, throwing its rider from the saddle. Hauling himself up from the dust, Rocloar cried out:

"Ajia, what is this miracle that stands before me!"

And the display that followed was, in truth, miraculous. Mythrian ordered the giant creature to copy everything he did. Lifting each limb up and down, the Troll copied each move exactly in its giant dimensions, so that the earth shook as it placed its weight down.

Being made of stone, the Troll was a little too stiff to perform some of the nimble routines performed by the apprentice. But it was still impressive.

In fact the Troll appeared very human in its movements, every posture following a similar shape to the boy.

The performance was a master class in the art of conjuring. Words could not describe the miracle they had witnessed.

However, Rocloar was worried. A creature of this magnitude could cause a great deal of panic. Some things, after all, are better said than seen.

"Mythrian," he shouted, "I've seen enough. Cast your creature away!"

Mythrian closed his eyes and returned to his heavy thoughts. As he did this, he ordered:

"Recall. Return from whence you came!"

Following his Master's orders, the Troll began to fold itself back into the rock from whence it came. Twisting and shrinking, the beast returned to its holding. Its features disappeared from view.

Within moments, it was no more. And as the boulder compacted itself down, it became a small rock again, lying softly, almost untouched on the ground.

Mythrian said nothing. His mind was filled with many questions, though one had been answered. His markings held more power than he could have ever dreamed. His wishes were coming true.

The audience stood still, stunned. They rubbed their eyes to check it wasn't a dream. They felt overshadowed by the presence of the Troll and the incredible gift Mythrian held.

An apprentice walked over to the rock, picked it up and held it tightly in his hand. For a moment, he thought he could feel the stone tremble to the touch, but then it was still and cold in his hand.

Gathering the apprentices, minus Mythrian, Rocloar congratulated them all on their hard efforts.

"First of all, thank you all for your participation. I've been extremely impressed with what I have seen from you here today. You should be very proud of yourselves. I'm sure you will have bright futures ahead of you. As a consolation for your fine efforts, if you walk over to Lynne by the gates, she will present you with a certificate for your exceptional efforts in our tournament. Once again, thank you and take care on your journeys."

As the apprentices walked over to the entrance, Rocloar gestured to Mythrian. "My young champion – follow me."

☨ ☨ ☨

After the crowd disappeared, a figure immersed in a dark, ragged cloak, crept quietly on to the tournament field.

It approached Mythrian's casted stone.

A long, bony hand, green tinged, wart-ridden, reached down and grasped it. The rock was put away hurriedly, inside a pocket in the cloak.

The creature quickly headed north-west, out towards the darkened wet woodland of Gwynan's Gorse, before anyone could catch sight of it.

CHAPTER 14 † THE SUMMONER
AND THE CROWN

ROCLOAR WALKED HASTILY towards the Mayor's house, deep in thought. He could not understand how the boy had been in a position to summon the Rock Troll.

Mythrian tried hard to keep up with him, and to avoid Rocloar's searching eyes as, from time to time, the older man turned to stare at him. He sensed that there was something special about this boy.

As the flags of the Mayor's house came into view, Rocloar muttered:

"I've been a scout in this village for seven years now, and in all that time, I have never witnessed anything of the magnitude and stature that you conjured back there."

He sounded irritated, perturbed. Rocloar stole another glance at Mythrian. He seemed uncertain, nervous of who and what he was dealing with.

He had never encountered someone with such a powerful, natural gift.

"Trolls are not even seen in this part of the world. And even they would be overshadowed by your Troll. How did you do it?" Again, his question was tinted with frustration, anxiety almost.

"I don't know," the boy replied. He was thinking of the tablet, of when he first held it, back at the Guild in Hamlynstone. "I just saw the rock by my foot and ..." Mythrian paused, choosing his next words carefully.

"Well ... it just happened. I never imagined the troll would grow so high and wide. I must have just got carried away with the moment."

91

Rocloar sensed the boy didn't want to be put on the spot. That perhaps he had simply underestimated his own ability.

Coming within the last few hundred metres, Mythrian was surprised when he found his head looking downwards towards the Mayor's household.

At first he thought of asking Rocloar, but thought he would figure out this peculiar sight for himself.

Usually, the Mayor's household sits above the village to state its authority. But here, the house sat below the settlement.

Perhaps it was trying to portray a different meaning. The most important people to the village are its guests, the young apprentices from across the kingdom. Maybe the fact that the Mayor's residence had been built below the settlement, was to emphasise the point that the students are the key to the village's power, not the Mayor or anybody else in charge.

"Here it is. The Mayor's house. May I remind you before we enter that you must be on your best behaviour? Modearn is not a very strong hearted man and he can feel intimidated very easily. Try not to ask him too many questions, allow him to post the topics."

The scout then continued in a quiet tone, "The poor man hasn't quite been the same since that incident in Emory Forest."

"What happened?"

Rocloar cut Mythrian short, raising a finger to his lips, silencing him.

"Never you mind."

Quite a large building, consisting of two storeys and painted white, the house was surrounded by flags and banners, just to keep the village theme running. There was a large garden to the front, with rows of plants forming the boundary.

Stepping through the front gate, there was a long walk down the pathway before they stepped up to the door.

Knocking several times on the door, they waited patiently before the door was opened by a servant. Before he could say a word, a man in his middle ages, lavishly dressed stepped up from behind.

"Hello Rocloar, good to see you. I see you have brought a

visitor."

Rocloar introduced his champion. "Greetings Mayor. May I present to you, Mythrian. He has won in the contest of summoners."

"Excellent, please come on in."

As they made there way inside, they followed the Mayor to his office.

Grabbing a couple of chairs, the three of them sat down next to the Mayor's front desk, which was overwhelmed by a large quantity of letters.

"Ah, yes. Our young victor. Many congratulations, Mythrian. I'm sure it will be only the beginning in a long and prosperous career for you." The Mayor looked closely at Mythrian, intrigued by the young apprentice and his profound appearance.

"Mythrian here is a very special apprentice, sire." Rocloar put his hand on the boy's shoulder. "Today, he performed a miracle. For no other word could describe what I and his fellow competitors saw. At first I was confused, because rather than using the customary crystals for his contest, he chose to use a small stone, barely the size of his hand. And then with his incredible gift, he transformed the small stone into a giant Troll."

"A giant Troll?" the Mayor returned, surprised.

"Yes sire, standing higher than any watchtower that keeps eye over our land."

The Mayor was impressed but unsure. What Rocloar was saying sounded more like the work of the Gods than of human hands. But he never liked to take away the spirit of the young and gifted.

Stroking his beard thoughtfully, Modearn congratulated the young boy.

"Wonderful. How very gratifying it is to see my tournament producing such heroes. You deserve your prize: the title of Summoner is yours, to carry with you wherever you go, so that all will honour you for your victory here at Avalin."

Behind the Mayor, was a series of boxes carrying scrolls. Leaning over his chair, the Mayor produced a scroll tied with a garland of eagle feathers. He handed it to Mythrian with a gentle smile. The boy studied his face. The Mayor's eyes were a bright sky-blue, his expression paternal, his admiration genuine and full.

Mythrian, shaking from the excitement, could not have expected to be greeted by such a warm and knowledgeable man.

But something was wrong. Something seemed to be out of place.

It took a moment for Mythrian to take it in.

"Your crown ..." the boy mumbled. "Your crown is gone ..."

The Mayor's face went white. There was a bleak silence. Rocloar quickly stepped in, grabbed the boy's arm, whispering too loudly:

"How dare you speak to the Mayor like that!"

But Modearn told Rocloar to ease off the boy. Scratching his curly mop of brown hair, he knew that unlike every Mayor in the kingdom, he was without his symbol of authority. His golden crown.

"It's alright, Rocloar. Be at peace with the child. He simply speaks as he sees – a rare quality in these unhappy days. To be honest with you both, I have no idea where my crown is. You see, the truth is, it is lost!"

The Mayor straightaway began to tell a curious tale of misfortune. Sitting back down on his chair, he continued:

"I was in Emory Forest examining the condition of the woods with a number of foresters. In recent years, sad to say, we have neglected the management of the woods. Well, I was just quietly wandering through the forest, when my crown was knocked straight off my head!"

"I'm sure it was nothing sinister, sire," Rocloar said. The Mayor merely shrugged his shoulders.

"It happened so quickly, I was ... I don't know, flustered. My men surrounded me, I was whisked into my carriage, the horses bolted and we were away. There was simply no time to figure out what had knocked my crown off. My people scanned the area later on, but in these times we live in and when evil still hides in the shadows of our land, I did not think it wise for them to stay there too long. I ordered an end to the search. A dark day for me. I don't think it will be long before the authorities find out."

"You left your crown in Emory Forest?" Mythrian asked.

"Yes," the Mayor replied. "But that place is vast and ... notorious for danger. The woods now are so dark and dense, who knows what might be hiding in them?"

Mythrian spoke boldly:

"I'll go."

Rocloar and the Mayor looked at each other in astonishment.

"That's too dangerous," Rocloar said.

"I'm sorry Mythrian; I wouldn't even let any of my royal guards go into those woods, let alone such a fine apprentice like yourself! No, no ..." the Mayor added, "... it's simply out of the question!"

"Please let me find your crown. I have a lot to prove of myself and I am relishing chances like this. I promise you I will watch every step I take and if I feel that the woods aren't safe for me alone, I will leave with haste."

Modearn smiled in the presence of the daring boy. This is something he would not assign to anybody, but he saw the ambition and eagerness in the boy's eyes.

"Alright Mythrian, I will let Rocloar take you down to the end of the woods. But take care. I do not want any injuries otherwise I am going to be in deeper trouble."

"Thank you, I won't let you down."

Just like that, Mythrian was out of the door, raring to go. Rocloar was about to follow him before he was pulled back by Modearn for a few words:

"Look after the boy. I don't want a casualty on my hands and neither do you. Stay by the outskirts and wait for Mythrian. Whatever you do, do not go into the woods. Understand?"

"Of course, my lord," Rocloar confirmed.

Chapter 15 ✝ The Silver Sword

EEP IN GWYNAN's Gorse, the cloaked creature was hiding. She was waiting for a messenger.

The forest was dark with shadow, the wind whistled eerily through the thin, spiny branches.

The messenger soon appeared, in the form of a bright light, its features impossible to make out. It was one of the elders from the Enchantment. But he was communicating with the witch through telekinesis, as he was not allowed to leave his home in the mystical forest.

Crouched down on the floor, the creature was gathering stones, setting them out in a small circle. At its centre she placed the rock from which Mythrian's Troll was created. It was then that the beam of light spoke:

"Did he cast the beast?"

"He did," the creature solemnly replied.

"Good work. You have completed your task."

"I did nothing," the creature muttered, looking down to the ground at her feet. "I merely oversaw him. He raised the Troll from the stone himself. I only placed the stone where you told me to. I performed no magic. It was entirely a spell of his own doing. The power flows through him strongly now ..."

"Elaborate?"

"When he noticed the stone, he connected with it. He sensed the power within it. He has a special fire, an energy, a spirit ..."

Silence. The Elder of light swerved slightly, inched closer to the creature:

"Tell me."

"His powers grow, alarmingly so. He is sensing new spirits daily. Within the trees, within the earth, within the elements. Somehow, he has utilised all that power … immeasurable force. This could be just the beginning."

"What will become of him?" The Elder of light grew suddenly intense, focused, sharp. It was as if it were irritated by what it heard.

"He will become a God!" the creature shouted.

"One of us. So this is Ajia's game, is it?" the spirit replied.

"Ajia never meant for this. He only placed his powers in the tablet so he could communicate with its chosen finder. However, this came with a heavy risk. The power was not to be utilised. Only to be held within its caster, until Ajia is freed and then he would retake his power to restore himself back to the Enchantment. The boy has connected with a force which has summoned the power. Soon he will become unstoppable."

"How could this have happened?" the spirit returned, frustrated.

"It must have taken something of great force, a strong natural power that could connect both the boy and the tablet." The creature paused before quietly hissing underneath her robe, "Lightning?"

"What was that?" the spirit asked.

"Nothing, just a thought."

The messenger of light snapped back, intense and scornful:

"I must see this power for myself. Re-cast the Troll from the stone. Let's see how confident he is of his own powers, when hundreds of lives are at stake around him."

The creature could not argue. She covered the stone with her hands, shielding it from the light above. Then, from underneath the palms of her hands came a bright emerald cloud of energy, engulfing the stone.

As the green light engulfed the stone circle, the creature commanded:

"The village of Avalin. Destroy it! Tear up the earth beneath it! Leave nothing."

The stone. It was awake again. It groaned with anger from within.

Rocloar and Mythrian had finally reached the outskirts of Emory Forest. It loomed ahead of them, full of dark foreboding. Mythrian, seemingly unperturbed, jumped off Rocloar's horse and was striding into the undergrowth when the scout called after him:

"Proceed with care, Mythrian. Keep your eyes peeled. Hide yourself when you see danger. Do not be foolish and try to confront it. Do you understand?"

Mythrian turned, and Rocloar saw him nod his head, slowly. A second later, he had disappeared from view.

Mythrian headed cautiously into the heart of the forest. The trees were so dense it was difficult even for him to make his way through. The ground was very uneven and soaked by water draining from the nearby lake so that he was constantly slipping and falling to his knees. On more than one occasion he had to cling to branches above to pull himself out of trouble.

"How on earth am I to find the crown under all this mud?" Mythrian thought to himself. Though his confidence was high, he knew that his chances were agonisingly low.

As he approached the heart of the wood, though he had lost his sense of direction, the ground became more firm. The undergrowth thinned. Fewer obstacles presented themselves.

The change in surroundings confused Mythrian, as he noticed the soil under his feet was made up from small rocks and rubble. It was curious. It looked unnatural somehow. As if someone had cleared it, and made the ground harder for a purpose.

Analysing the area around him, he realised he was climbing a slow gradient, and that this part of the wood must be on higher ground than the lower muddy parts. He was clear of the waterline; the land was drier, the way ahead more open.

Mythrian wondered, could this forest be concealing something?

One thing was certain. It would be far easier to find the crown in this drier region of land than in the boggy flats before.

He began to search the terrain, checking and double-checking every inch of the ground. He looked deep into trees and bushes, brushed branches aside, looking in and under and between giant leaves. He found nothing.

As the day was turning to late evening several clouds had begun drawing over the woods. Mythrian momentarily took shelter from the cold wind behind an enormous blackthorn tree. The thick, grey clouds now obscured the seventh sun from above and the forest grew darker. Shadows lengthened in the branches of trees, looming over the boy. They were like claws in the darkness, reaching out for their prey.

Mythrian was unsettled. He had just made up his mind to head back out of the woodland, when he overheard voices.

He froze, trying to work out where the noise had come from. It was close.

It was coming from the other side of the blackthorn tree.

He listened intently, trying to distinguish who or what it was on the other side.

Two voices, but not human. Their tones were too highly pitched and they appeared to be arguing over something.

Delicately, Mythrian moved the leaves in front of him aside.

He saw a figure in a small, open area, just a stone's throw from his place of concealment. Then he noticed the second creature to his side...

GOBLINS!

Mythrian, startled, fell backwards on to the earth. His hands lost hold of the branches. The blackthorn tree shook violently.

The noise sounded deafening to the boy. He covered his gasping mouth with his hands. He lay helpless on the floor, desperately trying not to make another sound.

His heart was in his mouth.

At any second, the grim faces of the goblins were going to appear over the rim of the bush. Their mouths would already be dripping, ready to feed on their prey.

He waited and waited but the faces never appeared. Curious and confused, Mythrian pulled himself back up.

He peered through the tree again. It seemed that the goblins had become distracted by something very precious.

They were quarrelling, poking and pointing at something Mythrian couldn't see. Whatever the item was, it had the two goblins bemused.

By now the Goblins did not seem so grim to the boy, he was more interested in knowing what it was the goblins were so intent on.

Reaching into his trouser pocket, Mythrian found the crystal that he had kept from his contest earlier in the day. It was exactly what he needed to scare the goblins away.

Casting a small light like a bright sun the size of his palm, he shot it into the air, over the heads of the goblins in the clearing. As the light trickled over their heads, fizzing and hissing as it evaporated in the air, the goblins looked up at the colourful spectacle, captivated. Their attention was entirely distracted from the object on the ground.

Suddenly, the light spontaneously exploded, startling the goblins.

The goblins sprinted out of the opening, screaming, their arms covering their heads.

Mythrian stepped into the clearing.

He was choked by the sight that he beheld.

There were rocks, forming a stone circle on the hardened ground. At its centre was an enormous, beautifully crafted silver sword.

He moved closer, and as he did so, the sword became luminous, lighting up in the clearing. The stones around it glowed like crystals. Light reflected from the sword's mighty blade.

Mythrian reached out and touched the handle of the sword with the tips of his fingers. He felt an almighty pull of energy drawing him close.

The blade of the sword was perfect, unblemished, yet warm to the touch as if it had not long been used.

He wrapped his hand tightly around the handle, and to his astonishment, was able to lift the sword with ease.

He held the blade perpendicular before his eyes. There were symbols carved in the steel there, words in an unfamiliar dialect.

Surely, it seemed to Mythrian, he had found a wondrous relic, perhaps placed there by the Gods.

Creeping up from behind, Mythrian sensed a figure from the darkness. It was tall, at least three feet higher than Mythrian. It was within arm's reach of the trembling boy.

He could clearly hear the sound of metal on metal, grinding. Whatever it was, it was wearing armour. Full protective body armour.

The boy's spine tingled as the cold, sickly breath of the creature wrapped his neck. He could neither run nor hide.

He knew he had only one option. To turn and face his foe.

He fell backwards when he saw it; he cowered into a ball on the floor. His voice cracked with fear as he waved his sword in front of him.

"Don't come any nearer! I'm warning you!"

His knees knocked together, his sword was shaking wildly. Then, he heard its voice.

"Please. Do not fear, young one. I mean you no harm."

A bright voice, a good soul. A Spirit, dressed in armour, stood before Mythrian. Relieved, the boy breathed in deeply, calming and steadying himself.

"Who are you?"

"I am Elrick, once humble knight to our kingdom's great leader, Aedorn. Upon my death, I was spirited here by Ajia, to guard the very sword that you have unearthed. For that sword you hold is the same sword used by Aedorn himself in the great battle against the forces of Draigorn's minions, four decades past."

The boy was speechless. To hold a part of his kingdom's greatest hero was something Mythrian could not believe.

"It's inspiring," he finally gushed.

"For so many years, I have had to guard it from many greedy creatures like the two goblins here before you. I have been waiting for a creature of good spirit to draw the sword. At least now I can finally be put to rest, knowing that it is in safe keeping."

Studying the boy as he lowered his sword, the ghostly knight kindly asked:

"I didn't frighten you too much, did I?"

"No, I'm fine. It's just ... these woods are very dark. It can play games with the mind," the boy replied.

"Indeed it can. Though I must admit that I see very few of your kind entering these woods."

"This forest is actually owned by the village of Avalin. I know because I came here looking for the Mayor's crown. He lost it here on his previous visit," the boy explained.

Without a word, before Mythrian had even finished his sentence, seemingly from thin air Elrick produced the crown.

"You found it!"

"I hope you have not been searching for too long. May I ask you your name?"

"Mythrian."

"Mythrian? Good. Please tell me, why have so few good soul been in these woods?" The knight was curious to know.

"The Mayor said that with other important tasks, they had had little time to manage the woods. After his last visit, in which he lost his crown, the Mayor deemed the woods too dangerous for anyone to enter."

"And so he sent you in." The spirit was confused by this.

"No. I came in of my own accord. I wanted to come to these woods to find his crown," the boy explained.

"That's very brave of you."

"Say, you must have been in these woods when it happened. Did you not see the culprit responsible for the Mayor's crown?"

"I did. But ... it is not important who it was. But now you have found your crown I would advise you to leave these woods, as they are not safe."

"Can I ask you something before I go? You told me that you once served under Aedorn?"

"I was one of Aedorn's closest Generals. His right hand man to be more precise," the spirit spoke loud and proud. "I was there at every battle he fought, for blood and glory. I stood by his side, proud to fight beside such a worthy nobleman."

"What was he like as a person?" Mythrian curiously asked.

"He was a man ahead of his time. Evil feared him. He feared nothing. Many have often said that there is a bit of Aedorn within all of us. He was a very disciplined and noble man. He was always wary of others too. A caring man for his own kind. He was the greatest man I ever knew. He is there, with you, right now. In that very sword."

Mythrian gazed intently at the sword, staring at his reflection in its blade. He wondered if Aedorn had ever held the sword exactly as he had then.

"Such a fine work of craftsmanship," the spirit continued, "so powerful was its strike, yet so light was its yield."

"This sword was made by man," Mythrian replied, amazed by Elrick's claim.

"Only with hammers and the skills of great blacksmiths. Aedorn would not have had it any other way."

Surely this fine sword was a gift from Ajia. How can man produce a sword of this calibre, free from damage, over all those years of use?

Mythrian could not believe what he was holding.

"That sword is yours now, young one ..." Elrick said, after a moment.

"Treat it with respect and honour and in turn, all creatures, large or small, will fall to your will."

Mythrian felt incredible pride as he swung the sword from side to side, mastering its feel and strength.

The knight, watching him, added:

"You remind me of Aedorn. You could always see it in his eyes. Pride, determination, desire. They say Aedorn's spirit lies within the sword. Look ..."

Elrick's massive thumb traced hidden writing in the blade: "May this blade never dull, so long as there is evil left to be slain."

The words were written in an encrypted speech. A code used by high Generals, to stop unwanted eyes reading their plans.

Elrick finished:

"Thank you, Mythrian. I am greatly honoured to have met you. Thanks to you, I can finally rest with all the other knights that I fought with so many years ago ..."

There was a refreshing element of calmness as they smiled at one another. But the tranquillity was broken by an earth-shattering vibration that rocked the woods they were in.

"What was that?" Mythrian immediately turned himself into an attacking stance, picking up on the sound as it echoed through the woods.

"Sounds like it came from outside the woods," answered Elrick, disturbed by the noise, fearing for the young boy's safety.

"Avalin. That sound could be coming from Avalin."

Mythrian instantly sensed fear as the thought of all the young apprentices at the village of Avalin came into mind. But there were hundreds of guards and scouts stationed at the village.

What could create such a thunderous sound, to shake fear into the boots of hundreds of guards? Mythrian began to feel giddy from the heavy thoughts that began to plague his mind.

"Mythrian, you must go back and look for help. I know you may feel nervous and afraid, but you have no reason to be. We all have a spirit and that spirit burns strongly in all of us, especially when our lives are most at risk. Believe in the power of your spirit, for nothing is stronger. And don't forget the spirits around you, we all have a purpose, even us that are deceased. We will all be there with you. But you must believe in yourself, Mythrian. Overcome your fears. Believe in your spirit. NOW GO!" he ordered.

"Rocloar," Mythrian remembered. "He's waiting for me outside the forest. I can seek help from him."

As the boy quickly retraced his footsteps through the forest to find Rocloar, the knight wished the boy farewell, before drifting off into the wind, till nothing more of him could be seen.

The run back was difficult for Mythrian. The densely packed forest made it impossible to run at speed, as he pushed branch and bush out of the way, tripping over along the water-drenched terrain.

The forest seemed endless and Mythrian began to wonder whether he was ever going to find an exit, or if he was just going round in continuous circles.

But he followed his gut instinct and was beginning to see a glimmer of hope as he noticed the trees around him were becoming more separate from one another.

He was nearing the edges of the woodland.

Standing by the edge of the forest, Rocloar was losing his patience.

His orders were not to enter the woods and thus he stood, just outside Emory Forest, unable to progress.

The loud crash had shaken him, just as it had Mythrian, and he felt helpless. He wanted to ride back to Avalin to help, yet he had to wait for Mythrian to come back from his search.

Suddenly, he heard a voice calling him through the trees.

"Rocloar! Rocloar!"

Mythrian came running towards him. He was holding the Mayor's crown above his head, like a trophy.

Rocloar greeted him and began straightaway to make their forward plan:

"We have to hurry, Mythrian. We must get back to Avalin."

When they rode into Avalin, the sight that greeted Mythrian and Rocloar sent shockwaves through their spines.

The Rock Troll that Mythrian had conjured had somehow been re-cast. It had been terrorising the village, destroying everything in its path. Guards and scouts, even some of the older apprentices, had been trying to repel it, but its immense size was proving overwhelming. Nothing was going to stop it reaching and annihilating the very heart of the village.

Rocloar and Mythrian watched from a distance.

"I'll take you to the southern fields," Rocloar told the boy. "Make your way clockwise around the village, round towards the gateway. The apprentices will be waiting there for transport back to Helianthe."

But Rocloar's orders simply bounced off Mythrian. He was staring hard at the beast that he had so recently summoned.

He spoke just one word: "No."

Mythrian rebelled, jumped off the back of his horse and began marching his way over to the Troll. Rocloar grabbed at his arm, shouting:

"What are you doing? We need to get out of here!"

Mythrian stood his ground.

"I cast this creature, therefore I can destroy it. I have no fear …"

"Mythrian, this thing is going to tear the village to the ground and us too if we remain here. We must leave and wait for back-up to arrive. This is too powerful for you."

"It is strong and powerful but it has its weaknesses. You may not be able to understand this, but I have the power to stop this creature. I can stop it right now!" Mythrian confidently returned.

"But I can't let you do this. You must get out of here. It's too dangerous. It's too great!"

Rocloar couldn't let the young boy risk his life against the Troll, but Mythrian was not to be reasoned with. The boy shook himself away from Rocloar, moving away, moving forward.

The scout could hardly bear to look at the boy who was heading towards a certain, deadly fate. Collecting his thoughts, Rocloar turned on his horse then rode off into the heart of the village, hoping to find Mayor Modearn.

Mythrian stepped up to his fate, heading directly towards the seething, violent Rock Troll. The boy was calm, systematic in his approach. His eyes, his body, his mind were alert, not scared. He may have been a mere boy, but a new strength had taken hold of him. He was very much in control.

CHAPTER 16 ✝ THE BATTLE OF AVALIN

ROCLOAR SLOWED HIS horse. He had been galloping through the fields on the southern fringes of the village; he spotted a scout who was checking the area for stranded or lost apprentices.

There was a terrifying, booming, stomping sound coming from the village. It was as much as Rocloar could do to steady his horse, which was getting spooked by the mysterious sound. Rocloar shouted to the scout:

"Where's the Mayor?"

"By the village clock." The scout looked scared; his eyes darted around, looking for danger. "They say he's trying to gather the apprentices, to get them out of the village."

Rocloar spurred his horse back into action. When he arrived at the heart of the village, he found the Mayor and a couple of apprentices sheltering behind a turned over table. The witch had cast Nymphs with the Troll, taking advantage of the chaos by pulling down tents and destroying valuables.

Rocloar reached for his sword and threw it from a distance, killing one of the Nymphs instantly. Another one charged directly towards him, hoping to knock him to the ground while he hastily tried to draw his second, smaller side-sword. The attacker was stopped in his tracks, two feet away from Rocloar by a spear, thrown from a nearby scout. It hit the creature just in time. It saved Rocloar's life.

Losing numbers, the other Nymphs fled to the far side of the village, chased by the guards who hurled any and all objects in their path, hoping to knock the creatures down.

Stepping down from his horse, Rocloar was approached by one of the guards defending against the Troll.

"Sir, we cannot hold the Troll for much longer and there are too many Nymphs around the village."

"Forget the Troll," Rocloar ordered. "Pull all your troops back, just focus on the Nymphs; I want every one of them burnt to ashes!"

The guard was hesitant to act on his orders.

"Well don't just stand there. Send for the others," Rocloar shouted harshly.

"Yes sire," the guard finally accepted.

✝ ✝ ✝

Only minutes had passed yet they had felt like hours to the scout.

By the village clock, at the centre of the settlement, Rocloar was close to breaking point. The distant screams from the Troll were cutting into his heart like a dagger. All at once he felt a rush of emotions: guilt; the anguish of betrayal. A searing fatigue almost overwhelmed him.

He muttered under his breath, and wiped cold sweat from his forehead. "What … what have I done?"

He had thrown Mythrian into the Valun's Den. To certain death. Rocloar tried to remain strong, but the pressure was growing too much for him to handle.

Mayor Modearn was trying to pull himself up from the table he had been hiding behind, when Rocloar made his way over, offering help.

"What evil is this that bears down on my village?" Modearn was holding his head, his hands over his ears to block out the agonising screams from the Troll only an acre away.

"We must go, Sire. We must get you to safety with all the apprentices."

"Indeed, the two with me here are the last two apprentices to go …" the Mayor spoke, until he suddenly remembered the boy whom the scout had brought to see him earlier in the morning. "Wait a minute ... where's your apprentice? Rocloar, where is Mythrian?"

Rocloar could hardly say a word. His eyes streamed with tears, his mouth quivered in shame.

The Mayor asked again: "Rocloar, where is he?"

Turning his head to the East where the Troll was making its move, the Mayor's stomach churned from the terrifying thought.

"You sent him to fight against that tower of evil?" Modearn's face was swelling a deep, plum-red. He stared angrily at his scout.

"What on earth were you thinking?"

"There was nothing I could do to stop him. He overpowered me."

The Mayor stared levelly at Rocloar, with powerful accusation in his eyes. He turned, and moved away.

Rocloar called after him: "Where are you going?"

Stopping and turning round to answer the scout, Modearn's last words were:

"I go to save Mythrian. I don't care if that thing kills me, if Mythrian's still alive, he deserves our help. I'm going to get that boy out of there."

Rocloar made no reply. He followed.

CHAPTER 17 † RETURN OF THE MASTER

THE GUARD CARRYING Rocloar's orders had finally reached the area where his troops were defending against the Troll.

"Everyone pull back. PULL BACK!"

"What about the Troll?" a guard returned.

"Focus on the Nymphs. Burn every one of them to the ground," the leader ordered.

Turning away from the Troll, heading back into the heart of the village, a guard caught sight of an apprentice, a young boy running up towards the beast.

"Young apprentice heading for the Troll!" the guard screamed, catching everyone's attention. "He doesn't stand a chance! It's suicide! He'll be completely crushed!"

There was nothing to be done. The situation was hopeless. "Our orders are to withdraw!" the chief guard cried. He thought quickly.

Pointing to a handful of his men, he ordered:

"You seven, stay here and watch over the boy. Don't interfere; you'll only make matters worse. Just … watch, alright? Hold your ground here. Enter only if the situation becomes critical."

The seven chosen guards hid themselves in defensive positions, keeping a close eye on the apprentice's progress. The remaining guards rushed back into the village to take on the Nymphs.

They moved quickly, like wild animals, in for the kill.

The Troll saw its chance to enter the village, to take it by storm, but was then stopped in its tracks. A mind-rattling whistle echoed loudly through its head: it startled the beast; it was painful, skull-splitting.

As the whistling became more intense, and pitched even higher, the Troll wrapped its hands over its head and bellowed loudly, trying to shake off the agonising and irritating ringing.

The beast turned its heavy, stone-clustered neck, catching sight of the young boy approaching. It looked down at the tiny frame at its feet, failing to recognise its old Master. It was definitely him that was making the painful noise.

Mythrian stepped even closer to the giant Troll, intensifying his high-pitched whistle, releasing violent sound waves that were intense and painful to the Troll's ear. They rang through the dense perplexity of the creature's body like the chimes rung from a giant, monastery bell.

Frustrated, aggravated, and enraged, the Troll reared up and away from the village. The dark voids of its eyes focused solely on the boy.

The Troll's next move staggered Mythrian.

Turning round to face the boy, the Troll released a strange, searing, bellowing call. It cut and echoed through Mythrian's soul. Without warning, the beast's giant fist crashed down on the earth with incredible speed and power.

Mythrian's world shook.

Violent shock waves and tremors were released through the earth from the Troll's massive blow. It was like an earthquake. Mythrian was knocked cleanly off his feet.

But the truth was that the Troll hadn't even intended to catch Mythrian with that blow. It hadn't even started on the boy yet. Stomping on the ground and shaking it, it was merely expressing anger, only trying to stop the irritating whistling noise in its head.

When it came, the sudden attack shocked Mythrian. How did a creature so massive move so quickly, with such great agility and momentum?

Mythrian had to think fast. He had not expected the Troll to be so quick and agile. But something was wrong.

The cloaked creature that had brought the Troll back to life had placed a spell over it, enhancing its powers. Suddenly, it looked less like a Troll.

It looked human.

But it was becoming increasingly difficult for the boy to think, as the beast relentlessly attacked. The Troll stamped and flailed its limbs frantically, trying to catch the boy with one of its deadly blows.

It was all happening too quickly. There was no time at all for Mythrian to think. It was as much as he could do to dodge the barrage of heavy attacks from the monumental beast.

He was beginning to regret underestimating the Troll's ability. He retreated quickly to the edge of the village, hiding behind one of the tents.

Leaning back against the canvas, slowing his heavy, quick breaths to a calmer tempo, Mythrian listened keenly. He could hear the Troll moving behind him.

And then nothing. Mythrian was confused and disturbed. The Troll couldn't have stopped moving and yet he heard not a sound. Only the wind shaking in the heavy cloth of the tents.

It was too quiet. Mythrian needed to know where the Troll was.

Suddenly, out of nowhere, he heard a guard shouting:

"Mythrian, look out!"

But it was too late. The brutal arm of the Troll swept through the tents around Mythrian, sending him hurtling backwards through the air. He gasped.

He landed heavily on the floor, and one of the tents collapsed on top of him. Mythrian quickly tried to drag his way out from underneath the tent cloth.

But the Troll was watching.

Mythrian was exhausted, his limbs ached, his body was tired and weary. He couldn't take much more.

The Troll towered above him, and then sent him shooting through the air again, but this time with the layer of earth beneath him. Mythrian felt desperate, close to death. He hadn't the strength or the resources to defeat a creature of this magnitude and power.

"We must help him now!" cried one of the guards. He's going to get killed!"

Modearn and Rocloar stopped in their tracks in the presence of the Troll. The sight of Mythrian fighting for his life stunned them.

Modearn instinctively moved to help him, but Rocloar held him back.

However much they wanted to save the boy from the Troll, it was just too dangerous to confront a creature of that magnitude. By foolishly running in to try and save him, they could place Mythrian's life in greater danger.

From the cover of an overturned table Rocloar, Modearn and the remaining guards watched the boy struggle, waiting for the right moment to intervene.

Back in the village, things were going from bad to worse. The guards had been attempting to kill the Nymphs with their spears, but now instead they were forced to take cover, as the creatures above were bombarding them. It caused them grievous delay: just when they needed to take down the beasts on the ground, one by one, they were being attacked from above.

One of the guards reached Modearn and Rocloar, sheltering behind the table. The Troll still loomed violently above them, taunting Mythrian. It would be soon moving in for the kill.

The guard broke urgent news to Modearn:

"Sir, the Nymphs are proving too strong. We've lost most of our ranged weapons. We simply can't defend ourselves with swords and spears, not from aerial attacks. They're just picking us off."

Suddenly, Rocloar screamed warning. The Troll slammed an earth-shattering punch to the ground in front of them. The impact of his fist was shattering to the ear, and it sent Mythrian flying through the air towards the distant tents.

Even from afar, Modearn and his guards heard Mythrian's torso crashing into the wooden struts supporting the structure. The sound of flesh and bone hurled against wood was sickening; stomach churning.

Mythrian tried to haul himself up from the ground. But he

was too tired and exhausted. He couldn't even lift himself to his knees.

Was this the end? Had he come all this way for nothing? Was the Troll just too powerful and strong?

Looking down to his left, on the ground, he noticed three emerald crystals. They must have been in the tent he'd been tossed into.

Picking up the crystals in his hand, he shut his eyes, quickly trying to think of a plan. A distraction. That's what he needed. Time to think and recover.

He opened his eyes, preparing to cast his spell. The immense shape of the Troll towered over him, ready to finish the boy with one final blow.

With all the strength left within him, he threw the crystals into the air, releasing three brightly coloured Nymphs, just like the ones attacking the village.

Swooping around the Troll's head, the Nymphs at first blinded it with sizzling explosions. The creature roared as it panicked and stumbled back, reeling.

The Nymphs were fast, agile and cunning: under Mythrian's direction, they pushed the Troll back, driving it steadily away from the village.

This was good but not good enough. Mythrian needed a plan that would finish the beast, once and for all. But what could he, a small boy fighting a titan monster, do?

Watching the creature stumbling backwards across the green sward, Mythrian saw the Troll was heading for a rough patch, roughly the size of a village tent. His mind flashed. His eyes darted towards his opportunity.

Roots. The bare patch of ground had networks of exposed tree roots, extending out in all directions.

What if he could trap the creature? Entangle and imprison it, tie it down and bring to an end its evil momentum, once and for all.

The troll stepped ever closer to the bare patch of ground. Mythrian drew out his sword, his guiding inspiration.

He lifted it high up into the air.

Searching deep down within himself, he could feel the power growing inside. It was like a key, turning. As the energy filled him, the cryptic markings on his body were brightening, moving, pulsating.

Mythrian felt invigorated; energised; healed. He felt invincible.

He faced the Troll. Mythrian was ready. Calling the Nymphs away, the conjurer began his spell, focusing hard on the area under the Troll's feet.

Modearn, Rocloar, all the guards watched with great anticipation as the boy began his attack.

As the wind picked up into a fast, powerful gale, the earth began to tremble underneath the Troll's feet. It looked down there, trying to understand what was happening, and what it saw made it stop and stare. The beast was transfixed. The roots were rising, serpent-like, up from the ground.

And as they rose, they became thicker. They coiled into circular spirals, crawling like serpents around the Troll's feet.

It was when the roots began to attach themselves to the creature's limbs that it panicked. The strength of the roots was immense. Even the vice-like grip of the Troll's massive hands couldn't lever the roots away.

The Troll tried desperately to tear the vines off. It kicked its legs violently, but the roots only tightened their grip. The beast was overcome, pulled and pinned down by a thousand thick roots.

Immobilised, both its legs were chained to the ground and the roots were still continuing to grow, not just in size, but in numbers too.

Leaning over itself, it used immense hands to try to prise the vines away, to no avail. As fast as it could tear at the vines, more roots grew back, pulling the beast's giant frame backwards, overpowering it, taking full command.

The more it struggled, the tighter the grip became.

Modearn and his guards dared to move from their defensive positions.

They couldn't believe what they were seeing. Mythrian not only had the Troll trapped, but he was humiliating the once unparalleled huge beast.

By now, the beast was struggling to escape. Its roars sounded like death throes: guttural, echoing through the soul of the surrounding landscape. Mythrian was no longer afraid. All the guards, all the other apprentices were cheering. He glowed with pride.

He felt a mixture of new emotions. An immense power and scintillating excitement in his mind; peace and resolution in his soul.

He felt exhilarated. A tremendous power surged through him, Ajia's power. It was unspeakable. He had total control over the completely exhausted beast.

Mythrian knew that it was time to finish the Troll once and for all.

It had its arms up in the air, frantically reaching out for escape. Root after root rose, coiling around its head and throat, gripping firmly.

Tightening.

The beast was growing tired of the fight.

Mythrian commanded the roots to strangle the giant Troll. It groaned loudly, helplessly. It raised its arms into the air, in one last frantic attempt to free itself. But it failed, as the root tightened firmly around its neck, cutting short its very last breath.

Slowly its eyes began to close for the last time.

The beast was beaten by the boy.

With his spell complete, Mythrian lowered his arms slowly down to his side. He dropped his sword back into its sheath. He tried to calm his beating heart.

The boy was overcome by pride and delight. He looked up towards the Troll, tangled, bound forever in its prison of vines and roots. He pitied the monster for he knew someone else was at work here.

But that could wait for another day.

Mythrian was surrounded by well-wishers. Some of them stood and applauded, others hugged him and others felt honoured just touching his suit. What he had achieved was unbelievable. He had conquered the Troll and defeated the Nymphs, who disappeared with the giant's death.

Mayor Modearn ran to congratulate him.

The boy took the treasure he had found in Emory Forest from his belt, and held it out to his lord:

"Your crown, Sire."

Modearn was speechless. He looked at the small frame of the boy in front of him, at the tattooed body, the wild hair, and the shining eyes.

"Thankyou, Mythrian ..." Modearn managed to say, after a moment. "... Words cannot describe what you have achieved today. Your victory will be re-told here for many years to come. We will leave the body of the Troll where it lies. Our victory is our symbol that good will always triumph over evil."

Turning back to the boy, Modearn said: "Now, I believe celebrations are in order. Don't you?"

In Gwynan's Gorse, the cloaked creature and the elder were reflecting on the boy's progress.

"Have you seen enough?" the creature spoke. She secretly bore a smile, having favoured the boy to defeat the Troll.

After a brief pause the elder returned, "I'm going to confer this with the others. There is much that needs to be discussed."

"Of course. But remember what you have seen today. In time, the boy will be even stronger than you."

"We shall see ..."

† PART TWO †

CHAPTER 1 † THE LAST IMAGE
OF AJIA

WITH HIS HANDS gripped firmly around the crystal ball, the Guild Master travelled deep within his thoughts.

So many questions were roaming his mind and he needed answers for them. One question stood out more than anything else. What had become of Mythrian's bodily markings?

Master Brennius was all too aware that something was being hidden from him. Mythrian was hiding something of great importance. But what could be great enough to physically change his appearance?

The boy's markings had for a long time eluded him of any explanation. But it became apparent to the old man that whatever it was that Mythrian had found, it must be a key of some sort.

Perhaps if he located the whereabouts of this key, it could explain the mystery behind his boy's unique feature.

But where could Mythrian have placed this key?

With his crystal ball in focus and ready for its reader's question, Master Brennius asked, "I'm looking for a key, perhaps of great importance. It belongs to a boy, with a secret yet foretold. I need some clues as to its possible position."

As the image began to take shape in the crystal ball, Brennius looked deep into its heart to find the image of a rough, darkened stone or tablet.

Master Brennius was slightly confused by the vision.

"Why has the crystal ball shown me this?" he thought to himself.

Through the eyes of the ball, he could not clearly see why the tablet was a key. Perhaps he needed a closer inspection.

"Where might I find this artefact?" the old man questioned the crystal ball.

His reply came with the image of an arched window, overlooking the village of Hamlynstone.

"Mythrian's bedroom. That's strange ..." Brennius suddenly thought, "Why didn't he hide the key if it was of great importance?"

Quickly rising up from his chair, Brennius headed up the long staircase towards the apprentice's room in search of the key.

Opening the door to Mythrian's room, he quickly set eyes upon the window which mirrored the image in the crystal ball.

He was in the right room, but where was the tablet? To his surprise, the tablet sat in clear view on Mythrian's work table, an easy target to steal, should anybody sneak into his room.

With the tablet, which felt unnaturally cold, in his frail and withered hands, he lifted it up to his face to inspect it closely. He saw nothing inspirational.

"Perhaps I am wasting my time," he quietly thought to himself.

His judgement was soon to be changed.

Turning the tablet over, upon the opposite side he noticed a very protrusive, dark line, running across the course of its structure.

Just about picking up the line with his fading eyes, he became fascinated by the cascading spirals that swept the surface of the tablet.

Brennius became intrigued by its unusual markings.

"These markings, they look familiar."

Placing his index finger on the line, he tried to use his insight to figure out what mineral or substance it consisted of.

But without warning a bright blue bolt raced across the line before it sharply struck him on his finger. Jumping back in shock, holding his hand over his faint heart, he dropped the tablet on to the floor.

The bolt was very powerful, though it was sudden, leaving his frail finger numb and tingly.

Nursing his sore finger in his hand, he stared down cautiously at the tablet. It appeared to be active.

Quick flashes of fluorescent light dashed across it while an aura of blue shielded its frame.

Suddenly he was seeing the tablet in an entirely different light. This had to be more than just an ordinary tablet, but what could it possibly be?

Grabbing the cloth off the table, he picked up the tablet and wrapped it in the fabric. This was serious but he needed more time to think before he came to any conclusions.

In heading back down to his quarters, he hoped he might be able to make some sense of the item through his vast array of books of knowledge.

Upon entering his quarters, he placed the tablet on a small table, which sat in front of his chair. Pulling back the cloth to get another look at the item, he began searching through book after book for answers.

The tablet was most certainly unique. There was no record or explanation of it in any of the books compiling information on various rocks, minerals and sediments.

Master Brennius was scratching his silky hair erratically, completely baffled by the find.

Gazing across the many shelves, studying the titles on the cover of every book, he came across one book which might just have the answer to his problem.

On one of the middle shelves sat a book which had been hanging loosely, balanced between two books on the edge of its shelf. Rather than pushing it back safely on its shelf, he decided to take a closer inspection of the book.

The book was a compilation of several well known authors, telling in great detail the story of the greatest hero there ever was; Aedorn, and what became of the world after his death.

A lot of the book seemed over-emphasised, possibly to attract more readers and to heighten the General's fame among the common folk. It was more like a tale than a fact-based novel.

But towards the back of the book there was an interesting article by a lesser-known author called Lindley Glonenbloom.

It gave a brief but fundamental account of what Ajia had left behind after his exile:

"As the God of all creation gave his last and final words to his people, he placed into a tablet his unprecedented power, in the hope that one day, a chosen soul would find that power.

"He gave no name, no location of this tablet. Only his solemn promise that one day, he would return."

As Brennius turned the page to read more, his eyes came to meet the tablet in full illustration, its alignment of bright azure markings alight.

The book fell to the floor.

He stood motionless, refusing to turn and face what he had discovered.

How did Mythrian obtain this artefact and more importantly, what would become of Mythrian in the future?

Though acting as a guardian for the boy, Master Brennius had seen himself as more of a father figure towards Mythrian. Like most fathers, Brennius was sometimes a little bit over-protective, despite how cleverly gifted he knew Mythrian was.

If Mythrian had somehow unlocked the secret behind the tablet, it would mean that he would be the chosen one. He would have to go in search of Ajia, to free him from his exile.

Not only could there be great danger in this, but Brennius himself would refuse to let Mythrian leave for such a dangerous task. He couldn't bear for anything to happen to his special pupil.

But he knew that it wasn't his choice.

Picking the book up from the floor and placing it back into its place on its shelf, he walked over to his big armchair and dropped back heavily into its easing frame.

Picking up his long, hazel cut pipe from the small table next to him, he took in a couple of big, deep puffs before calmly exhaling, releasing all the anxiety and stress.

For the remainder of that night, Brennius sat deep within his thoughts, his eyes staring coldly at the artefact, which still had momentary flashes of blue light along its string of indented lines.

Perhaps it was that light that had triggered Mythrian's markings to brighten in their appearance.

"So you're what's left. I am staring at the last remains of our God. The man who created us all from his great tree in the Enchantment. Look at you now. Empty. Powerless. Useless!"

Taking in another few puffs of his pipe, he continued

"Can you hear what I am saying to you now? How does it feel when someone asks you a question and you cannot answer back? As you know I have never been a true believer. I only believe in what stands before me. And your decision to choose Mythrian as your finder has further cause me to question my faith in you."

Knowing Mythrian would arrive back from his tournament soon, he needed time to speak openly with his pupil about the truth behind the artefact.

It was not going be a very easy conversation for him or for the boy. But Mythrian's future already hung in the balance of others to guide him and Master Brennius knew he had to be cautious with his words, to make sure that he started on the right path.

The days were going to get very long for the old man. His special student was soon starting a very long journey, travelling far from his Guild and his teacher.

"Don't think I won't be watching over him. You might be able to tell him things others cannot hear, but I will not let you lead him to foul trickery. You just look after my boy. If any harm comes, I will make sure nobody frees you from your exile, you hear me. Nobody will take Mythrian away from me. Nobody ..."

CHAPTER 2 ✝ WELCOME HOME

"WAKE UP MASTER Brennius, wake up," the voice repeated, as the old man slowly opened his eyes to find one of the Guild assistants awakening him.

He held an urgent message:

"Master Brennius, the carriages with our apprentices are arriving back from their tournament in Avalin. We request your presence outside the Guild doors."

Stiffly and awkwardly, Brennius lifted himself up from his armchair, with some helpful assistance. But as he was making a couple of quick and easy stretches, loosening up his bony frame, his eyes quickly set upon the tablet on the table.

Shielding the tablet from the assistant's vision, hoping that the one failed to spot the artefact before he was awoken, he quickly wrapped it in its thick cloth and placed it comfortably under the safety of his robe.

Picking up his hat off its stand, he walked out of his quarters, mouth firmly shut, as he made his way towards the Guild doors.

Standing beneath the entrance to the Guild, his fellow teachers beside him, Master Brennius watched the rows of carriages arrive through the village gates.

The first sun had moved high into the sky and brought with it a new week of excitement and prosperity.

As the villagers cheered on, their encouraging roar greeting the heroes back home, the apprentices couldn't get out of their carriages quickly enough.

The atmosphere was infused, so much so that the hairs stood up on the back of every teacher's neck. They were all very proud of their students and were equally anxious to talk to them on their return.

As all the carriages passed the gates, several guards walked up to the doors and opened them. Streams of students stepped down from the wagons, breathing in the refreshing air around them while gazing around at the large crowd drawn to greet them.

As they formed a large group in front of their tutors, Master Brennius stepped forward and congratulated his heroes.

"Welcome home, young heroes. You have made us and I'm sure yourselves very proud. And I'm sure you can't wait to tell us eagerly of your time at the tournament in Avalin. All in good time. For now, we have a surprise for you. In light of your efforts to your Guild and to your kingdom, we are honouring you with a feast, as a gesture, for all your many years of hard work and countless patience."

As the villagers began to organise themselves, preparing food and tables for the exhausted apprentices, they began the feast. The apprentices were all getting very excited, as various large trays carrying meats, fresh breads and crunchy fruits were placed on the set tables.

Endless rows of barrels carrying delicious beer were being displayed around the site. This pleased the older apprentices, who began to groan from the anticipation.

It was a welcome which made the apprentices feel much appreciated. They themselves felt proud of what they had achieved, since beginning their apprenticeships in the Guild.

For now, they would be placed on assignments around the various villages across the kingdom, fulfilling much needed tasks. Some of them would stay in Hamlynstone, but the majority would travel far away from their secure upbringing.

It simply depended on who needed them the most and how useful they were at their given skills.

But for now, that was not on the mind of any of the students, nor their tutors, as they eased down to enjoy their time of rest, back in Hamlynstone.

While the apprentices were tucking into their feast and enjoying the produce provided for them, Master Brennius had called Mythrian for a quick converse in the Guild.

Sitting on a ledge by one of the windows to the front of the Guild, the old man firstly asked the boy, "Well come on then, how did it go?"

"I won," Mythrian spoke proudly, before pulling out the certificate from underneath his suit and handing it to his tutor, who opened it up and quietly read the writing inside.

"Well done. I knew you would do it. So go on, are you going to tell me how you won?" Brennius spoke enthusiastically, keen to know more about his pupil's success.

Speaking in a slow, clear voice so that every word rang in the old man's mind, the young apprentice spoke, "I performed a miracle."

"A miracle? How?"

"When I was given a crystal with which to perform my contest, I noticed a small pebble by my feet. I don't know why, but something in the back of my mind told me to pick up this stone. I felt this incredible power run through me, as though someone was with me, standing by my side, calming my body and soul. And then I threw it, placed my hands out before me and released the power from my fingers. In no time at all, the small rock had grown into a Troll, three times the size of any cottage in this settlement."

Master Brennius said nothing. With the recurring thoughts of the tablet haunting his mind, the old man was understandably unsettled with his pupil's story.

Briefly pausing as he looked out of the window at his fellow apprentices who were laughing and cheering in the uplifting sunlight, Mythrian continued. "I don't know how to say this, but I've been given a very special gift. A power so great, that I can create that which others can only dream. I've been blessed by the Gods."

Master Brennius knew he had to tell the boy about his

knowledge of the tablet. But he was hesitant, knowing great care was needed in his words. The boy might feel uncomfortable with the fact that others knew of his powers.

"Mythrian, I was concerned for you after you left the chamber hall during Riener's performance and ever since I have been worried that you have been hiding something from me. Something very significant. When you left to go to Avalin, I went up to your room and found this on your desk."

Placing the tablet on the windowsill, the boy studied its structure, recognising it instantly. But Mythrian did not feel uncomfortable. In fact he felt rather calm about the situation.

"I'm sorry Mythrian, but I needed to know, as your guardian. What happens to you affects me. I know you wouldn't want me going through all your important belongings, but this tablet is not a blessing. It has put you in great danger."

"What do you mean?" the boy returned, listening to his Master's words with caution and concern.

"You have found Ajia's mystical tablet. You have been given his supreme powers, but you have also been given a task. When Ajia placed the tablet in its secret location, he told the people who stood before him on that victorious day, that whoever finds it will be the chosen one. The one who must rescue him from his exile. As you hold the power to the stone, you have been given the task of finding him."

As the boy scanned his hands and up his arms, searching the markings that stained his body, he looked at Brennius and replied, "What if it was my task all along to pursue this Mission? Why else would I be covered in these unusual markings? The mystical tablet is a key and I am the finder. I must do this, this is my destiny."

"It is dangerous. It is pointless. It is suicidal," Brennius shot back, refusing to believe the boy's claim. In his view, Mythrian was not going on this journey and that was final.

But as he looked into the eyes of his pupil, he knew that he had raised his voice too high and the boy was upset by his Master's apparent lack of confidence in him.

"I'm sorry Mythrian, but I can't let you do this. Ever since the day you were put into my arms as a child, I have cared for you like a father. And like any loving father, I am afraid of losing you before my time goes by. This quest is too dangerous, who knows what evil might be waiting for you in the shadows of your journey? I cannot let you go on this quest, Mythrian."

Perhaps Mythrian was not seeing the reality of the danger he was facing. But his mind was disagreeing with his Master's views.

"Do I have a choice?" Mythrian returned. There was no movement in his face. When Mythrian became focused on an argument, he became impossible to deter.

Brennius fell silent with regret. To think it had come to this, that his prize student had been placed with the sole task of finding the unknown location of their supreme God Ajia.

He didn't know what to say. There was nothing more to say, except to offer the boy advice on his journey as it unfolds.

Unsure of his path, the young boy asked his Master, "What should I do?"

"Has Ajia not been calling you?" Brennius questioned.

"No."

"You've heard nothing?"

"Not a sign or a symbol," the boy replied, scanning his mind for any clues, but coming up empty.

"Really, how odd," the Master rubbed his chin. "I would have thought that Ajia would be trying to communicate with you somehow, with you being the bearer of his tablet."

It was an interesting question that eluded the two of them, but Mythrian returned with the only knowledgeable answer he could come up with and said:

"Maybe he is trying to, but his messages haven't either reached me yet or he might be having trouble reaching me."

Taking a deep breath, the tutor told his pupil, "Yes, well anyway, I think for the moment you should stay here with us. We'll wait to see if anything occurs and then we'll make our move. Until then, get some rest and try to put all of this out of your mind. You don't have to start this quest right away."

As Master Brennius looked at Mythrian, who briefly stared down at the tablet before looking out of the clear window at the beautiful blue skies above, the young boy replied, "I'm not afraid."

Brennius drew a calm smile across his soft face.

"I'm sure you are not. I'm very proud of you and always will be. And I will always be there when you need me. Don't forget that you have many people looking over your shoulder. Many who will be there to guide you and keep an eye out for you in times of trouble."

As Mythrian nodded to his Master's easing words, Brennius continued, "Now come on, let's head back to the feast."

As they walked out of the Guild, back into the sunshine, they joined in with the apprentices and tutors, enjoying their feast.

CHAPTER 3 † THE LIGHT FALLS
INTO THE DARKNESS

To the East, past the dark forests of Hollman's Hollow, lies the pinnacle frame of the Eidoros Mountains.

A series of sharp, practically unclimbable mountains clustered across miles of terrain, shielding Siren's Gore from the land to the West. In the light, the sediment of the Eidoros Mountains reflects an indigo-purple. It makes them appear mystically entrancing, despite their harsh environment.

It was here, nestled in a small area of the mountains' lowlands, that activity was taking place. In the entrance to one of the caves running underneath the mountains came the sounds of intense conversation.

Standing under the brightly lit torches aligning the many miles of tunnels beneath the mountains, stood a figure cloaked in a dark, crimson robe. His face was hidden under his hood, only his lips were uncovered.

Though his identity could not yet be recognised, there was evidence of him being human. His beard was visible, as it lay wispy and curled on to his chest.

Though what purpose a human creature had in these lands of evil was unknown. It seemed that he was awaiting something? A gift? A treasure of great importance?

Walking into the entrance of the cave, three bandits led by the leader of their gang stepped forward into the view of the masked creature.

Two of the bandits were carrying with them a large wooden chest, which would usually be used for holding stolen goods.

"Step closer," the creature ordered, standing almost motionless on his spot, watching the bandits cautiously move closer. "I do not wish to shout at you from a distance."

"We've brought you your reward, now where's ours?" the bandit leader demanded, not willing to stand and chat too long with the cloaked creature, knowing he was not to be trust.

"Patience, patience. You'll get your reward. Just as soon as you prove to me that that box you have brought bears my treasure."

The creature was lightly grinning under his cloak, at the element of fear and uncertainty that was shading the bandit's face.

Looking over his shoulder towards his fellow members, the bandit leader ordered them with an air of caution:

"Come on lads, let's make it quick."

Placing the chest on a giant stalagmite that had been cut into a flat table top, the cloaked creature eagerly stepped forward to view his prize.

As he opened the chest, the creature was instantly confounded by the rays of blue and purple lights that were being ejected by the treasure within.

Excited and enthralled with his treasure, he congratulated the bandits on their find. "You have done well. I am very impressed with your efforts ..."

He cut his words shortS.

Just as he was about to close the box, he noticed something was wrong with the treasure:

"Wait a minute. Why is there a crack down one side of this artefact?"

The bandits were stunned. They had no knowledge of this and they were beginning to pay the consequences, as the creature's voice began to echo loudly:

"I should have known. You cut off half of my prize just so you could keep it to yourselves, because you can't live without your precious treasures. You greedy swines! You will pay if you do not hand me the rest of my prize."

The bandits were on the back foot. They could feel the anger burning within the creature and they soon felt isolated, as though his rage was wrapping them in an invisible web, pinning them down while he moved in, closer to his prey.

"But it's just how we found it."

"LIES!"

"Please, my lord, you must believe us," replied the leader, begging the creature, "We just found it on some villager, as we chased him and others out of our forest."

"Hhhmmm..." the creature went into deep thought, every second holding the hearts of the bandits in their mouths, as they waited to hear the creature's next response.

"You didn't find anything else on any of the other villagers?" the creature continued, angered that the other half of his treasure may be in somebody else's hand.

"We swear," the leader spoke, his hands in the air in surrendering fashion.

The creature went quiet for a minute, before looking over his shoulder and calling out to a couple of small goblins. They themselves held a chest though this one was filled to the brim with gold.

Dropping it in front of the bandits, the leader bent down to open the chest. But just as a rim of gold appeared along the opening, the creature slammed his foot down on the chest, closing it shut.

"I want the other half of my treasure. I don't care how you get it. Just find it."

"Yes, my lord," the leader assured.

The cloaked creature had had enough and headed back into the darkness of the cave depths. The bandits left the cave with a valuable chest of gold.

After the feast, Mythrian went with Master Brennius to his quarters. They were awaiting the arrival of Salen, who had been asked to join them for a talk on the tablet. Mythrian needed a friend to trust. Salen was the perfect candidate.

But when Salen arrived, walking into Brennius' quarters, his Master noticed that Rinen was standing with him. The Guild Master was unhappy with this.

"Did you really have to bring him?"

Unfortunately, Brennius did not favour Rinen very much. Brennius was a man who believed in strict discipline. Rinen was one student who often failed to abide by his rule.

"Oh, don't worry," Rinen returned quickly, "I can keep my word."

Looking around the room, an air of uncertainty flooded the quarters.

"Honestly. Mythrian has saved me from a lot of trouble. I owe him one."

Looking down towards Mythrian who was sitting in his Master's chair, not the least concerned by Rinen's arrival, the old man replied:

"Alright, you can stay. But if I hear anyone else talking about this outside this room, I will hold you personally responsible."

"Of course."

Rinen understood the situation. He knew all too well that Master Brennius was not one to get angry with.

"Gather round and make sure the door is firmly shut behind you," the Master told his students, so he wasn't shouting across the room; their conversation needed to be secret.

"What is it, Master?" Salen questioned, anxious to know what was worrying Brennius and his friend.

As they stepped closer to him and the boy, Brennius paused to think about how he was going to word Mythrian's story to them.

"What do you know about Ajia's tablet?"

"Only what you have told us," Salen spoke, unsure of what relevance this had to Mythrian. "It is the last remains we have of our God. It was secretly hidden in an unknown location. The one who finds it will be guided by Ajia to rescue him from his exile."

"Somebody once told me that it is believed to be held in the undergrowth of Ajia's tree, in the Enchantment," Rinen said, hoping to add some more depth to Salen's answer.

But the wise old man was quick to cancel Rinen's unfounded comment.

"I'm afraid you've been mistold the truth, Rinen."

As the cloth which wrapped the tablet on the table in the centre of the room was removed, the two apprentices looked on in amazement and some uncertainty.

"Ajia's tablet ..." Salen stood a gasped.

"That's got to be an illusion," Rinen responded.

"I assure you it's no illusion," Master Brennius replied, allowing the apprentices to breathe in its mystical allure.

"Where did you find that?" uttered Salen, completely stunned by the sight of the tablet. For a minute he was unsure whether this was the absolute truth. But he knew that his Master and Mythrian were in no mood for silly games.

"It was given to me by a friend of my father," Mythrian explained to his friends who began analysing the tablet.

"My father was the one who found it and so it has been handed down to me to look after, as a family treasure."

Rinen, who had crouched down to get a closer look at the tablet, spoke back, but with a twist of his light humour.

"Some family treasure. Most families tend to want to keep hold of theirs."

But as Rinen looked closer at the tablet, he noticed the dark lines that were sweeping the artefact.

"Hey look, there are markings on this tablet. That must be where the power is held."

"Wait a minute," Salen paused, trying to slow his mind down from the spin it was in. "If Mythrian holds Ajia's tablet, then surely he is the chosen one to take on its power."

"He already has the power," Master Brennius replied. "Those markings on the tablet once held Ajia's power, but the power now flows through Mythrian."

"What? You've unleashed the power? But that means ..." Salen was not comfortable with where this was heading.

"Yes, Mythrian is the chosen one," the old man responded.

"So this is why Mythrian's markings appeared brighter. I knew there had to be an explanation."

"Yes, well that's what we believe," Brennius spoke, "but we don't want to rush to conclusions before we have a thorough understanding of the tablet itself."

Rinen had many questions to ask. He was not uncomfortable with the idea like Salen or Brennius; however he was very intrigued by it.

"Hold on. Mythrian had these markings before he had found the tablet. Why do they appear the same?"

Brennius and Salen were baffled as to how to answer that comment.

Mythrian explained to them:

"Because it is my destiny. When my father found the tablet, in theory, he should have been the chosen one. But after he was killed, that responsibility must have been passed down to me. So when I was born, I must have been given these markings to specifically house the power that was awaiting me."

Continuing in a lower tone he said, "In essence, and though I hate to say it, I am Ajia's pawn in his attempt for his freedom. And it was only a matter of time. I am sure my father never wanted this for me, but his finding and passing has placed me in this awkward situation. I must go on this quest."

"No you don't, Mythrian. Have you not seen what we have achieved since he left us? We have learned to look after ourselves. His return would bring nothing," Master Brennius tried to explain.

Mythrian was not so easily persuaded.

"It is evil that I fear more than anything. Evil was stronger than us when Draigorn led his campaign to destroy our race. And I fear they will be stronger when they return. Only Ajia can help us rid this world of evil."

Master Brennius countered, "If Ajia was capable of wiping out all evil, then why did he not destroy evil when it arose before letting all the carnage that followed take its due course?"

"I don't know," Mythrian replied, "but something tells me that he was being falsely led. Someone or something could have been hiding the activity of Siren's Gore away from him. Blinded, until Draigorn's destruction came to the West."

The room fell silent. Nobody knew what to say. But crouched down by the tablet, Rinen had made an important discovery.

"I don't want to cause any panic but ... a part of this tablet is missing ..."

The room was lifted out of its silence.

"What do you mean a part is missing?" Master Brennius questioned, shocked by Rinen's astonishing find.

"There are fracture marks down one side of the tablet as though it has been cut by steel. Perhaps by a sword or an axe," Rinen replied, carefully brushing his fingers across the stress marks.

Mystery was clouding the tablet and Rinen's new find was casting more doubt and scepticism.

Mythrian, moving forward in his chair, compelled by Rinen's comment, added:

"My father was a woodsman. When he found the tablet, he must have cut off a part of it, when he cut through the tree in which it was held."

"But the man who gave this to you, he knew nothing about this. You don't think he could have possibly been hiding a part of it?" Salen asked.

"Gwyn, no. He would have handed the other half to me had he found it," Mythrian replied assuringly to Salen's question.

"Then your father must have held on to the other part in secrecy," Salen presumed. His answer sparked a new question. "Did anyone find it after his death?"

"But my father was killed in Hollman's Hollow by bandits," Mythrian replied.

"Well then, we've got a problem," Rinen confirmed. "If they killed your father, they may have the other part of the tablet. They would try to sell it for gold. An artefact like this could raise a lot of money. But who would recognise its worth"

Mythrian paused to think to himself for a minute. If the task of finding Ajia in his exile wasn't hard enough, it seemed the other part of the mystical tablet was missing. In the wrong hands, it could cause a lot of chaos and destruction.

"Hold on a minute, I've got a question for Mythrian," Salen interrupted, "If you've only got a part of the tablet, does that mean you only have a part of its power?"

Suddenly answers began to click in Mythrian's mind. Turning to face his Master he asked, "Maybe that's why Ajia has been having trouble contacting me. Maybe because the tablet has been broken, his communication is broken."

"That seems feasible," Brennius admitted, stroking his long white beard as he looked down upon the tablet.

"Then our first goal should surely be to find who has found the tablet," Mythrian responded instantly.

"Definitely not." Rinen spoke on behalf of Master Brennius. "There's only one thing that bandits would talk or trade to and that is anything as black hearted as they are. Whoever has it will only use it to bring evil into our lands."

"He's right, Mythrian," Brennius added, "Nothing is going to be easy in your quest and nobody except the four of us in this room can be trusted. When rumours arise in our lands, while their stories are often exaggerated, their basis may be true. Evil is rising again. You can sense it in the air and it is growing. Rush into things hastily and you will pay the price. But if you stay patient, the opportunity will arise."

As the tutor looked around the room at his pupils, they were all deeply immersed in the unfolding answers behind the mystery of the tablet.

However, Master Brennius was cautious about the three of them getting too carried away with their ideas and decided to call it an evening.

"Anyway, I think that's enough for now. Well done to all of you, especially you Rinen, for your remarkable discovery. It's a good job you came after all. It has at least given us some sort of lead with this quest. If any of you gain any more news, we'll meet up in here again."

As Rinen rose and stood next to Salen, Brennius continued:

"Remember, none of this must leave this room. As of now, all our lives are at stake. The best thing to do now I think is to get some sleep. Try to ease your minds and I will see you tomorrow morning."

As the pupils disbanded, heading up the stairs off to their rooms, Master Brennius took one final, long look at the tablet. This treasure was to change the lives of thousands forever.

Chapter 4 † A Distant Call

THE NIGHT WAS difficult for Mythrian.

With the thoughts of the tablet rolling through his mind, he was finding it impossible to get to sleep. What's more, it was raining heavily. Being by the coast, Hamlynstone tended to pick up more heavy weather as the clouds rained down upon the Cronian Mountains behind them.

He sat by his window watching the rain scatter down its frame, counting the bolts of lightning as they shaped the night sky.

For many years he had looked out of this window, dreaming of adventure out in the far lands. But he had not expected that he would be tasked with the most daring and dangerous adventure of them all.

To seek out Ajia and to restore the world to its former glory.

So doubtful was anyone's chance, so far away Ajia seemed to be from his people, that the adventure had fallen into folklore.

But like all stories told, there needs to be a hero. Mythrian was to be that hero and nothing would make his life more meaningful than for his feats to be told in generations to come.

Succeed or fail, Mythrian would be a hero throughout the land, just like Aedorn was during Draigorn's downfall.

But what was worrying him now was that someone else had another part of the tablet. Who knows what evil power could be enhanced should it fall into the wrong hands?

Rumours had been growing for the last few years that the skies to the East were darkening. New blood was rising.

A new wave of evil was growing and this time it would be greater and stronger than ever before. Alas, the people of this land would not speak of this, until the first drop of blood had been spilt.

But what Mythrian was waiting for was a message or a sign to start him on his trail. For a moment, the boy wondered whether Ajia was listening to his thoughts as he noticed a messenger, bearing information. He was heading for the Guild, running through the torrential rain.

Heading down the stairs, Mythrian hastily walked into the Guild entrance, where the messenger, soaked from head to toe, stood talking to one of the Guild tutors.

As the tutor noticed the boy over his shoulder, he pointed to Mythrian as the messenger walked over to hand him the letter.

"Are you Mythrian?" the messenger questioned.

"Yes, I am," the boy answered.

"I bring an urgent message, Mythrian. The Mayor of Fayrmayden wishes to speak with you on a matter of concern, involving you," the messenger said, handing the boy the note.

Thanking the messenger for the message, the boy walked back up to the warmth of his room, while an assistant brought a drink for the tired and drained messenger.

Entering his room, Mythrian opened the note before jumping on to his bed and reading it quietly to himself.

The note was written by the Mayor of Fayrmayden, the only female Mayor in the kingdom:

"Dear Mythrian.

I write this message in need of your help. We've been suffering from a disturbance which has been frightening my villagers. To the back of our village lie our gardens, where all our residents and visitors go to unwind from their hectic lives. But recently, witnesses have spoken of a voice coming from within our garden. We need your help for this matter, because the voice has been calling out for you. We will arrange for your transport which will be with you in two days, when the third sun has risen to its highest point. We await your arrival.

Yours sincerely, Mayor Eliza Heathcot, Fayrmayden."

At first, Mythrian was unsure what to make of the letter.

Who would be trying to contact him and why in the gardens of Fayrmayden?

Had Ajia passed his messages on to someone close enough to reach him? The only spiritual voice that Mythrian had spoken to was Elrick, in Emory Forest, but there was no reason for him to communicate again.

It could be a trap. But Mythrian knew that there might be the chance that this voice could give him some help or guidance with his quest. Surely nothing would be trying to contact him unless it was urgent?

Knowing that his Master should be told about this, he headed down the stairs towards his room. He couldn't wait till morning.

Approaching the door, he knocked on it several times. It echoed loudly through the wooden door into Brennius' room, waking the tired man from his sleep.

"Hold on, hold on," Brennius shouted, rubbing his eyes, while he walked up to the door in his long sleeping robe.

Upon opening the door he instantly recognised the young boy, wondering what had brought him to his room at this time in the evening.

"Mythrian, it's just gone past midnight, why aren't you asleep?" Brennius asked, leaning his weak body against the door frame.

"A messenger from Fayrmayden gave me this note. They've already organised the transport, I am to head there in two days time."

He handed Master Brennius the note, who let him into the room, while he walked over to his desk to read the note thoroughly.

Closing the door behind him, Mythrian looked around the room, taking in the atmosphere. Like any room Master Brennius worked or rested in, everything was neat and tidy and out of the way. He believed that having more space around you increased your level to think more clearly.

There were certainly a lot of similarities between Mythrian and Master Brennius and the need for space and tidiness was one thing they shared in common.

Carefully reading the note, Master Brennius was cautious of Mythrian's safety. There was no telling whether this voice was of good tongue or evil.

Turning round in his seat to face his pupil, he replied, "Well I can't stop you from going. But I'm still cautious of your personal safety. This has been sent as a call of emergency and while I'm sure that you're very capable of handling a situation like this, it still appears very dangerous. I would like to send a scout with you, as extra protection"

"Will the scout travel with me from here?" Mythrian asked, making sure he knew the situation thoroughly.

"No. I know of a couple of scouts who would be good for this sort of task, but they unfortunately are not from around here," the Master replied, while he assessed the other possibilities.

"On the way to Fayrmayden, you will find the mining village of Mignmedia."

"I know the way to Mignmedia, that's in the hills of Twyndall," Mythrian replied.

"Good, you can meet him there. It will give some time for the scout to make his way north to meet you."

Running the plan through his mind, the young man was satisfied with the idea and thanked his guardian for his help.

Opening the door to leave, Master Brennius stopped him to offer a final comment.

"Mythrian, take good care of yourself. If there is any information you can get that may help you on your search for Ajia, obtain it, however small it is. This voice may just be the answer to your quest. But don't forget there might be the element of danger. Be aware."

"I will," Mythrian assured his Master before he wished him goodnight and walked back to his room to try to get to sleep. Master Brennius tried the same, though his worries were drowning his thoughts.

As the molten lava bubbled and spit around the red rock inside of Siren's Gore, activity was growing. Thousands of minions were hard at work, cultivating their home to ensure more development to their civilisation.

In the many caves that layered the inside of the volcano, preparations were being set for a big occasion. Their Master had brought back a gift, a key to their efforts of revenge against the kingdom to the West.

In the main chamber, where all the evil souls rise to create new spawn, the cloaked creature entered from his meeting in the Eideros Mountains, his goblin assistants carrying the chest behind him.

One of the goblins asked, "Where do you wish the treasure to be placed?"

Their Master took off his cloak.

"Place the treasure upon the central pillar," he directed, as he watched the goblins carefully lay the artefact on a stalagmite, that had a flat, smooth top. Light from above, channeled down onto the pillar, intensifying the fiery colour around the site.

"Anything else you wish for us to do, Master Mordryd?"

"That will be all for now," Mordryd spoke, as the two goblins left to join the minions in their development.

Mordryd appeared of human origin, but he had a heart as evil as the minions around him, if not more evil. Though for a human, his level of power was unprecedented and few dared test his patience. But his background was unclear. Nobody knew who he exactly was or where he came from. But more importantly, why was a human controlling the forces of evil? All that is known is that he was a dark sorcerer who only used his powers to corrupt.

His face was pale and drawn, with some mild wrinkles detailing some age. His hair was long and wavy with streaks of grey, as was his chin beard, which stretched down to his chest. Behind his beard sat his sinister smile, which always added to the suspicious character, always draped in black. But his most significant feature was his right eye, though it had been covered by a black band, wrapped tightly around his head. What was it hiding? Was he more than he appeared?

Opening the box, Mordryd smiled with great pleasure as he looked at the gift inside, the other half of Ajia's tablet, his mind dreaming of possibilities. He had searched so long for this and now it was his. The first stage in his campaign was complete.

As he stared at the purple rays that danced across the mystical artefact, another figure, cloaked under a long robe, appeared behind him. It looked like the creature that had cast the Rock Troll against the village of Avalin.

"So you have found the tablet, or what is left of it," the cloaked creature approached.

Mordryd closed the chest, cautious of the safety of the tablet, even from his own followers. Turning to face the creature, he soon recognised who it was and welcomed her return.

The creature was actually a witch from the wild woods of Anthelstone, which had long thought to have held witches deep within the forest. It seemed she had news on the tablet, always seeming to have a third eye on the young conjurer and his development with the powers.

"Where is the other half?" Mordryd asked impatiently, hoping to hear good news on the missing link to his tablet.

"It has been found by a young boy who goes by the name of Mythrian," the witch replied, any expression hidden under the hood of her cloak

Disgruntled that his plans had been foiled, he hoped that the boy had not yet worked out the meaning of the artefact.

"Has he unlocked the powers within?"

"He has; with powers beyond a mind's imagination."

"Tell me more of these powers," the sorcerer asked eagerly.

"I can only tell you as much as I have seen," the witch responded. "To the west, by the village of Avalin, stands a rock troll, trapped heavily in vines risen from beneath the ground. This was the work of Mythrian – and to think that the Troll was once a simple rock that could fit in the palm of your hand."

Mordryd was enthralled at the powers of the tablet and could not wait to use them for his devious plans.

"Excellent. My minions are making the final preparations for the tablet. Many years ago, the mighty Draigorn led my forces into battle against the kingdom to the West. His soul may be lost, but his memory remains strong. Inside the depths of Siren's

Gore's molten core, that memory remains and with the power of the tablet, I plan to resurrect our great leader. To create a creature as powerful as the Gods. He will be my disciple and under my orders, he will crush the enemy in his grasp."

"Beware the power of the tablet. You only have a part of it. Its powers could backfire."

"There will be no problems with my plan," Mordryd responded sharply. "No man will be foolish enough to stand before his awesome might."

"What about Mythrian?"

Mordryd fell silent. He was already becoming angry with just hearing his name. He knew this young boy was going to be a thorn in his campaign, but he knew he could be spied on.

"I want you to keep an eye out for this Mythrian. I want to know where he is heading and when," the sorcerer demanded.

"He is heading in two days' time to the village of Fayrmayden," she replied confidently.

Stepping closer to the witch with interest, Mordryd continued, "How do you know this?"

"Because there is a voice calling him there," she spoke, "The voice of a spirit I once knew."

"Who?" Mordryd replied, wanting answers to every question.

"I cannot tell you. But all I can tell you is that Mythrian will be heading across the land known as Gyda's Pass, on his way to Fayrmayden. If you wish to catch him, you can catch him there."

"Hhhmmm...I don't have enough minions to assemble a party quick enough to counter him," Mordryd rubbed his beard, thinking of a plan to stop the boy from reaching his destination, but with the heavy work beginning with the creation of his disciple, there were few opportunities."

"What about your goblins? You have an army's worth of them to the south." The witch tried to offer another option.

"Yes, but it will take at least a day or two to get them assembled here and another few days till they reach Gyda's Pass," Mordryd answered.

"Then send for them. It will take Mythrian a few days to get there and back anyway. Assemble them now and launch them to strike Mythrian at nightfall on his return from Fayrmayden. He will not be expecting it."

"Very well. Kobar, your presence please." Mordryd called one of the goblins in charge of the activity inside Siren's Gore. "Send for a group of goblin infantry. I want them here quickly."

"Of course, Master," the goblin replied.

Just as the goblin was about to send his Master's orders, Mordryd asked for one final favour. "Kobar, do we have any Goblin assassins in Siren's Gore?"

"Yes Master, what would you propose?" Kobar replied, obeying every order his Master spoke.

"I want you to send one to Gyda's Pass right now. I want him to try to halt the young boy in his tracks; he'll know who I mean when he finds him. This will give time for the goblin infantry to catch up, so they can capture him. And don't forget to tell your infantry that when you catch him, I want this boy alive. In fact," the sorcerer paused, "Tell your assassin, that if he suspects anyone aiding Mythrian on his journey, deal with them appropriately."

Turning to the witch, he asked, "As for you, I need you to continue to keep watch over this boy. Tell me everything you find out about him."

"I will," the witch said, leaving Mordryd to watch over the continuing development of his great plan.

CHAPTER 5 ✝ THE JOURNEY
BECKONS

TWO NIGHTS HAD quickly passed as the third sun came into view above the hills. Mythrian's transport was only a mile away from the village and Master Brennius was wishing safe travel to his pupil.

But they were to have an unexpected arrival.

As Master Brennius, Mythrian, Salen and a couple of other apprentices who were on guard stood by the Guild doors, watching the transport moving down the central path, they instantly spotted something very peculiar.

The transport wagon was travelling very slowly, which seemed odd considering it was on an important mission. The coachman who was controlling the tempo of the horses seemed unaware of it.

In fact, the coachman looked cold and pale, his eyes staring straight forward while his hands remained tightly gripped on the ropes of the horses. Something was visibly wrong.

As the horses stopped in front of the apprentices, one of the nearby villagers noticed that the coachman had not moved a muscle since his arrival.

As he carefully approached the frozen soul, his body fell clumsily on to the villager's shoulder, who shrieked as he pushed the body off him on to the floor.

As the body lay lifeless, face down on the floor, all the villagers screamed with fear as they noticed an arrow pointing out of the coachman's back.

Shocked by the incident, Mythrian rushed to the wagon, but was stopped by Salen. With the help of the two other apprentices,

Salen removed the cover over the back of the transport, to make sure there wasn't a trap.

As the cover was ripped off the top of the wagon, the apprentices were instantly repelled by the horrible sight of dead corpses, their faces as pale as the lifeless coachman.

With flies swarming across their skin, one of the apprentices rocked each body one by one, just to check all of them were dead.

All were but one.

To the front of the wagon, one figure was covered from head to toe in the cloth. As the apprentice nudged him, he trembled, muttering cries of help as he hugged the skirting of the wagon.

Firstly looking towards Salen, who gave the orders to remove the sheet, the apprentices prepared themselves for a trap. When the cloth was pulled back, a figure leapt out from underneath, shouting at the top of his voice:

"DON'T HURT ME! PLEASE! SPARE ME!"

"It's alright," Salen assured the man, holding him tightly to stop any sudden attacks, while the survivor tried to calm himself down, relieved to have found a friendly face at last.

After the survivor had settled down, sitting in a chair with a warm drink and a blanket over his shoulders, Master Brennius and his apprentices needed to know exactly what had happened to their transport.

"Can you tell us what happened on your way here?" Master Brennius asked.

Taking a moment to regain his thoughts, he recalled:

"All I remember was that it happened somewhere in the middle of Arlyne's Drift. We were quietly travelling on our way here, when arrows appeared out of nowhere, hitting every inch of the wagon. With the coachman being the first one to be hit, many of the other travellers jumped off the back and ran for their lives. They didn't make it far. Soon, I was the only one left on the transport, and the only one left alive. Peeking through the bottom of the cover, I caught sight of a figure which I had trouble making out. At first it looked human and it was dressed pretty similarly as well, until I caught sight of its hand and noticed its dark green tinge. I had never seen a goblin before and it was quite a disturbing sight. As I watched it placing the bodies back on to the transport, I hid myself under one of the cloths we had in the back. Luckily he failed to spot me before he kicked the horses on to here."

As they all took a moment to take the words in, Salen wondered, "What do we do now? If those goblins are still out there, they will be looking out for the wagon on its return. It will be an easy target for them, since they've already intercepted it."

"True," Mythrian agreed. "But we still have the horses and in good shape. If I was to just take the horses to Fayrmayden, not only might they not catch me since I will be without the visible frame of the transport, but I will be moving far more quickly. It's a risk but a risk worth taking."

Turning to the survivor, Brennius asked, "How far were you from Mignmedia?"

"About half an hour short of Mignmedia in the transport," the man replied assuringly.

Focusing on Mythrian, who looked confident that his plan would work, Master Brennius placed his hand on his forehead, fighting against his will. Finally he agreed with himself to let the boy go, ordering one of the villagers:

"Saddle up the horses, we plan to leave now."

Focusing on Mythrian, Brennius continued, "Whatever you do Mythrian, don't stop until you get to Mignmedia. Only then will you be in safe hands. Look out for yourself."

"I will. Thank you, Master."

With his horses set, Mythrian jumped upon the saddle, while he made his final farewell before he began the long journey to Mignmedia.

Galloping across the Lochrian plain, with the third sun sending down its rays of light, Mythrian focused only on what stood before him.

Crossing the calm, gentle streams, riding through the shaded cover of the woods and sprinting across the emerald greens of Lochrian, Mythrian was unimpressed by the beauty around him. Not even the quietest of areas was going to be safe on his journey.

Exiting his home region, Mythrian entered the land of Arlyne's Drift, a land separated in two by Gyda's Pass, which divides the land from the North Sea.

To the west, the land was boggy, unprosperous and difficult to cross quickly, whereas to the east, the land was fertile and budding.

If the sticky ground did not help Mythrian on his way to Mignmedia, the famous crystal hills that surround the west side of the village were going to be another set obstacle to get round. Though, should he be able to reach them by nightfall, they could offer him some useful cover till the morning.

Half an hour had passed since he had entered Arlyne's Drift. The long, flat plains of Lochrian had disappeared. Miles of rough bog land stood before him. An unwelcoming sight for the boy, knowing he had to take extra special care with every step.

Carefully avoiding the bubbling pools of moss covered ponds and the unpredictable banks that shaped the unstable land, Mythrian was cautious of his pace, carefully watching everything unfolding in front of him.

Visibility was poor. Over many of the pools, a thick mist covered the surface, hiding their position like traps. The odour of the bogs was sickening. Mythrian limited his breathing, so as not to take in too much of the vile stench.

But while Mythrian was passing through the boggy terrain, a head popped up above one of the pools behind him, its infested skin matching the greens around it, invisible to the naked eye.

As it watched the boy and his two horses slowly making their way across the bogs on their way to Mignmedia, the creature rose out of the depths.

Standing calmly still in the pond, so the top half of its body was free to manoeuvre, the creature – a goblin – reached over his shoulder to take hold of his bow. Drawing a blunt arrow intending only to knock the boy unconscious, he quietly drew aim.

In the final seconds before the bow was unleashed, the boy would have had no idea of the position of the creature, had it not been for the birds above.

Circling the ground from above, a group of dark birds had been following the boy since he had entered the region.

Few travel through these parts of the kingdom. Few make it through. Many are killed by inhaling too much of the potent fumes or drown in the hidden pools. There is often plenty of food for these carnivorous birds.

As the birds caught sight of the green creature, they suddenly sprang into action, releasing distress calls at the presence of the unfamiliar figure.

Looking over his shoulder, Mythrian caught sight of the figure in the pool. It was a goblin; he appeared heavily equipped. No doubt, he had been sent to capture the boy. But the goblin had become distracted by the birds, who had given away his position.

While his attention had fallen from the boy, Mythrian made a quick break for it, galloping as fast as he could against the uneven ground. But even Mythrian's quick momentary escape was not going to be enough to out-speed the goblin.

Watching the boy trying to make a stealthy break, the goblin pulled out from his quiver three arrows, which he lit.

Around the site, hidden in the thick marshes, posts had been planted by the goblin, holding within them flammable materials. Aiming his arrows at the posts, the weapons connected with their targets. The chemicals fused, lighting the boggy terrain up in a series of flames, acting as barriers to halt the boy.

There was no escape.

So quick was the creature's release of his arrows, that Mythrian hardly had time to think of a route out. Soon he was surrounded by a ring of fire.

The flames were simply too high to jump over and the horses were refusing to leave the centre of the ring. But the fires were drawing inwards and they were moving in quickly.

As the flames drew closer, Mythrian could only just about see his foe through the flickering flames. He was walking up to the fire, to get a closer look at his prey.

Quickly looking for an escape, he noticed a small pool, on one side of the flames. The fires were sweeping around it, leaving a gap, just about big enough for him to slip through.

It was the only option he had.

Leaping off the back of his horse, while covering his head with his arms, he threw himself through the gap, diving into the murky pool.

Trying to open his eyes, Mythrian struggled to see through the dark water as its contamination was burning his eyes.

Without the ability to see and getting very low on oxygen, Mythrian had to find some way out without giving his position away.

Placing his right hand on his forehead, he used his powers to create a third eye above his head. As a luminous blue eye appeared on his forehead, it lit up the pool, enabling him to see underwater.

His search needed to be quick, as there was no way of telling whether the goblin could see him from above. Finding an exit through some weeds which led through to another pond, Mythrian closed his third eye and swam through.

Meanwhile the goblin had reached the ring of fire but as he peered through, he could only see the two horses, panicking in the centre of the circle.

Suddenly, the tables had turned and now the goblin felt like the captured one.

Was it a spell? Had he really disappeared? He couldn't have gone far. But scanning round the area, looking into some of the nearby pools, his search came to no avail.

Suddenly his ankles were caught by a pair of hands from a pool behind him, pulling him down. The goblin lost his balance and fell face down on to the marsh.

Clutching the blades of grass, fighting against the very strong pull of the boy, the goblin lost his grip as he tried to reach for his blade. In his panic it fell from his belt, sinking into the pool.

Taking his chance, the boy dragged the creature underneath the surface; the goblin did not appear so deadly now he had lost his equipment.

Wrapping his arms around the creature's neck, Mythrian denied the goblin any air. As he wriggled and squirmed, Mythrian's arms were tightening ever more.

As his movements weakened, Mythrian grabbed his own dagger and stabbed it into the creature's chest.

The goblin instantly fell limp. As Mythrian relinquished his grip, the beast slowly sank to the bottom of the pool, his task failed.

Crawling out of the pool, Mythrian, tired and exhausted, took a couple of much needed breaths of air. He was thankful that the danger had cleared, but he had a new problem.

Lifting himself to his knees, he saw the wall of flames in front and his horses trapped within. The flames had become too intense and there was no chance of Mythrian freeing them.

As he sat stranded, miles away from the closest village of Mignmedia, watching his only means of transport trapped and helpless, Mythrian needed nothing short of a miracle. But perhaps luck was on his side.

Holding out his hand, Mythrian noticed droplets of water hitting his palm, increasing in numbers rapidly. Looking up towards the sky, Mythrian could not hide his delight as he saw great clouds of dark grey intensifying, raining showers down upon the land where he stood.

Focusing back on the horses, the boy thanked the skies as the rain calmed down the fire around them. As the flames died down, the horses were all too happy to skip through the smoke, freed at last and able to rejoin their Master.

Was this luck? Not if you're such a strong believer as Mythrian. He knew that Ajia had helped him here, maybe sensing his danger from far away.

Either way, Mythrian was free and was able to make his way over to the approaching mountains, sitting west of the village of Mignmedia, better known as the Hills of Twyndall.

Approaching the hills, Mythrian allowed the horses to take a drink from one of the pools at the base of the hills, the water high in quality, having run through many forms of minerals and crystal within the mountains.

Leading his horses up the mountainside, Mythrian sat upon a ridge, on one of the hills where he was to rest for the night. Lying on his back, admiring the full moon above, Mythrian was reflecting on his long day.

For sure, it was eventful and it certainly proved that nowhere was going to be safe for Mythrian. Whoever had the other part of the tablet must know who he was.

But who that was so far remained a mystery to the boy. However, the incident with the goblin was a reminder to Mythrian to remain cautious, no matter where he travelled.

CHAPTER 6 ✝ REFLECTIONS

A S THE NIGHT clouds swept the darkening sky, bringing with them cool breezes that picked up as they ran up the mountainside, Mythrian slept peacefully under the full third moon.

He had been sleeping for roughly two to three hours before he was suddenly woken up by a strong beam of light, coming from nearby.

The light from the moon above had caught something within the mountains and its reflection was dazzling.

Rubbing his tired eyes, Mythrian couldn't make out what the light was. He decided to take a closer look.

Waking himself up and clambering to his feet, Mythrian took his time approaching the light. After the incident earlier, there was no judging whether this was another trap, but he knew that he couldn't run from everything that confronted him.

Slowly approaching the light, occasionally looking around in case of danger, Mythrian noticed that the light was coming from inside a hole on the mountainside.

The hole was big. It baffled Mythrian as to how it came to be of that size.

Moving ever closer, Mythrian's curiosity had overstepped his caution.

As his foot slipped on some loose ground, the forward momentum threw him down the hole. Sliding through the endless tunnel, he was heading into the heart of the mountain.

Shooting out of the bottom of the tunnel, Mythrian hit solid ground hard on his front. Re-catching his breath after landing heavily on his ribs, the boy firstly began to wonder how far he had fallen.

Rising to his knees, Mythrian had to pause to behold the spectacular sight around him. It was, without doubt, the single most beautiful place he had ever seen.

"Wow ... so this is where all the crystals are dug up from," Mythrian spoke as his words echoed around the hollow cavern.

Crystals; rubies; gems; emeralds; packed in their thousands, lining the walls just centimetres apart. The pack of bright colours reflecting rainbows of light against each other had Mythrian spellbound.

He had stumbled into the depths of the hills of Twyndall, where all the crystals used for casting spells are found buried within its rocky structure.

To think that this cauldron of beauty was hidden away from the outside world. Mythrian could have been the only person ever to stumble into the depths of Twyndall.

He felt very proud and enthralled with his discovery.

This was a gold mine for any caster of magic and Mythrian could not help but take a couple of the crystals for himself. It would be silly not to take a few while he was there.

Picking out a couple of lush, ocean blue crystals from the side of the wall, Mythrian thought he was doing no harm, tucking them safely under his shirt.

But as he continued to admire the mesmerising sight, he began to wonder how he was going to get out.

The hole from which he had fallen was too high to reach and there didn't seem to be any tunnels within the site.

Mythrian then thought of climbing the walls to reach the tunnel, but they didn't look safe or stable.

For a moment there seemed no obvious way out. He couldn't stay here for the rest of his life. He needed to find a way out and quickly.

Suddenly an idea flew into his head. The pools at the bottom of the mountain, where his horses had drunk from its rich, clean water. The water must come through hidden chambers within the mountain. Perhaps the tunnel, through which he had fallen was caused by water.

His eyes caught sight of drops of water leaking from behind one of the crystals. Perhaps if he released the crystal there might be enough water to fill the cavern so he could reach the tunnel above.

It was a risk, but he had no other ideas and he couldn't spend any longer in this undiscovered labyrinth.

Having lost his dagger after the battle with the goblin, Mythrian had to make do with his sword. Chipping away at the sediment around the crystal, trying to loosen the gem, thin cracks appeared behind it.

As the water began to flow more freely, Mythrian placed his sword back into its sheath and pulled the crystal out. Water gushed out on to the floor, spreading across the labyrinth.

As the water covered the floor's surface and rose to ankle height, Mythrian was worried that there wasn't enough pressure and more importantly not enough water.

Finding another couple of crystals nearby that appeared to have water behind them, Mythrian opened them, revealing more water as it rose to his knees, spinning clockwise around the cavern.

His plan was going well but as he opened another hole, two big cracks appeared, spreading quickly across the wall. Ripping through the interior of the cavern, they formed an arch, twice Mythrian's height.

Suddenly, the huge area collapsed, as gallons of water rushed in, throwing the unsuspecting boy backwards into the water. Trying to remain above the water level, Mythrian was fighting the strong levels of current and losing.

As the water rose till the boy's feet were lifted off the floor, the motion began to swirl the boy round in circles.

The speed at which he was spinning made it dangerous as well; his hands scraping against some of the sharp edges of the crystals.

Managing to look up towards the tunnel above, Mythrian knew that with the speed the water level was rising, he would only have one chance to reach for the tunnel and crawl out to safety.

Trying his best to keep to the outside to give him a better

chance of reaching it, his chance was soon to come.

With the tunnel now in arm's reach, the boy waited as he spun round for the last time, the crystals on the wall trimming like blades through his blue suit.

As the hole approached, he reached out with his arms as far as they could be pushed, while his fingers clenched tightly around the skirt of the tunnel.

Holding firmly on to the edge of the tunnel, fortunately, the sediment was strong, as he lifted himself out of the water.

He had reached the hole successfully but the water was still rising and it was heading up the tunnel.

It was a race, as Mythrian crawled as fast as he could up the steep tunnel, focusing only on the light above.

Leaping out of the edge of the tunnel, Mythrian grabbed his horses and stood in a safe area.

As he watched the water run down the mountainside, it eventually came to a halt. Mythrian drew a deep sigh of relief. He was glad to have got out of an awkward situation, but at the same time was proud of his discovery.

Mythrian was learning many valuable lessons along his journey and he hoped this was to be the last time that his curiosity would put him in danger.

In one of the pits outside Siren's Gore, work was constant with the burning of metals and other useful resources.

The many thousands of minions, digging and carving through stone, were building bases, armouries, housing for their growing numbers.

But most of the work was going into a new project, a castle, to be built on top of Siren's Gore. This monumental fort would be the pinnacle of their fast development, in their second wave of destruction.

Not only acting as a viewpoint into the distant lands to the West, it would also be the fortress for Mordryd's new disciple.

But while they were beginning constructions down below in the caverns, an important message was being returned.

Through one of the chamber openings, a goblin bearing information cautiously approached Kobar, one of the main goblins in charge of Mordryd's work.

Kobar was a respected individual. He had served his Master well, in both preserving Siren's Gore and efforts in the field of battle. In fact Kobar was once in one of the heavy infantry groups, but his knowledge and profound ability quickly shone above the rest.

Goblins are split into two groups; goblins used for battle or warcraft and goblins used for knowledge and teaching minions the ways of the world. There is a distinct line between the two, with infantry goblins being stocky, oily skinned and very grotesque facially.

Those used for knowledge are very thin, covered in warts and are heavily wrinkled and yet they tend to be very human-like in their features.

Kobar himself was far larger than the average goblin. In fact he was probably twice the weight of many of his counterparts. A jack of all trades, he was abundantly strong, intelligent and very, very quick tempered.

Few dared disobey his orders, for many of them did not last very long. Their teeth were plucked and set on a piece of string which he held round his neck, to warn others not to do the same.

Though being strongly admired by his Master, Kobar was often in the firing line for any mishaps that occurred so he made sure they didn't go wrong that often.

Watching the work of his minions closely, Kobar was only hoping for promising news from his approaching messenger.

"Kobar, I bring news of your assassin," the messenger began. "He found the boy known as Mythrian but he was unfortunately slain by what I can only describe as a very powerful individual."

Throwing his arm out and grabbing the messenger round the throat, Kobar lifted the goblin up with ease, choking him while he remained focused on the activity in front of him, so as not to startle any of the workers.

"I did not ask for excuses," Kobar screamed. "I make the orders and I expect them to be completed. Your comments have angered me. Why should I not crush you in my grasp right now? You know these minions need to eat fresh. Their appetite makes them stronger."

"I beg you, have mercy," the goblin pleaded, trying to free Kobar's powerful grip with both hands, before stating, "It was not me who failed you, Master."

"In combat, we were always told to act as one. It made us stronger, more fierce. Anyone stupid enough to disobey that rule was executed," Kobar replied, before staring at the breathless creature in his hand and continuing.

"We are on the forefront of becoming an unstoppable force. Soon the world will be ours to regain once again, but first we need to eradicate the ones who don't belong. And you don't belong."

As he finished his comment, he slashed his claws across the goblin's chest, drawing blood before he threw him over the edge, into the chamber below.

As the smell of blood tickled their noses, rushes of minions were quick to feed on the fresh victim, a gift for their hard work.

Watching his minions from above, crowding round their prey, Kobar welcomed another goblin, Gloro, who had moved out of the shadows behind him.

Having watched his response to another failed mission, the goblin kept his distance from Kobar, though this goblin had come with a more positive return.

"Kobar, the infantry group you requested is here."

"Let me see them," Kobar ordered.

"Certainly, right this way."

Taking Kobar into a small chamber carved into the mountain, Gloro introduced him to a line of goblin infantry. They stood still as if carved out of marble; the band of light infantry neither blinked nor flinched in the presence of Kobar. He was very impressed.

"Troops, I wish to send you on a mission. One of my assassins was killed by a little vermin known as Mythrian. He is very powerful and very dangerous towards our campaign. I do not want him dead. So you'll have to figure out how you will tackle that one yourselves. He will be travelling across Arlyne's Drift. Find him there and bring him to me."

Stopping halfway down the line, without warning Kobar threw his hand at one of the infantry, hitting him sharply on the side of the face.

"Is that understood?"

The goblin stood still, his eyes unmoving. Focused on the wall in front like his fellow units, he showed no pain.

"They have been trained well, but are they the right troops for this task?" Kobar questioned.

"This sounded like a very important task so I assembled the finest troops around. They will complete your task," Gloro confidently answered.

"I have no time for your words," Kobar replied. "Just do your task. That is all."

As Kobar left the room, Gloro ordered his troops to the front gates. Their calls were deafening.

CHAPTER 7 † OF HAMMER AND ANVIL

TROTTING DOWN THE side of the hill, Mythrian and his horses had scaled across the hills of Twyndall. They were now in arm's reach of the village of Mignmedia.

Patting his horses for their great perseverance, Mythrian was relieved to have finally made it safely to his first stop-off point.

Being a mining town, Mignmedia was very dark and dull. The once scarlet pillared walls that surrounded the village had been dyed black by the fumes and dust ejected through the mines.

The tall turning wheels that stood as the main feature of the settlement, bringing up water for the local mills or materials dug up from mining, stood very cold and plain.

Unlike most villages, the atmosphere was very quiet. It wasn't until Mythrian reached the gates that he began to hear the sounds of the villagers filling the air.

Tying the horses to one of the posts along the stables by the entrance, Mythrian began his search for the scout waiting for him.

Though the village was reasonably quiet, there were a lot of people wandering around the various shops. Mythrian found the distant atmosphere unwelcoming.

As Mythrian began to unwind from his treacherous journey wandering passed the many shops, he felt as though he was travelling in a loop. Next to the shops were blacksmiths and tailors; both being the main suppliers of the town.

There were no houses in the village. Most of the workers lived in rooms above their workshops. Most of the visitors were traders.

As more and more shops opened up, as the fourth sun rose higher above them, Mythrian soon noticed that the village was becoming more lively and populated.

The clock had chimed midday. Soon the area around Mythrian was filling with traders and workers coming into the village.

It was quite a sight to behold for Mythrian, watching the many traders and workers coming into the village, whether they were buying goods for their work or exchanging conversations on the crafts.

Just watching the blacksmiths hitting sword and shield against the anvils showed these were true craftsmen and Mythrian was moved by the great skills of a lot of these workers.

But as the crowd of workers swelled, the unsuspecting threat of thieves was heightened. Coming from such a quiet village as Hamlynstone, Mythrian was unaware and this made him an easy target.

Quietly taking in the sights and sounds from the nearby furnaces, their bellies burning precious metals, exhaling breaths of dense, blackened smoke, Mythrian was unaware of the mysterious figure creeping up behind him.

Untying the sword from Mythrian's belt, the figure, whose face was hidden by his cloak, took his prize and headed off to one of the traders to cash in on his find.

Thinking to himself as to where to head next around the village, Mythrian placed his hands casually on his hips only to notice his sword was missing.

Turning around to face the crowd behind him, Mythrian failed to spot anybody suspicious enough to have taken his sword.

Heading around the village, looking for Aedorn's sword, Mythrian knew this was the last thing he needed at this time. He was stunned to find it in a blacksmith's shop and even more so to see he was presenting it to an interested buyer.

Racing over to stop his possession falling into a new pair of hands, Mythrian shouted, "Wait ... that's my sword."

"Excuse me young sir," the blacksmith stopped him, "Just who do you think you are?"

"That is my sword," the boy replied, before he caught sight

of the hooded man behind the trader. Not only was he standing by the stool holding Mythrian's sword; his discreetness and his refusal to make eye contact with Mythrian, made him a prime suspect as the thief

Pointing towards the man, he continued, "He stole it from me."

"This man you are pointing out happens to be my assistant and he told me he acquired this sword from a trader," the craftsman argued.

"What type of trader is going to hand an artefact like this to a suspicious figure like that?" Mythrian tried to argue back, but his response was falling on deaf ears.

"I'm sorry, sir, but I'm going to have to ask you to leave," the man spoke, as he looked over the shoulders of the boy towards the guard, who was alerted and made his way over towards them.

Spotting the guard behind him, Mythrian continued to testify, "I'm telling you, that is my sword. I found it in Emory Forest, by the lake."

"Oh, now you are lying. Nobody goes into Emory Forest. Nobody's been in there for years."

Everybody was beginning to lose their patience with the boy and as the guard approached and placed his hands on the boy's shoulders, Mythrian knew that he was in trouble and all for the wrong reasons.

"What seems to be the problem?" the guard muttered, leaning over the boy.

"This boy is stopping me from selling my goods to this customer," the blacksmith replied.

"But it's my sword," the boy continued to state his argument, but to no avail.

"Right, you're coming with me ..." the guard spoke before a hand landed on his shoulder, moving him aside.

Stepping into the conversation was a man who stood very tall, head and shoulders above the others.

"I think you all owe this boy an apology. That is his sword that you are holding."

Mythrian had no idea who he was, though he was thankful of

his intervention.

"Who are you?" the guard questioned.

"I'm the original owner of that sword. This boy bought it from me, when was it ..." the anonymous man returned, looking down at the boy to make the conversation appear more real than his comments were. "About a week ago now. I firmly suggest you give it back to its rightful owner."

Embarrassed to say the least, the blacksmith handed the sword back to Mythrian, who showed some gratitude by offering his thanks.

Watching the conversation with disgust, the wealthy customer shunned the craftsmen. "Well, I see my business isn't needed here."

Turning to the thief, the blacksmith looked in a vile mood, as Mythrian and the anonymous helper moved quickly away from the scene.

Thanking the stranger, Mythrian was keen to know who he was.

"Thank you ever so much for getting my sword back for me, but may I ask who are you?"

"Is your name Mythrian by any chance?" the man spoke, bending down slightly, so the boy didn't feel too intimidated.

"Yes it is; you must be the scout sent to meet me here."

He was pleased to have found the scout and knew he could now rest a bit easier.

"The name is Thain," the tall man replied, before he pointed to a local tavern, saying, "Fancy a pint?"

"Sure, I'm dying for a drink," the boy hastily returned before they headed off to the tavern, which was nestled between two large barns holding transport.

As Mythrian sat patiently by a table in the tavern, Thain came back from the bar with two mugs filled with cold, overflowing beer.

Placing them under Mythrian's nose, he began sniffing the arising aromas, guessing the flavours in his head.

Drawing the beer closer to him, Mythrian lifted the mug to his mouth and gulped a large quantity of its refreshing taste. Placing the mug back down on the table before easing back into the chair, Mythrian enjoyed his moment of relaxation.

"Has it really been that bad?" Thain asked, noticing the boy looking tired and drained.

Opening one of his eyes, catching the face of the young man who was keen to know of the boy's journey, Mythrian pulled himself forward. Leaning over the table, he told the scout of his journey.

"We started off on the wrong foot getting here. The transport sent from Fayrmayden to Hamlynstone was ambushed. All were killed except the horses and one very terrified man. The transport itself wasn't in a condition either."

"Of course, but how did you make it to here?" the scout continued the conversation.

"The horses weren't too bad considering what had happened on their journey. So I took them with the thought that if the danger was still out there, travelling light and fast, there was a chance that I would avoid contact. Unfortunately, that wasn't to be the case."

Scratching his head as he tried to recall the events that followed, he explained as well as he could remember.

"I was travelling through the west region of Arlyne's Drift. Due to the unreliability of the terrain, I had to slow the horses down."

"You know there is a longer but safer route to Mignmedia from Hamlynstone? It is very protective, but would add at least half a day on to your journey. Travelling south to Helianthe, there is a small woodland, half a mile before the settlement, turn left directly there and you enter Everlyn, the capital of Hagenherde. There is a path from there that leads up towards Mignmedia. It's the path I took to get here," the scout explained.

The boy was unaware of this.

"Unfortunately I've never travelled as much as some of my

compatriots, so I would not be aware of routes like that. But I wanted to get to Mignmedia as quickly as I could, so it seemed the obvious route. I thought the boggy lands of Arlyne's Drift would give me some cover, though it wasn't I who had best used the landscape."

Focusing on Thain, making sure he had his full concentration, Mythrian told him of the creature that attempted to stop him on his journey.

"I was ambushed by a goblin of some sort. I have very rarely seen them and none of them as, well ... as human-like as this. The way it moved, the way it thought."

As Mythrian paused, conjuring up the face of the enemy in his mind, Thain, who was compelled to know more, said, "Go on."

"After it was distracted when it was aiming an arrow at me, I quickly tried to flee the area, but it had set traps. It had been expecting me and there were posts in the ground, set across the boggy field. One by one he lit his arrows, firing them at the posts before they set alight. It had me trapped. But how did it have me trapped? Since when has a creature of evil known the understanding of traps or of using resources like fire? Our fathers fought off Draigorn's minions with the ability of siege and artillery which they were not accustomed to. But they have learned this somehow."

"My God, this is terrible news. I'm sure you haven't told anyone of this?" Thain posted the question.

Mythrian answered a firm "no" to which the scout continued:

"Good, because this type of news could send the kingdom into disarray. I went to Hagenherde recently as part of my business. I tell you, they are worried up there. You can sense it now that fear is spreading across the land, village to village. We've never been comfortable since we reclaimed our lands some four decades ago. Just of late there has been a lot of unwelcome activity, especially to the south."

"Why, what's happening there?" the boy was keen to know.

"I shouldn't say too much. But to the south, by the Mountains of Morbian, they say creatures are being found every day and we're not just talking about one or two at a time. To be honest, there has always been a lot of activity down there, but now the numbers are growing at a rate never seen since the rise of Draigorn."

"You think it's starting all over again?"

Settling back into his chair, the scout was not particularly comfortable about answering questions on this topic but replied:

"I don't know. But as these rumours grow, you tend to make up your own theories on what might happen. All I've learnt is that you can never trust anyone or anything, no matter how close you are. But anyway, we're straying from the subject," the scout laughed, knowing that they were initially talking about Mythrian's journey.

"So tell me, how did you escape from this goblin?"

"There was a pond which opened up a small gap, just about big enough for someone of my size to fit through. I fell into the pond and swam through the various pools until I was behind the goblin. I then pulled him under and killed him with my dagger. I would have lost my horses too, had it not rained and put the fires out."

"Well, I'm just glad you made it. Your journey will be a lot safer now."

Mythrian felt a lot more at ease to hear those words. He didn't think once about telling Thain of his trip into the hills of Twyndall.

The conversation between the two of them continued as midday drew closer. Thain was thinking about making a move.

"I think we ought to head off now. The land is flat and straight. Leave now and we should get there by the afternoon."

Nodding his head as he drank the last few drops of his pint, Mythrian agreed to the scout's words. Untying their horses, they set off on the journey to Fayrmayden.

CHAPTER 8 † REGRETS

ACK IN THE Guild in Hamlynstone, Salen was standing by
the door, watching the bustling activity before him. He was
actually on guard, though he didn't believe that anything,
of consequence was going to happen.

By midday, with the third sun beaming down from the sky,
Salen was growing tired of watching the same old repertoire of
activity. He reconciled himself by looking for another task.

But as the messenger bringing post to the village stepped up
the Guild steps, he handed a series of letters to Salen. Searching
through the letters, he was hoping to find something addressed to
him.

In amongst the letters, he found one from the Arena Fort of
Aldremayne.

Letters were only sent from there if they were of importance or
needed quick attention.

Placing the other letters under his arm, he opened the envelope
on behalf of Mythrian and read the note within.

"To whom this may concern, I write this letter on behalf of
the great Arena Fort of Aldremayne, which is hosting its annual
festival, five days from now. Those who claimed victory in
their competition at the tournament of apprentices in Avalin,
are requested to join this festival to compete inside the arena.
They will participate in front of the many scouts searching for
gifted pupils to hire for vacant positions. All attending must send
confirmation two days prior to the event. All competitors will stay
in one of the many rooms in the welcoming village settlement of
Falstone. We wish all attending a safe journey and keenly await

your arrival.

Yours sincerely, the Board of Aldremayne."

This message posed a problem for Salen as he wasn't sure how long Mythrian would be on his current journey to Fayrmayden. It could well take a day for him to get there and a day to get back, assuming that no other incidents take place on the way. Best to look for Brennius; he would know what to do.

Asking people around the Guild if they had seen him, they all pointed to his quarters. At first Salen thought this was odd as with another new year approaching, he would have thought Brennius would have been in his class or study, making sure all was in order for his new students.

Opening the door hastily, entering his Master's quarters, Salen grabbed the door with his other hand to slow it down, as he caught Master Brennius hard at work.

But as Salen watched his Master closely, he noticed that he was not working at all. In fact he appeared to have lost something; judging by the distressed look on his face, something very important.

He was pulling drawers to and fro to no end, searching through stashed papers and items, behind the books on the bookshelves, on top of every work table.

Salen wasn't sure whether this was really a good time to speak with his Master but the letter was important and it needed prompt addressing.

"Master Brennius," Salen timidly spoke, hoping not to surprise his tutor but Brennius paid no attention.

He tried again, likewise to no avail. Knowing subtlety was not going to catch his attention, Salen raised his voice so it sounded clear across the room, "Master Brennius!"

As Salen spoke, Brennius jumped up in shock, knocking over part of an apparatus that was sitting on his study desk. As glass beakers smashed, the chemicals made a considerable amount of mess across the wooden floor.

Luckily none of the apparatus was carrying anything potentially hazardous and the equipment itself was fairly basic but to Salen's surprise, Master Brennius was unusually timid in his approach to the incident.

"Oh dear, what a terrible mess," the old man muttered into his robe as he picked up a small pan, brushing the glass and throwing it into the bin.

Salen stood rather bemused by Brennius' nervous approach. Any other day, Master Brennius would have gone bright red with anger and would have been quick with his punishment. Today however, the old man did not seem comfortable and looked very vulnerable.

Both Salen and Master Brennius knew of the danger facing Mythrian. While Mythrian was positive about his quest, Brennius was having difficulty containing his concerns.

Recently events were making the old man very worried and, quite possibly, unwell physically.

Watching his Master trying to pick up the broken pieces of his work, Salen apologised for his entrance but stated his reasons:

"I am sorry, Master Brennius; I did not mean to startle you. I bring important news. Please let me help you ..."

Salen reached for the chair as he helped Brennius into its comforting frame.

"I had received a letter and I was looking for your guidance."

"Ok ..." Master Brennius tried to calm himself, taking in a couple of deep breaths as he opened the envelope handed by Salen, "Let's see what we have here."

Leaning over his study desk, Brennius muttered the words to himself. Salen stood by his side patiently, awaiting his guidance.

After a thorough read, Brennius returned, "Good, I will let the other teachers know of this as soon as I'm finished in here. Thank you for reminding me," Brennius laughed at his forgetful memory. "I had totally forgotten about that event."

"I think you miss my point, Master," Salen stated, taking the letter back from him. "I was speaking on behalf of Mythrian. He won his contest in Avalin and is expected to go to this. But I don't know how long his journey will take to Fayrmayden. What should we do?"

"Ummm ... Just put it to one side, I'll deal with it later," the old man pushed Salen's question aside. He obviously had more important things to do at this current moment in time.

Angry and shocked by his Master's blatant rejection, Salen could understand his current worries but knew that he needed his word on this quickly approaching event.

"Master, we need to sort this out now. We don't know what might turn up within the next few days. This is a very important event and one that I know Mythrian would not want to miss. But I need your clarification on whether I can assign him to this competition ..."

"I DON'T KNOW!" Brennius shouted, banging his arms on the table in an unprecedented burst of rage. "I don't know."

Salen leaned back to avoid the old man's unexpected outburst.

Holding his hand on his head, Brennius tried hard not to draw a tear. The pressure was becoming very strong and he was not coping well under it.

Knowing he needed to apologise to Salen, the old man said, "I'm sorry Salen. I didn't mean to offend you. I just ... feel so tired, so old. I don't think I can take too much of this pressure."

Placing his arms around Brennius' shoulders, Salen comforted the man, knowing by his words his Master was feeling very unwell and needed all the help he could get.

"I apologise myself. I understand what you're going through. I know it's hard, but ... if you need any help or if you have too much on your shoulders, just tell me and I will help you."

Placing the note on the desk, Salen continued, "Just give a yes or no as to whether I should sign this on Mythrian's behalf."

Drawing a deep breath, Master Brennius tried to feel confident of his boy's safe return and answered, "Yes."

"Thanks," Salen returned before he headed for the door.

Brennius quickly added before he left:

"Salen, I do apologise. I am thankful for all your work. I'm just under a lot of pressure at the moment. I'll be alright. If at any time you have a problem, just tell me. I'll help you out, I promise."

Salen thanked his Master before leaving the room. Easing back into his chair, he knew there was much to think about, concerning himself and the others around him.

After leaving the meeting, Salen headed out of the Guild, seeking Rinen, who he knew was in the area. He needed to tell someone about Brennius' fragile state.

Heading round to the side of the Guild where there was a large playing area, Salen caught his long known friend throwing a ball with some young toddlers, no doubt looking after them while their parents were trying to find time to tidy up their households.

Walking over to him he stood beside Rinen, watching him throw the ball back and forth, while Rinen laughed occasionally as their stubby fingers dropped the ball.

As Salen approached, Rinen noticed his friend was in deep thought. "Drifting off again Salen?"

Drawing a sigh, Salen mumbled, "I just had a rather difficult conversation with Brennius."

"Why, is he getting muddled with his words again?" Rinen asked.

"No," Salen paused before he spoke, reflecting on the situation. "I just wanted his word on an important message that involved Mythrian. But he seemed very sensitive, very fragile."

"Well," Rinen continued to look on the bright side, "He is an old man. People have moments when they get like that. Just forget about it, he'll be alright. He's probably just getting worked up over Mythrian's departure."

"While I agree with your words Rinen, I think something needs to be done about it ... and now!"

"Why, what do you mean?" Rinen became more intent on the conversation. Salen's words were serious and Rinen was concerned as to where this was going.

"Rinen, I think we need to take care of Master Brennius."

"WHAT!" Rinen was shocked by the remark and as he stared at Salen, lost for a reply, one of the toddlers threw the ball back, smacking him on the side of the head. Understandably all the toddlers thought this was hilarious, rolling over in laughter on the grass.

Pulling a sarcastic grin at the toddlers, Rinen turned back to his conversation with Salen. "Are you serious?"

Salen nodded to his question. "He needs to rest. His health is rapidly deteriorating and the pressure is mounting on him. He needs to be somewhere he can rest and regain his strength."

"But where?" Rinen was quick with his questions.

"I was thinking about Alvocanen. It is the grand fort of magic and spirituality. He will be in safe hands, plus he will have many like-minded heads around him."

Picking up the ball and continuing his game, Rinen admitted, "This is bad news. What should we do about Mythrian?"

"I'll talk to him when he returns. But we have to make a decision on Master Brennius first. It is for the best," Salen spoke as he closed his eyes and wiped his head. The decision was tough but needed to be done.

"When are you going to speak with Brennius?" Rinen asked.

"Later, when he isn't busy. It will be difficult to convince him but I'm sure he will understand."

CHAPTER 9 ✝ STRAIGHT TO FAYRMAYDEN

A S MYTHRIAN AND Thain headed for Fayrmayden, their pace slow and steady, they cantered across the fertile greens of Arlyne's Drift, both feeling calm and relatively safe. The open fields gave them clear visibility for miles ahead. Nothing could hide in this shallow turf.

As they approached the halfway point of their destined journey towards Fayrmayden, they came towards a little brook. A calm stream, surrounded by thin reeds which cleansed the water as it came through, it was the ideal spot to rest and drink some water.

They tied their horses to a nearby tree, its foliage shaped like a mushroom, with its long, thin branches pointing downwards, creating a cool ring of shade underneath.

The horses certainly didn't mind lying in the shade after a long, tiresome journey in the basking fourth sun.

Crouching down by the edge of the stream, Thain took his flask from his belt and placed it against the flow of the river, filling it with clean, fresh water.

He took a thorough swig of the water. It was perfect. The reeds had taken all the unwanted sediments out of the stream and had left the water enriched and full of nutrients.

Calling Mythrian over to take much-needed refreshments, he had to shout quite loudly, as Mythrian was looking out towards the far plains.

"Mythrian! Come here and have a drink, the water's lovely."

Jogging over towards Thain, the boy took the flask and drank the water. It was very pure and Mythrian felt quickly regenerated as he examined the area around him.

"This is brilliant. I feel replenished already."

"Drink as much as you can. There isn't a cloud in the sky and the air isn't going to get any cooler. We still have a fairly long journey ahead of us."

"How far away do you think we are from Fayrmayden?" Mythrian queried.

"About two to three hours away. Could be shorter than that, just depends on how the conditions change," the scout replied, scanning the distance while his hands blocked the sun above.

As Mythrian continued to take in the comfortable scene around him, he moved away from the stream, closer to the shade of the tree.

Strolling across the grass, Mythrian was enjoying the peacefulness of the surroundings.

"Lovely area, isn't it?" Mythrian spoke.

"Yes. These plains have always been very fertile and popular, though it has always surprised me why people don't make more use of this region. Very odd," Thain returned.

"Mind you, I guess you can't graze every area. You have to leave some of it to nature."

"Yeah, guess you're right," Thain backed Mythrian's statement.

Thain was a very tall man and with his short, shaven head and sharp, boisterous face, he could easily be mistaken for having a very hard, edgy persona. In fact he was quite the opposite from that. He was cheerful and bubbly, someone who enjoyed a lot of company. He was also very trustworthy, focused on any given task, until it was fulfilled.

Having lent his flask to Mythrian, Thain used his hand to drink from the stream. Though there was no element of nearby danger, Mythrian followed the stream south, looking out for anything suspicious while Thain was in a vulnerable position.

Along the stream, Mythrian became nervous when he noticed footprints embedded in the ground.

Looking over towards Thain who was crouched down by the stream pouring water over his shaven head to cool himself down, Mythrian decided to investigate.

Moving his hand across the footprint, it soon became apparent that these were not human prints. The feet were large an there were claw marks at the end of each toe. Judging by how deep the prints were, the creature responsible may have been carrying a large amount of weight. It could have been on the run as well.

Looking over towards the stream, he noticed numerous tracks. Following them, they lead to the other side of the stream and beyond.

Looking over towards Thain who was splashing water continuously over himself, Mythrian was thinking of yelling but knew that was a bad idea, should anyone else be nearby.

At his loudest whisper, Mythrian called out, "Thain! Thain!"

Picking up the shrill tone, he noticed the boy calling him over with a worried look on his face.

Staying within the river, unsure why the boy was panicking, he called back, "What's the matter?"

"Sssshhhh!" Mythrian told Thain to lower his tone. "I found some tracks in the ground. They look like gob..."

But just as he was about to finish his words, they both heard the sound of a twig breaking nearby.

As they looked around the stream, Thain noticed that something had was causing movement within the reeds.

"Quick, hide yourself," Thain ordered, as Mythrian jumped behind the closest tree he could find.

Thain bravely chose to follow the hidden creature. Slipping silently into the shallow stream, he crouched down so his head sat below the reeds.

Carefully moving the reeds aside, he tried to see who had caused the noise.

The hidden creature was playing a similar game, although it was peeking through on to the green where the tree stood. It saw two horses, tied round the trunk, but nobody else in close proximity.

The creature was cloaked and did not appear to be carrying any weapons. In fact the creature felt more nervous than Thain or Mythrian, its hands were shaking on the reeds, while its breath was held.

Was this creature here to catch Mythrian or was it trying to steer clear of them? Perhaps it was on other duties but had to hide from the approaching pair.

As Thain quietly shifted the reeds aside, he found himself behind the figure. It did not seem to be goblin-like; its figure was rather more human but he took no chances.

Standing tall over the cloaked figure, he wrapped his arm round the stranger's neck, pulling backwards into the water as it splashed wildly for help.

Poking his head around the side of the tree, Mythrian could not see either Thain or his attacker, only the cries of desperation could be heard as each individual tried to gain the upper hand.

"Thain?" Mythrian called, thinking about jumping in the river to help the scout, but the man was quick to respond.

"Get out of here Mythrian. Take both the horses."

Mythrian could only see hundreds of reeds rattling violently on their end as waves of water were lifted five feet into the air.

"But how will you leave?" Mythrian insisted.

"Don't worry about me. JUST RUN!" Thain ordered the boy as he gained the upper hand in his entanglement with the creature.

Quick to his word, Mythrian hastily untied both horses from the tree, before he raced off as quickly as he could, not looking back until he reached his final destination of Fayrmayden.

Holding the creature down into the water, Thain questioned it, "Who are you? What do you want from us?"

As no reply came except a quiet squeal for help, the scout shook the stranger wildly, demanding an answer, "TELL ME! Who are you? Or I will squeeze the air right out of you."

As the creature begged the scout to stop his onslaught, its hood dropped, revealing its warty, pale face.

"A witch?" Thain was shocked by this sighting. "What do you want? What are you hiding in Arlyne's Drift?"

"Never say what it isn't yours to know," the witch returned as she cast a spell from her fingers, shocking the scout who momentarily lost his grip. The creature took her opportunity to flee.

"Hey!" the scout ordered the creature back. "Come back

here. I'm not finished with you," he replied, giving chase to the creature down stream; determined to whether her intervention had anything to do with Mythrian's journey.

CHAPTER 10 ✝ SPIRIT OF THE GARDENS

SCAPING THE CLUTCHES of danger, riding across Arlyne's Drift, Mythrian was approaching the village of Fayrmayden. As the walls of the village came within sight, Mythrian drew a sigh of relief as he entered the settlement.

Vibrant and intoxicating were the colours of the flowers that swept through the peaceful village. There were even flowers in amongst the wooden walls around its border.

Fayrmayden was a peaceful place, mainly because it was here where women were taught how to be maidens. Only traders, craftsmen or people requested by the Mayor were allowed to enter.

Knights or heroes were forbidden, as they had a strict policy on any communication with the maidens.

As Mythrian tied the horses by the entrance, he began his search round the village which was buzzing; most of the villagers in front of him were maidens, who appeared to be taking a break from their work.

"That's strange," Mythrian thought, looking around the area in front of him. "Where's the rest of the village?"

The only building in front of him was the school from which all the maidens came, but he could not see past this, as there was a lot of foliage blocking the view.

He noticed a couple of paths which seemed to lead around the school, but they all had hedgerows which were formed in an arch, making the path appear from a distance very dark and restricted.

Confused and unsure who to ask, Mythrian received help from a young girl, roughly the same age as himself, who noticed him walk through the entrance.

"Can I help you?" the young girl asked, intrigued by the unusual features of the boy.

"Yes, hello, my name is Mythrian. I was looking for the Mayor. She has sent me a letter of urgency which needs attending to."

"Follow the left path round the school. Her house will be signposted on the left."

Just as the girl finished, what looked like one of the teachers stood on the top of the stairs, in front of the school entrance and began to ring the bell, ending the break for the maidens.

"I've got to go. My name is Lyana by the way," the girl spoke, shaking Mythrian's hand.

"Lyana?" Mythrian thought to himself, "is this Rinen's sister?"

Knowing how much Rinen missed his sister, he thought about telling her of his situation in Hamlynstone, but he knew that it probably wasn't the right time or place to say. Perhaps they might cross paths again in the future. He would like to re-unite Rinen with his sister.

"Pleased to meet you," the boy replied, before the young girl rushed off to join her classmates.

Momentarily looking back towards the village entrance, wondering deep within his thoughts whether Thain was ok, he took the left path round the school. Behind the school stood the main part of the village itself.

Walking down the path, Mythrian analysed intently the neatly cut hedgerows that wrapped around the side of the path. Above him long, wispy plants lightly tickled the top of his head; its leaves shining brightly from the sun glimmering through.

Coming to the end of the path, he entered a round, open area where the floor was made entirely of smoothly cut stone slabs.

In the centre of this circle stood a beautiful fountain with water as pure as silk.

As he walked up to the fountain looking at his reflection on its surface, Mythrian saw not the tired face he expected but a lively, replenished face.

Moving away from the fountain, Mythrian looked up at the

picturesque village in front of him. The houses looked cosy, warm and like most of the village, they were covered in lots of flowers.

They all looked very expensive compared to what the houses were like back in Hamlynstone.

From here, it looked like there were two more paths wrapped around the village. The one to the right looked like it led to another area of the village, but the one to the left had a signpost, addressing the Mayor's household.

With no hesitation, Mythrian took this path, which took him towards a very large, white brick house.

Tucked away in amongst a haven of pristine foliage, Mythrian stepped up to the strong, wooden door and gave it a good couple of knocks.

The door was opened by one of the Mayor's servants, and a middle-aged lady, dressed ideally for her position as Mayor, welcomed the boy into her house.

"You must be Mythrian. I'm so glad you're here. Please come in."

Wiping his shoes on the mat before he entered the home, he followed her into the lounge where they sat down to discuss matters of concern.

Sitting down on a wide, lavish sofa, Mythrian was handed a hot herbal drink. It was just what he needed to calm done the tension from his journey.

"I take it you had a safe journey down here?" the Mayor spoke, judging by the boy's calmness and composure.

"I had a few minor setbacks but all in all it was a lively journey," the boy replied, reflecting on his long and tiresome excursion.

"I apologise for calling you at such short notice but ..." the Mayor paused, almost too nervous to state her words, "... several of my villagers said that they heard voices, spirits coming from within our garden, just to the back of us. I sent for help because ... well ... the voices were calling for you."

Mythrian moved back slightly into his chair. Who would be trying to call him here, in Fayrmayden? The only spirit he knew was Elrick, the knight he met in Emory Forest, but he had no reason to request the boy's presence.

"You say voices. You mean there is more than one?" Mythrian clarified. He needed to be sure of his position.

"As far as the villagers have told me, yes, more than one."

Mythrian took a moment to think. Spirits do not usually attack the living, so he was assured of that, although in these dark and dangerous times, you can't be sure of anything.

But there was no reason as to why these voices were evil. Perhaps these people weren't used to seeing anything of the supernatural.

"Ok." Mythrian was now ready for action. "Did you say the gardens are to the back of here?"

"Yes, take the right path round the village; it will take you directly into the gardens. But be careful. If you want I can send some guards in with you."

"No, I'll be fine," the boy knew assistance would cause more trouble. "It will be better if I go in alone."

"Once again, thank you for your help. The village has been very quiet from the fear caused by these spirits. Break my people's silence."

"I will," the boy assured the Mayor as he bowed politely, before he left the house for the gardens.

Leaving the house and taking the right path leading round to the garden at the back, Mythrian was poised for anything suspicious.

As the foliage grew and the fourth sun shone only through holes in between the rows of plants, hanging in an arch over the path, Mythrian made his way through a series of openings wherein each sat a statue, surrounded by a carefully selected group of plants.

There was no telling whether these statues were of anyone in particular, but they must have all shared some meaning with the village.

After passing half a dozen of these openings, Mythrian was growing tired of his search and the repetitiveness of the areas around him. Perhaps these spirits could see Mythrian and weren't going to answer to him, knowing of his presence.

But as he walked past the statue of a relatively young woman, holding a bowl filled with water, Mythrian watched the statue closely.

Just as he was about to walk away, he unexpectedly heard a voice call him, "Hello."

Stopping, before turning round to face the statue, Mythrian stood still, staring straight forward to show the hidden spirit that he was not afraid.

The voice laughed, but not in a sinister way. In fact, its tone seemed rather gentle, far from the voice of anything evil.

"A very courageous young man, just like your father!" The voice sounded clear to Mythrian.

"Who are you?" the boy threw the question back, uncomfortable with the spirit talking freely about his family members.

The voice sighed, "I guess you were too young even to hear your mother's voice as well, you poor thing."

"Mother?"

Mythrian fell quiet, unsure whether to believe the hidden voice, but deep down inside, Mythrian knew that this voice was not lying.

"Mother ... where are you?" Mythrian asked, as he moved closer to the statue. "Is this statue of you?"

"No, I don't look that bad. But ... I'd rather you didn't see me anyway, as I am now."

"But I've never seen what you look like," the boy mumbled, wanting to see the face of the mother.

"You don't need to see me. Even if I did show you my appearance, you would not see the face of your mother, only a bright light of her burning spirit. Just remember me by my voice … Mythrian?"

"You know my name?"

"Yes, a strong name for a strong child; God bless Vispa."

His mother was keen to know more of his childhood, for she was now, like all spirits, a part of the earth and had only risen to aid Mythrian in his quest.

"I'm so happy to see my young boy all grown up. Where have you been living?"

"I was found by a scout in a wooded area, next to the Cronian Valley. I was placed in the hands of the Guild Master, Brennius, in

Hamlynstone. He has been my guardian and teacher."

"My boy is an apprentice. I knew someone would find your gift. Tell me, are you doing well at your Guild?"

"I have excelled in many subjects," Mythrian boasted. "... and I won my competition at the tournament for apprentices at Avalin."

"Oh wonderful!" His mother was glad that no harm had come to him. "I'm so very proud of you. In those brief moments I held you, I knew you were a special child."

"Yes. But ... I wish you were here with me to enjoy these moments," the boy said, feeling as though there was a great wall separating him from his mother.

"I know my dear. I wish I was with you too. But we cannot change the past." His mother sighed. "I have so many questions to ask you, but I have very little time."

"Please Mother, tell me what happened to you."

"NO!" the voice shouted, before understanding that she had raised her voice too loudly and spoke lightly. "No ... sorry, Mythrian, I can't."

"But I know what happened to my father," the boy insisted.

But his mother knew this. "I know. I was informed."

"By whom?" the boy was curious.

"Ajia."

The boy said nothing.

"Yes, Ajia," his mother continued. "he cannot communicate with your people and he is limited in what he can say to us, the spirits because of his exile. But he managed contact me and sent me here to speak to you. He knows of your situation..."

"Do you know?" Mythrian interrupted.

"No, Mythrian. He just sent me with the message that ... he needs you to look for someone."

"Who?"

"A witch, called Vispa."

"Vispa, you mentioned that name earlier," Mythrian was unsure as to how a witch was going to help him on his travels. He thought they were all evil.

"She has the answers to many of your questions."

"Well, where can I find her? I don't know what she looks or sounds like ..."

"Do not worry, my child. In time, she will find you," his mother stated.

"But why? How does this witch know the answer to my questions?"

"She is closer to you than you think."

Mythrian was not comfortable with this situation, "Are you hiding something from me, Mother?"

"No, Mythrian. Trust me. She will try to contact you soon. Be ready, but be warned, for there may be others near her who could be trying to lead you into a trap."

"Ok, I will."

Mythrian paused to think about what had been said. While being meaningful and useful, Mythrian was still upset that he couldn't be with his mother.

"I'm sorry, Mythrian, but that's all I can say. I must go. I cannot stay here for long but I am truly proud of you and I will be watching over you wherever you go."

"But Mother ... I don't even know your name," the boy implored.

"My name is Leida."

As Mythrian repeated the name, trying to put a face with her voice, his mother fell silent. Her presence faded.

Mythrian had one more question to ask, but as he called, "Mother, Mother?" there was no reply.

Her time had passed.

"Goodbye Mother ..."

CHAPTER 11 ✝ A NEW JOURNEY

A s Mythrian walked back out of the gardens and into the village, he was emotionally drained. Head down, shoulders hunched, Mythrian was deep in heavy thought, not in the least suspecting the crowd in front of him.

"Look, he's returned from the gardens," one of the villagers spoke, awaiting the news.

Almost every villager stood patiently behind the Mayor, who was positioned at the front of the large group. With smiles addressing their faces, they didn't seem to be too concerned about Mythrian's depressed state.

The only worry on their mind was whether the voices in the gardens had been banished by their hero.

"Well, has evil been dealt a thorough blow?" the Mayor crossed her fingers.

Drawing a deep sigh, knowing these people would not have the slightest idea of what the had been through, nor would they be able to understand, Mythrian just answered:

"The voices you fear have gone. They will never trouble you again."

A huge cheer swept the crowd as they knew their nightmare was over. As they clapped in their appreciation for Mythrian, the Mayor spoke to the tired apprentice:

"Thank you, Mythrian. Words cannot express our gratitude. Thanks to your help, my people can now rest at night safely and in peace. But you must be tired from your great efforts. Come, let us get you something to eat."

As Mythrian sat down by a free table, placing a bowl on it with a varied selection of meat and vegetables, he tried to push the events of earlier in the day, momentarily out of his mind.

It was difficult though for Mythrian to feel relaxed. Villagers, though hard at work, were constantly looking over towards their hero.

Over his shoulder, girls from the guild were whispering to one another, taking a lot of interest in the young man.

All of a sudden, Mythrian was the centre of interest.

"What is wrong with these people? It's as if they've been locked out from the outside world," Mythrian thought to himself.

Mythrian had never expected a village to be so ... so unprepared.

Guards were few. Defence was nothing but a wooden wall of no great height. Guilds ... for maidens?

No wonder they feared the voices from the gardens. This village wouldn't last two seconds if evil laid siege to its garrison.

To Mythrian, it was surreal. But it was far the least of his worries.

Spotting the apprentice by the table, Lyana, who had spoken to Mythrian earlier in the day, walked over to see how he was.

Placing her food on the table, Lyana sat down opposite the boy. Mythrian was so far away in his thoughts, he did not notice her arrival.

Lyana just stared at him with her bright blue eyes, waiting for him to make the first move.

Finally returning from his thoughts, Mythrian instantly noticed Lyana smiling in front of him. Surprised by her arrival, he greeted the maiden:

"Hello."

"Hello again. I hear the village is in awe of you," she replied.

"It was nothing, really."

"It might be nothing to you, but it means a lot to us. We have never been attacked or threatened by the east, or from activity outside our own," Lyana explained.

"No, why not?" Mythrian was curious for an explanation but Lyana did not have a suitable answer.

"The east wouldn't gain anything from taking this settlement. That is why we were so frightened of the voices coming from the gardens. We are not use to such activity. Have you ever been involved in any confrontations with the east?"

"Unfortunately I have and I am sure I will be involved in many more," Mythrian answered.

The conversation paused for a minute, until a strange looking creature jumped up at Mythrian, wagging its tail at the unfamiliar face.

"What the ...?" Mythrian was shocked by the sudden appearance of the creature.

"Oh, this is a Pen-dragon. He's the Guild's pet," Lyana returned, clicking her fingers to call the creature. But it was far too interested in the apprentice.

Studying the creature, which was no bigger than a dog, Mythrian saw that its head was reptilian and it was scaled head to toe. On its back it bore wings and had an unusual line of thin, bony spines, which were like sensors, reacting as its facial expressions changed.

"I see he has wings. Can he fly?" Mythrian was indeed intrigued by the creature, though unfortunately he was not in the mood to play with it.

"Not at his age, he is very young. But in five years' time, he will be twice his size and strong enough to fly. Much like its larger relation, the dragon."

"Going to be quite a handful then," Mythrian spoke with a smile. "I didn't think dragons existed. Well not in these parts of the world anyway."

"They're very rare. But he's very friendly," Lyana returned.

"I can see that," Mythrian replied, fighting the dragon who was pulling on his shirt, begging him to play.

"So where do you come from?" Lyana changed the subject.

"Hamlynstone. It's a quiet little village, close to the western ocean."

"Hamlynstone ... Hamlynstone, that name rings a bell," the

young girl searched her memory for the answer, but came up empty. Mythrian was unsure of what to say. He wanted to re-unite Rinen with Lyana, but something inside was telling him that it still wasn't the right time.

"You should come visit sometime Hamlynstone sometime," Mythrian offered. But the young girl refused.

"We're not usually allowed to visit other villages. We have a strict system here."

"No worries. Anyway, I'm afraid I must be heading off. I have a long journey ahead of me."

"Can I just ask you one more thing?" Lyana added.

"You're asking about my markings. It's a birthmark," he replied.

"Just a birthmark?" Lyana smiled in return. She knew he was lying.

"Nice to meet you Lyana," Mythrian finished the conversation, offering to shake her hand.

"I hope we meet again," Lyana spoke.

They shook hands.

"I'm sure we will," replied the boy, before he brushed aside the dragon and headed towards the main gates.

‡ ‡ ‡

Walking into the stables by the main gates, Mythrian was just untying his horses from their posts when a man walked up behind him.

"Excuse me, are you Mythrian?"

The boy turned round to find a man who was very smartly dressed, no doubt from somewhere very important. However, he also looked very impatient.

"Yes, I am. Why?"

"We have a carriage waiting for you. Unfortunately there has been some unwelcome activity near Gyda's Pass and the area has been quarantined. We will take you safely around the border, past Hagenherde to your home village."

"Quarantined?" The boy immediately thought of Thain. "When I travelled down here, I came with a scout called Thain; we got caught up in a minor skirmish ..."

"I'm sorry young sir, but we haven't searched the area as of yet. We're just restricting people from entering the region."

Mythrian stood silently. There was still the chance that Thain was safe. He just hoped that Thain had not been led into a trap and had left the region and the danger within.

Pulling his horses with him, Mythrian and the man walked to the carriage. It was large, holding at least six guards. When Mythrian stepped into the carriage, he noticed there were no beds, bu there were seats and to Mythrian's delight; they were very comfortable.

Glad to see the back of the village and the end of his journey, Mythrian rested, as the carriage rode on to Hagenherde.

CHAPTER 12 ✝ ACCEPTANCE

STANDING BY THE door of Brennius' dormitory, Salen drew a big, deep breath before entering. He was unsure as to how he was going to tell his old Master about his plans, or how he was going to react to him.

Stepping into the room, he called, "Master Brennius ..."

But he came to a halt, seeing the old man sitting on the ledge by his window, watching the activity outside.

The atmosphere seemed non-existent in the room. Usually Master Brennius had a very warm, kind soul that always enlightened the people with him. But the room felt so cold, so empty.

Brennius knew he was there and knew why he had come. "Greetings, Salen. You have a message for me?"

Watching the old man swivel round on the ledge to face his apprentice, Salen spoke, "Master, I know you may disagree but I think it may be best ..."

"If I take time out from my post as Master of the Guild," Brennius finished Salen's comment. While his eyes looked sad, his smile still shone.

The apprentice didn't know what to say. He had not expected his Master to give up the fight so easily. It seemed Brennius had finally accepted that the pressures around him were too much.

"Master?" Salen returned, encouraging Brennius to explain his true feelings.

"I'm not going to lie to you, Salen; I am getting too old for this. I understand that it must have been difficult for you to approach me, but you've done the right thing. I think I need some time to regather my strength and focus."

Looking back out of the window, the Master looked back on his time at the Guild. "You know Salen, I've been here sixty-three years. Not a lot has changed since then, only the colour of my hair. But through all I have taught and all that I have done, I guess there comes a time when the small things around you eventually catch up."

"You know, Master, it's only for a short while. You can return any time. We're all very worried about you and together, we believe that maybe just some time away from matters concerning both Mythrian and the Guild, would give you time to regain your strength."

"Yes. May I ask what you have planned for me?" the old man tried to perk the conversation up.

"Alvocanen."

"Ah, the fort of magic and spiritualism. Yes, I am sure I will like it there."

"I thought that it would be the perfect place for you to settle in. Also, when he returns, Mythrian will be heading in the same direction towards Aldremayne. I thought the two of you could meet up down there," Salen answered.

"That's a lovely idea, Salen," Brennius agreed. "Have you heard anything more from him recently?"

"No. But I'm sure he's doing fine," Salen returned.

"I'm sure he is. So when do I leave?" Brennius asked the apprentice, who was more comfortable with the conversation now.

"Two days' time."

"Good. You've done extremely well, Salen. It takes a lot of courage to do what you have done today, but you have achieved it successfully. I have been really pleased with your progress over the past few years. You've come on in leaps and bounds," Brennius praised his apprentice.

"Thank you, Master," Salen replied.

"I know you may have other plans but since I'm going to Alvocanen, my spot as Master of the Guild will be available."

"I'm not sure if I am ready to take that sort of leap, Master.

What about one of the other tutors in the Guild, will they not take your place?" Salen responded.

"Salen, I didn't become Master of the Guild just because I was talented at many subjects or because I was very clever at teaching others to pursue their gifts. I was chosen because I brought new ideas to the Guild. I taught differently than all the other teachers at the time. I didn't just teach my students of the many skills that convey our modern world. I sought after that special gift within each and every one of my students. Everybody is different and everybody has their own special abilities. And so I started to build special classes designed to hold students who shared similar abilities. That's what made me Master of the Guild. And that is why I want you to be Master while I'm gone. The other teachers won't bring anything new. But you will. You've already shown me how bright and willing you are. This is the perfect opportunity for you."

The positive answer gave Salen confidence to rise to the challenge. It would only be till Master Brennius returned and there was much he could learn and achieve from the position. Besides, he was no longer an official apprentice. He already had learned a lot from Brennius' guiding wisdom.

Salen accepted the position. "Ok, I'll do it. I'll stand as Master of the Guild until you return."

"Well done. I am pleased you agree. You'll do a great job," Brennius replied.

"Thank you, Master. I had better go. Now with your permission I can contact Alvocanen and let them know you will be heading to them."

"Take care," Brennius added as Salen left the room.

CHAPTER 13 ✝ JOURNEY INTO THE DARKNESS

AS A COUPLE of guards led the way, carrying with them lanterns to light up the road, the carriage bearing Mythrian followed closely behind. The skies were dark. Clouds had hidden the fourth moon and swept the land into total darkness.

Inside the carriage, Mythrian sat awake, but was restless. Beside him were two guards, who occasionally looked out of the window; wary of any distant movement within the darkness.

The journey so far had been quiet, but the guards protecting the carriage were nervous. Visibility was poor and, wielding torches, they were an open target.

Travelling on a path that was taking them directly towards Hagenherde, they were to be stopped just ten miles away from the capital.

Something was lying on the road blocking their pathway. It was big and it was covered by a large blanket.

"Why have we stopped?" Mythrian asked the guard next to him.

Leaning out of the window, the guard posed the same question, "What seems to be the problem?"

"Something's blocking the road," one of the guards responded, carefully approaching the blockade.

Grabbing hold of the cover and moving it back, there was nothing sinister – only a collection of large stones. But they had been placed there for a reason.

Several of the guards began to pick up a noise, coming from nearby. It was gradually getting louder, intensifying to a great thunderous sound.

The guards swallowed hard. Surely nothing had broken through their quarantine in Arlyne's Drift? They were in a vulnerable position and they only had eight guards manning the carriage.

Trying to look through the endless darkness for any movement or sign, one of the guards was hit by an arrow. The word passed around quickly:

"We're under attack!"

Jumping out of the carriage, one of the guards looked at Mythrian and ordered, "Stay here."

As the seven guards ringed the carriage, they looked ahead to see a long line of fire approaching them. The fire was from torches and the torches were from a pack of goblin infantry, heading straight for them.

As the goblins got closer, their appearance raised fear in their enemy. Grins broadened their faces as they charged at the guards. Their armour looked heavy and yet they were running at a very quick pace.

The guards were heavily outnumbered.

Drawing their bows, a couple of the guards sent a signal into the air. A flare to hopefully catch the attention of nearby units.

But as the goblin infantry charged at the guards, they bravely threw everything they could at the great number of enemy troops.

Their numbers dropped quickly.

From his carriage, Mythrian attempted to make a quick escape, but one of the goblins caught him from afar.

"Over there. After him!" he called to his fellow troops, pointing at the boy.

As a couple of the goblins chased after the fleeing boy, a wave of human guards came rushing into the area; answering the call for help, as they charged at the goblin infantry.

As swords clashed, good and evil released their battle cries with deafening blows to their enemies. The goblin infantry were stronger and better equipped but more and more guards were rushing in to repel the falling units.

While the battle was taking place, the creatures chasing Mythrian were catching up. Knowing he couldn't out-run them, he had to turn round and fight.

Drawing his sword, Mythrian faced the creatures. As they stepped closer, Mythrian could feel them towering their imposing will over him. In the thick darkness, only their sinister faces shone through.

Knowing he needed the boy alive, the goblin aimed for Mythrian's sword, hoping the impact would knock him down.

Hiding behind his blade, Mythrian had never been taught how to fight with the sword. Every attack from the goblin was becoming harder and harder to block.

His feet were stumbling beneath him. His arms were too tired to continue fending off the goblin's attacks. Help was going to be the only way out.

Frustrated as to why the boy hadn't been knocked down, the goblin lost his temper and lifted his sword high into the air; in the few seconds before it headed for a devastating blow, Mythrian spotted an opening.

Spinning to the side of the goblin, the sword missed and gave Mythrian a chance to strike back. Throwing his sword in sideways, it struck the goblin through a thin gap in his armour.

The first beast was down. But there was still one more to pass. Watching his compatriot fall to the sword of tiny human, the second goblin came forward with even more anger.

Launching into a blistering assault, Mythrian was repelled further and further backwards. The nearby torches were becoming too distant to see and the darkened creature in front was merging into the surroundings.

Mythrian was battling on pure reaction. It wasn't to be enough.

Falling on to his back, exhausted from the barrage of attacks, Mythrian did not have the energy to get back up.

As the creature approached, it pulled out a club, intending to knock the boy unconscious. But just as the goblin drew near, a guard came to Mythrian's aid, tackling the creature and wrestling it to the ground.

With the creature down, Mythrian rushed off again to find a place to hide until the battle was over.

Heading further to the west, he came to a little patch of hedgerows. Sitting down, taking in a few deep breaths, he watched the action from afar.

All he could see were the flames from the torches dancing across the plain. Though most of the torches were wielded by the guards, as the goblin infantry were losing numbers heavily.

Soon they were outnumbered and the remaining units quickly made their escape, back towards the East.

The battle was over. But had the chase finally finished?

Mythrian, resting against the hedge, hoped so, breathing in safety. Or so he thought.

Creeping along the hedgerow, heading back to the carriage, Mythrian paused to check the area was clear.

As he was leaving the area, an arm suddenly swiped around his neck:

"Got ya!"

✝ ✝ ✝

When his eyes slowly began to open, Mythrian wondered where he was.

The surface below him was scarlet in colour and the smell of burning came from nearby.

Looking to his side, he saw two pairs of feet. They were very large for human feet and had a terrible odour to them as well. But whoever they belonged to, they were dragging the boy across the floor.

Stopping abruptly, the boy was laid on to a bench. His arms and legs were tied tightly. The faces remained concealed.

Facing upwards, his eyes caught the skies through a gap. They were dark, with purple fusions, but they did not rain though thunder was evident in the clouds.

As the bench was moved vertically upright, Mythrian became more adjusted to the area around him. It appeared like a cavern, but there were thousands of tunnels, like a hive.

In front of him was a long path, the same one he had been

carried across. To the side was a river, but it was still and it oozed the colours of the sun.

As his eyes looked dead ahead, he saw a figure emerge in a black robe. His servants had gone; only he stood before Mythrian.

"Welcome to my chamber," the creature spoke. Its voice was slightly muffled under the robe, but the boy still heard clearly.

Looking around the chamber, Mythrian, who still felt light headed, muttered for help:

"Salen ... Brennius ..."

The cloaked creature laughed at the feeble attempt.

"You're a long way from home, boy."

Mythrian could see the creature's smile under its hood. Such an evil grin, its silvery reflection seemed far from human.

Looking down at his limbs, he noticed the chains pinning him down.

"What are you going to do to me?"

The creature stood silent. He kept the boy waiting for his answer.

"You have been causing quite a lot of trouble to our plans. As heroes pass, the name I hear constantly is Mythrian, Mythrian. They say you have a gift, a great power. I am intrigued by this."

The creature edged closer. Mythrian's heart skipped a beat as he nervously watched the figure approach.

"Tell me, out of all the people in the West, why did you find the power? Why were you blessed with his powers?"

Laughing in a sinister fashion, he continued:

"You don't appear very powerful in front of me. Are you afraid? Oh, Mythrian, fear is a terrible thing. You fear me, because you don't know the monstrosity that hides behind this robe. What if I was to reveal my true self to you? Would you still fear me?"

Grabbing his robe, he threw it up in the air, before it rested on his back like a cloak. As Mythrian stared at the creature he recognised the terrifying image clearly.

"DR ... DR ... DRAIGORN!"

The creature laughed so hard, it leaned back, sending echoes around the chamber. Mythrian tried to shrug himself off the board. He turned his head away, closing his eyes tightly.

"That won't save you Mythrian. You're never going to learn to face me if you can't even look me in the eyes."

Mythrian mumbled to himself, "It's not real. It's just a dream."

The creature was in total control. He didn't want to kill the boy. Not yet. He just wanted to see him beg.

"What must he be thinking, Ajia. There isn't much hope for him. For you: for your kind. Look at me Mythrian. Look at your foe."

As the boy opened his eyes, he slowly turned his head to face the creature. But Mythrian still refused to believe what was before him.

"You're not Draigorn. Draigorn was killed by Ajia."

"You're right, I'm not Draigorn. I am his successor; I am the next in line."

The boy shook his head.

"Lies. Tell me, who are you?"

Taking off his helmet, he looked the boy straight in the eyes:

"Mythrian ... I am you!"

"NO!" Mythrian screamed as before him stood the mirror image of himself. His exact face stood on top of the skeleton armour. He dared not look at this impossible image.

"Mythrian, it is time!"

CHAPTER 14 ✝ IN THE PRESENCE
OF HIS MAJESTY

"**N**O!"

Mythrian shot up forward in the bed. His ears were ringing, his throat was dry and his head felt heavy upon his shoulders.

Placing his hands over his head, he tried to gather his thoughts:

"It was just another nightmare. But why do I keep getting them?"

Sunlight was aplenty as it shone through the open window. Barely adjusting his eyes to the environment, the room he was in was warm.

The room was primarily white. The walls had been painted with a lime wash, while the wooden beams within the room were of a rich, maroon shade.

The floor was made of sandy beam strips, as was some of the furniture in the room.

Wrapping himself in his blankets, Mythrian was in shock by the sudden twist of environments. The image of Draigorn burned in his mind and he struggled to shake it off.

As he sat deep in thought, studying the room around him, a visitor opened the door and entered:

"You've woken up. Great. How do you feel?"

Looking up at the tall man, Mythrian studied the calm, collected face. As the light dashed across his face, he appeared like a bright spirit. But as the sun moved behind a large cloud, it dimmed the light to reveal a recognisable face to the boy:

"Thain! You're alive."

"Of course I'm alive," the scout returned, as if it was ever in doubt.

The boy was pleased to know no harm had come to the scout, but he admitted his concern:

"What happened to you? After I left you for Fayrmayden, I heard nothing more from you. Even the guards surrounding Arlyne's Drift said they had not spotted you or anyone else in the area."

"I had to keep a low profile," the scout returned, looking down at the floor boards, while he recalled the events leading up to their position now.

"The creature I encountered by our stopping point somehow escaped me as I went after it. Turning back to head for Fayrmayden, I overheard a large clash of sounds coming from nearby. Hiding in amongst a large shrubbery, I saw a group of goblin infantry, heading south. I knew this was trouble and I feared for your return so I headed for Hagenherde to alert them of the situation."

Moving closer to Mythrian, the scout smiled.

"It's a good job I did alert Hagenherde, otherwise you might have been caught by those goblins."

"I thought I had been caught by goblins," the boy remarked. "When the infantry attacked our carriage, I managed to escape, hiding within close proximity to the battle by a hedgerow. But just as I was about to rejoin the guards, something grabbed me and knocked me unconscious."

"Yes, that was me."

The boy was shocked. "Why did you do that?"

"Because it was for your own safety. I'm not sure if those goblins were specifically targeting you, but there were bound to be more around. When I found you hiding behind the hedgerow, I feared you were going to run off in the confusion. So when I caught you, I knocked you unconscious so you didn't run away."

"I see." The boy sat quietly, keeping his thoughts to himself.

"I know it was a bit rash and I know you have had a difficult journey to and from Fayrmayden. I just did what I felt was right at the time."

The boy was still slightly uncomfortable with Thain's approach, but at least he was back in safe hands, though he was unsure where he actually was.

"Thain, where am I?"

"You're in Hagenherde, the safest place in the Zodiac. You're in one of the recuperation rooms used for ill or injured soldiers."

"When will I be transported back to Hamlynstone?"

Mythrian wanted to get back home. There was much to be discussed, but Thain was still cautious of his safety.

"Soon, Mythrian, soon. We will take you back when we feel that the area is secure. But for now, just get some rest and get your energy back."

Turning around to leave the room, Thain suddenly remembered a note in his pocket. Pulling out the note, he faced Mythrian and told him:

"When I chased after our spy, the creature dropped this note on the floor. The note was written for you. Do you wish to read it?"

"Yes, please."

Handing Mythrian the letter, Thain left the boy to read the note.

"I'm needed for duties, but if you ever need me, you can find me by the courtyard. My station is situated there."

"Thanks," the boy replied, as the scout left the room.

Mythrian was eager to read the note. Who was this spy and why was it trying to make contact with Mythrian? Opening up the note, it became clear who this had been written by.

"Vispa …"

In the great hall of Hagenherde, nervous discussions were being made about the flurry of recent attacks from enemy forces. From both sides of the hall, arguers were raising their tones. It seemed everybody who was anybody had a question on this topic.

His Majesty sat casually as always on his throne. Unlike the previous two majesties who always seemed to be more on the ball with the activities around them, the reigning monarch, Elgrator, was very laid-back.

While he was concerned about the growing problem of activity to the East, he never seemed to look as though he was interested in the erupting commotion.

Self-centred arrogance doused his burning flame.

Standing to the side of His Majesty, two of his most important figures listened in on the conversation.

They were his leading General in the artillery range, Gethen, and his second in command and possible successor, Galenor.

Moving into the middle of the hall, a speaker introduced a General from Hierheldon, a great fort built to the north of Mignmedia:

"Order, order please. If you don't mind, we can begin discussions. Your Highness, let me introduce you to Hugor, High General of Hierheldon."

Stepping into the middle of the hall, the General bowed to His Majesty, who pulled an almost reluctant smile in return.

"Your Majesty, I am thankful for your concerns, in light of the high number of threats we have recently received. We have had fourteen separate attacks in the north within the last few days. These have not been minor skirmishes by any means. We have already lost fifty-three men in the process."

The General momentarily paused to honour those that had died protecting their lands. Many in the hall did the same, for these were horrific numbers, on a scale never seen before.

Hugor continued his speech. "We believe that they have travelled down Gyda's Pass on boats, where they have landed in the southern area of Arlyne's Drift. We cannot be sure of this, but we have had a large number of scouts surrounding the northern proximity and they have found little sign of enemy movement travelling on foot."

His Majesty spoke, "But as far as we know, these creatures know nothing of the seas. Are you proposing the idea, that they are now capable of building boats and are raiding our lands from coastal routes?"

"As far as we know, yes, Your Majesty," the General

returned.

"Well, I'm sorry Hugor, but I just don't believe you on that. These creatures may be strong, but I doubt they have become so advanced that they match our level of development. The coastline to the north holds back a very rough sea. It would take a lot of effort to produce a boat, substantial enough to carry a raiding force and strong enough to compete against the harsh northern seas."

"I wouldn't be so sure of that Your Majesty ..."

A figure stepped out from the crowd.

"As long as the boat is stable enough, it will carry a large weight over the northern seas. And at this time of the year, the seas near the coast can often be quite calm."

"I understand that a boat does not have to be complex in its design to withstand the force of the sea, Revan. But the thought of those evil creatures to the East, building boats with their stubby hands and primitive tools. Who taught them to build boats, capable of withstanding the might of the oceans?" Elgrator responded, bluntly as ever.

"Nobody, Master. Nobody but themselves. In the same way that we have mastered the sea and learnt how to combat it, they have equally followed."

"But Revan, they would have had to ... evolve, to equal our level of development."

"That they have sire. Just look at how much we have evolved since the last war. Everything evolves over time. After all, they would need to if they wish to defeat us, with how strong we have grown."

This young man was called Revan. An odd fellow, he was in fact His Majesty's personal informer, at times acting as a speaker for His Majesty, for he had always been good with words.

An extremely clever man, Revan was equally a very simple man. He was polite, well mannered and knew his place and when he was needed. Though he was strong with words, Revan was a follower, not a leader, speaking only when required. Facially, he was light skinned with long, dark hair and deep brown eyes. Though he was a very confident man, he often appeared very timid, perhaps even a little suspicious of people around him.

He was indeed a very strange man but he was perhaps the most intelligent of them all.

"But has anyone ever proven this? Has anyone ever seen a creature of this level? A creature which can match our intellectual abilities?" His Majesty uttered, standing firm on his side of the argument.

"Actually there is ..."

Turning their heads, the crowd looked towards the door where Thain stood casually, leaning against its frame.

"Sure, there is someone. In fact he is in our capital right at this moment."

"Bring him here. We would be pleased to meet him," Elgrator replied to Thain's statement.

After a short wait Thain returned with Mythrian in front of him. Walking through the hall, with hundreds of wide eyes cast upon him, Mythrian was still feeling the effects from his long journey.

Standing before His Majesty, gossip was running wildly through the crowd. All were taken aback by his original appearance.

"Look at those markings," they all quietly muttered to each other.

His Majesty was interested.

"Welcome, Mythrian to Hagenherde and to the great Hagen hall. It is a pleasure to meet you."

Mythrian looked nervously around the hall. The crowds were intrigued by his appearance. There was a silent hush as the observers held their words, waiting for Mythrian to speak.

"Why have I been brought here?" Mythrian asked His Majesty.

"Over the past few weeks there has been a lot of activity in Arlyne's Drift. Our men have been under heavy attacks from waves of enemy troops. And you, Mythrian, have apparently been in the thick of it. That's why we have brought you here, you know more about them than any of us. We are in need of your help," Elgrator responded.

"I am pleased to tell you everything I know," Mythrian spoke, watching His Majesty's grin move ever so slightly wider.

"Excellent; Revan, inform this young man of our situation."

Stepping closer to Mythrian, Revan took caution in his steps. He was unsure of what to make of the boy. He remained suspicious about his cryptic markings, even slightly sceptical. Were those markings holding a great power or was he just trying to catch a lot of attention?

But in a world where races are set far apart and any mutations are considered outsiders, how had this boy been accepted into the community? He had not just grown under their influence, they were influenced by him.

"As you know, there have been several attacks across Arlyne's Drift. With little sign of them travelling on foot, we have reason to believe that they have landed on boats through Gyda's Pass. However, there is one problem with this; as far as we know, they don't know how to craft a boat. Or so we think. Can you say, having been close to the enemy, that they have the capabilities of building these resources?"

Mythrian was unsure of what to say. He knew the truth had to be told, but he didn't know how it would be taken.

"It is possible, yes."

"Well then, can you tell us of any incidents that may back these claims?" Revan continued.

"I will tell you of one. On my way to the village of Mignmedia, I travelled across the western boggy plains of Arlyne's Drift. Riding across the marshes, I had no idea that behind me, in one of the pools, was a creature waiting to strike me. But it did not attack me with the sword. This creature attacked by stealth. It aimed at me with a bow and arrow. Luckily he was distracted, but as I tried to escape, he released the arrows at posts set into the ground. They became ablaze. I was trapped, in a ring of fire. Only my ingenuity saved me. I could not fight this creature back."

"Bows and arrows. Are you sure?" Elgrator was shocked by these claims.

"I am sure."

"You say this creature had placed traps around the grounds as well. That means it must have been waiting for you. Someone or something must have been spying on you. If they are doing that,

that means they could be spying on any of us," Revan posed the question.

"We have been spied upon," Thain answered. "When I travelled with Mythrian, escorting him to Fayrmayden, I intercepted a creature who was spying on us. Although I initially caught it, it slipped out of my grasp. I could not catch up with it."

A tremor of fear passed down the spines of all in the hall, as apprehensive words were passed from ear to ear.

"Order, order," the speaker called for silence.

His Majesty was discontented with the distress that was filling the hall. He knew his people were not ready for another attack from the East. He needed to calm down the rift before it leaked throughout the land.

"Let me just remind you of the entire situation. Yes, there may be enemy troops spying on us, but there have been creatures hiding in our lands since Draigorn's first attack, some four decades ago. Their attacks might have increased just of late, but that doesn't mean they are beginning a second wave to conquer our lands. And I will tell you why. It's because they don't have a leader. Their only leader has gone. Deceased. They are only throwing these attacks to try to scare us. But believe me, people, beyond the valleys of our lands, into the darkness of the East, lies nothing but the remains of a fallen race. They have no leader and they will never return to our lands."

"You are wrong," Mythrian stepped forward.

"Well then tell us, if you know better. What do you know about the East?" Elgrator asked, unhappy with Mythrian's disagreement in his statement.

"I have had dreams. Visions of the East," Mythrian spoke aloud.

"Dreams are make believe and your mind is young. I expect what you have been through lately may have placed some fear within you. Fear is a dangerous emotion and your imagination may be dwelling on it."

"Dreams and visions may not always be true but they all have meaning. But I believe mine are true, because I have a gift. You see it, for it has left its mark on my frame. The markings that scar me are my gift to the world. In return I bear its consequences, for it has shed light on to the East. There I have seen him."

"Him?" Elgrator inched closer on to the edge of his seat.

"The man with no name. He has returned. With a new body, a new life. His time is drawing closer. When his armies were defeated four decades ago, the one known as Draigorn was slain. His evil soul was vanquished but his memory remains. In the core of Siren's Gore, that memory is being stored. Soon he will arise again and I fear he will be more powerful than before. We cannot overlook this situation, Your Majesty. We have to be ready now."

"Mythrian, you frighten me with your knowledge of the East. Nobody should have such dark visions. How am I sure that I can trust your word?" His Majesty spoke, twitching heavily as he scratched his neatly trimmed, auburn beard.

"You must."

"Why?" Elgrator demanded.

Mythrian reached under his shirt, pulled out Ajia's tablet and held it high above his head, for all in the hall to see.

"Because I am the one …"

Hands were clasped to stop the gasping that swept every mouth in the hall. His Majesty moved backwards, sinking into his chair, covering his eyes to shield the disturbing sight of the stone.

Mythrian had taken the tablet on his journey. Though he was proud to bare his gift to the world, he did not know the danger he was falling into.

Though its surface was dull, it still bore enough light to capture the imagination of the crowd. Many of the onlookers turned away. It was just too much of a powerful sight to take in.

Revan too had seen enough, quietly creeping backwards into the crowd, before disappearing through a door in the corner of the room.

After a long pause, Mythrian finally placing the tablet back under his shirt, before Thain led him back out of the hall.

Elgrator removed his hand from his sight to watch the boy leave the hall. The image of the tablet still burned in his mind as he thought of the consequences this meeting had brought.

They were now at war with the East.

Chapter 15 ✝ The Fortress of Fire

"PLEASE, NO!"

Inside the cave he could see the shadows of a giant beast, a Gorgoroth. The skulls by its feet were apparent as its hands reached out for its prey.

Its arms were very long, almost the size of its awaiting prey, and incredibly muscular. Like pillars of marble, they appeared unbreakable.

The goblin trooper tried to retreat but he was pushed nearer to the entrance of the cave by two of his fellow kind.

As the beast groaned, its jaws opened to reveal an unnatural amount of teeth. Row behind row, teeth the size of ice-picks; they still bore some of the remains of previous banquets.

"Please, forgive me," the troop begged, but there was no escape.

"Not this time," one of Kobar's servants told him, before throwing him into the depths of the cave.

As they watched the shadow of the troop seeking for an escape, the monumental frame of the beast approached. Suddenly, the beast appeared, as the troop screamed for help, covering his face with his arms. But the beast destroyed the troop in seconds, throwing its arms down heavily on to the goblin, breaking it bone by bone.

From afar, the rest of his unit was crouched down, tied with chains, shaking from the disturbing sounds echoing out of the cave. They did not want the same fate.

Kobar stood in front of them. While he seemed relatively calm, his hands were gripped in an enclosed fist. In his grasp he tightly held his whip, which was made from several layers of horse skin.

While the goblin troops would prefer the cold sting of the whip, than the claws of the Gorgoroth in the caves, the marks of Kobar's lashes would remain forever. It spells dishonour and failure.

"I hope this teaches you all a lesson. Failure is unacceptable. And you were hand picked as the finest goblin unit, capable of handling this situation. You're a disgrace to your race and to our lord, Mordryd," Kobar addressed them.

"But we were ambushed ourselves. There were too many of them ..." one of the troops pleaded but his words were cut short.

"Silence! You failed because you couldn't travel through the western land undetected. For years we have adapted to the darkness. We have learned to hide ourselves in the shadows, a gift which has enabled us to trespass through any form of landscape we choose. But you failed. Miserably!"

As the troops held their heads down in shame, Kobar continued.

"You're lucky; Mordryd has decided to keep you for future tasks. I hope you don't fail him again, because the next time it will be your heads. But just to make sure you don't fail again, I'm going to torture you one by one. So the message sticks in your mind."

Grabbing one of the troops by the jaw, he lifted his face up, so eye contact was made.

"Do you understand me?" Kobar questioned.

"Yes, Kobar," the trooper replied, before Kobar loosened his grip, letting the head fall back down in shame.

While Kobar stared down angrily over his troops, one of his servants approached him.

"Kobar, Master Mordryd wishes to speak to you. He is in the council chamber, below the castle."

"Very well," he said to his servant, before giving the troops one last look to fear. Kobar always preferred to use body language to impose his dominance rather than through speech.

Before Kobar entered the council chamber, Mordryd was in conversation. The figure was difficult to make out but it appeared like a bright spirit. It was the elder who had meet Vispa in Gwynan's Gorse, though Kobar knew nothing of this. Once again, he was communicating through a telekinesis.

"I hear you have found the tablet, or half of it anyway," the spirit spoke.

"Yes, but it seems the other half has been found and drained of its power. We have a foe," Mordryd returned.

"He is no foe. I have seen him. He is strong and gifted, but I should not worry. He is only a boy, he still fears the dark and all that dwell inside."

"I refuse to believe that. He has already proved his worthiness as a foe. And he will grow stronger, with each and every passing day," Mordryd answered.

"Yes, he may be growing stronger, but so are you. Don't forget who you are, Mordryd. He is not immortal. You have the power but you must use it. I am impressed with your development but it will take more than this if you wish to conquer the West."

Looking over Mordryd's shoulder, he looked at the stone pillar in the centre of the chamber, which held Ajia's tablet.

"There he is. Our once true leader, trapped within stone. Are you ready to join forces with hearts of evil?" The spirit laughed before continuing, "When am I to meet this disciple of yours?"

"Soon," Mordryd responded hastily. "He may be ready for us, but we are not so ready for him."

"Will he not correct that?" the spirit returned.

Mordryd said nothing in return.

"Now I didn't come to argue. I came with an important message. It seems that when this boy activated the powers of the tablet, he was hit by something of incredible power."

"You're saying that to unlock the tablet's powers, I have to find an unnatural force to open it?" Mordryd replied.

"Not unnatural. Apparently at the time when the boy unlocked its powers, there was a lot of disturbance within the atmosphere."

"Lightning?"

"It may just be enough force to unlock the power from within the tablet," the spirit explained.

"Excellent, I will make note of that," Mordryd added.

Still focusing on the tablet, the spirit noticed Kobar entering the chamber.

"One of your Generals is approaching. Farewell, Mordryd. I will head back and talk with the elders. We await the arrival of your disciple."

"Of course," Mordryd spoke before the spirit disappeared from sight.

Turning round to face Kobar, Mordryd instantly drew a smile to welcome his favourite assistant.

"Kobar, welcome to my council chamber."

The goblin had his eyes feasted purely on the tablet. He had never seen it before and yet, even through his darkened eyes, he could see the inner beauty within.

"You wished to speak with me Master," Kobar spoke in his deep, gurgling voice.

"Yes Kobar. In fact I wish to show you something. Follow me ...

Leading him out of the council chamber, they exited the mountain near its peak. There in the open, on the highest peak of the volcano, stood the final developments of the new castle.

The castle was imperial and against the crimson red skies, its walls lit up in a bright, fiery orange. Like the suns above, it brought life and a new horizon for the creatures of the East.

Kobar stood silent behind his Master. He was pleased with his minions' work though with such an evil heart, he drew no emotion.

"Beautiful, is it not?" Mordryd spoke. The setting could not be more delicately placed. From the castles high watchtowers, Dremenon; the entire north eastern region, which holds the volcano of Siren's Gore could be seen, even through the darkest shades of its surroundings.

Imposing; dominating; impregnable. It adapted well with their tastes and surroundings.

"I do not picture beauty, I picture opportunity."

Kobar was blunt in his words, but Mordryd could see the sparkle of optimism in his eyes.

"Kobar, my recital will begin on New Year's Day. I want you to be there when our Lord rises again. You are my strongest and most trustworthy General. His Lordship will honour your presence."

"Of course Master, but the new year begins in four days' time. What do you wish me to do before then?" the goblin asked.

Kobar loved to work. Rest was for the weak, and the short-fused goblin was quick to expel those who showed any weakness.

"Send for my army. I want every soul of evil to witness this memorable occasion. This will be the greatest event in our lives. The event will take place in the main chamber. It is large enough to hold the majority of our army."

"I will follow your orders, Master."

"Thank you for your time, Kobar. I understand that you are very busy," Mordryd thanked his General.

Kobar bowed to his Master, before he walked back into the mountain. Mordryd remained where he was, dreaming of the future ahead of him, while he watched his minions preparing the finishing touches to his Lord's castle.

"Beauty: unprecedented. Opportunity: Endless."

Chapter 16 ✟ The Arena Awaits

AFTER HIS DISPLAY in the great Hagen hall, Mythrian was sitting quietly on his bed resting, gazing out of the window at the fifth sun and its maroon spectre.

He would be leaving soon for Hamlynstone, but he was not in the mood to look around the kingdom capital. Instead he thought solely of the journey back to his home. Until Thain knocked on the door:

"Only me?"

Stepping into the room, Mythrian noticed the scout was carrying another letter in his hand.

"Another change of direction, I don't doubt," Mythrian thought to himself, rubbing his tired, drained eyes.

"Alright Mythrian, just to let you know there's been a change of plan. A man from Hamlynstone called Salen has sent you a note. Would you like to read it?" the scout offered the letter to the boy.

He turned it away:

"Can you read it for me?"

Mythrian did not want to go on another journey. He had been through quite enough on his last journey.

"Certainly," the scout said, before reading the note aloud:

"Dear Mythrian.

I hope you have had a safe journey. I am glad to know you are in safe hands. I am addressing this letter to you because I have been asked to register your name for the arena fort of Aldremayne. Your victory in Avalin has gained you a place in the arena. Myself and Master Brennius both agreed that you would wish to compete in this event. You have been given accommodation in the Village of Falstone. Heading there from your current position in Hagenherde, you should get the settlement within a day's journey hoping all goes well.

I also wish to tell you that while he is well, we have agreed that Master Brennius will momentarily step down as head of the guild. We have been worried about his health and so he will stay for a short time at the fort of Alvocanen. He will visit you in Aldremayne for your tournament.

Best Wishes, Salen Mandel."

Mythrian placed his hands over his face and shook his head uncharacteristically. None of this seemed like good news to him.

Even the thought of competing in the most prodigious tournament around was not exciting the boy. He was too tired to fight or compete. The few days that had passed since leaving Hamlynstone had felt like a month.

"Are you alright Mythrian, you seem slightly down?" Thain asked the boy.

"I'm tired. I don't want to go on another journey. I just want to go home," the boy answered.

"Hey, look I know you're tired. But this is a great opportunity for you. Something that I believe you would regret if you don't go," the scout tried to perk up the young apprentice. "Besides, your Master will be down there to meet you."

"Yeah. I guess so," the boy sighed.

Tousling the boy's head gamely, mucking up his stringy, wispy hair, Thain stood up and ordered the boy out of his bed.

"Come on Mythrian, let's get you ready for your journey."

After being helped by Thain to gather his belongings and get a rough bearing of his intended journey to Falstone, Mythrian stood by the main gates, preparing his horse. He wanted to travel alone. Thain was still cautious of the young man's safety, but he knew the lands down to Falstone were safer than those to the north.

Moving round to the right of the horse to attach a flask of water to the saddle, Mythrian heard a voice halt his actions.

"That was quite a show you put on for us today."

Turning round, Mythrian spotted Revan standing casually against the wooden walls of a local shop. His long hair was coolly swept back, revealing his bird-like face, with his unusual beak-like nose.

He had been heavily interested in the boy's markings since Mythrian had entered the hall. He just could not get his head around them, remaining mystified by them.

Before, he was unsure of the boy, but now, he seemed intrigued and obliged to greet Mythrian more personally.

"Well I'm glad you enjoyed it," Mythrian returned bluntly.

Revan smiled. "Look Mythrian, I'm not here to issue you a warning. I am here because I wish to help you."

Mythrian turned away from his horse and walked up to the General.

"Thank you, but I don't really need any help."

Rubbing his hands over his forehead, Revan tried to explain to the boy:

"Look, I know this may not be the best time for you to talk but we are entering a very dangerous time. You may not quite understand the situation yourself. Your actions in the hall have cast a lot of questions over our position in this world and a lot of doubts as to whether we are ready to confront these challenges."

"What are you trying to say?" Mythrian was slightly unclear on Revan's comments. He tried to make it clearer for the boy.

"Elgrator was not pleased when you revealed the tablet to the council. Although it shocked many, the tablet had long fallen into folklore. While it may recapture the hearts and spirits of our people, the memory of Ajia long restored, its sight comes with a grave warning. One that I feel has come at a bad time."

"Are you saying that I should have hidden the truth?"

"No, Mythrian. It is not what you have said that has caused such a stir amongst the high order, it is what has begun. Mythrian, we are at war!"

Mythrian paused as the words pushed him back. Revan continued:

"If what you said is true, the East is beginning their second wave, with a new leader at their helm. These words will pass through the land quickly and will send fear into every heart of good. Though you should never hide such knowledge from your people, I fear we are not ready for such an event."

"But isn't it better that I told His Majesty, rather than keeping it a secret and placing thousands of citizens at risk?" Mythrian replied.

"Yes, but I know Elgrator very well and I fear that he will be reluctant to call for an assembly of his army quickly enough. Though he is strong and guides his men well, Elgrator is resilient on letting other people dictate his actions. Until the enemy throws an attack, he will not make a move."

"But isn't there anybody below him who can order the movement of troops, should the time arrive?" Mythrian asked.

"There are many Generals within Hagenherde, controlling many units. They have full control over their units, yes, but only Elgrator can issue the engagement in a war," Revan returned.

"Is there anything we can do? Would it not be best to issue a letter to our surrounding settlements to warn them to be prepared?"

"No. I fear it would have a negative effect. We have a strong army already in waiting. Half of our force remains hidden in secret, in the northern fortress of Hierheldon. The threat of the East has long burned in our minds and I hope that our numbers in the forces have increased. But I have little more knowledge on this."

Mythrian nodded at his words, before going back to his initial question:

"Is this why you wish to help me?"

"Partly; consider me as your inner link with the higher order. If you need any help or if situations change and you need urgent assistance, address your problems to me and I will help you. I doubt Elgrator will listen to any more of your questions, but I will. I do not hold enough power to grant many actions, but I will do my best."

"Thank you," Mythrian returned.

"I am pleased to help you. After all, you hold a high position in these times of crisis," Revan spoke.

"Thank you, I am grateful for all your help, though I still fear that you are unsure of me and my background. Does my appearance offend you?"

"No. It's just in the world we live in, where those born differently are not allowed to live amongst regular folk, it has amazed me as to how you have fallen in so socially amongst the crowd," Revan replied.

"I've never really taken that into consideration," the boy added.

"I'm sure you haven't. But your appearance does not startle me, in fact I think you bear a very strong image. My only concern is that you have got to be careful. There are people in this world who do not like people of your appearance standing close by them. It's hard to say because you probably don't feel any threat from others when you travel to foreign villages. But you should be careful who you talk to, because some will try to get you banished from their villages. You don't deserve the life of a Halfling. None of them do," the young man stated.

"I understand," Mythrian responded. He did not feel comfortable listening to Revan's views. They seemed very harsh to him but he knew the young man was only trying to help.

"I'll leave you to get on your way now. You've got a long few days ahead. But just remember, if you ever need help from Hagenherde, forward it to me."

"Of course," the boy returned, before mounting his horse. "Oh, and one more thing. When I'm gone, could you keep an eye on Elgrator for me? From your words, I fear he may be cautious of letting me travel too far from his sights."

"Don't worry. I'm sure he wouldn't do anything to put your life at risk. He's probably just shaken from a lot of the recent events," Revan assured the boy.

"Good day, Revan."

"Good day, Mythrian," the young man replied, watching the apprentice dash across the drawbridge and out of the capital.

Revan felt as though he had eased a worry from his back, as he calmly returned back to his post in the throne room.

CHAPTER 17 † THE EAST TRAVEL NORTH, THE WEST JOURNEY SOUTH

T HROUGH DARK VALLEYS and solidified molten paths, Mordryd's army marched in their millions towards Siren's Gore. In the region of Melodia, where black dragons swarm the violet skies and desert serpents roam the arid land, the sound of thunder sparked from thousands of feet in unison.

Wave upon wave of goblin infantry, archery and even cavalry divisions marched to the crackling whip of goblin legionnaires, creating the banter from above.

"Come on you filthy lot, we haven't got all day," Valor, one of the legionnaires spoke, before turning to another in his unit. "I've never seen an army move so slow."

"That's alright, it just makes our job more amusing," one of the other legionnaires returned, before cracking his whip on several of the troop below.

Goblin legionnaires are the brains behind the development of all goblin units. Superior in knowledge and uncannily human-like in image, legionnaires have unprecedented control over their troop. However, sometimes they overstep their authority and many goblin infantry troop have tried to overpower their rivals, only for Mordryd to step in and stop any action.

Mordryd had learned to trust their commitment and it was through them, rather than their Master, that a new wave of stronger units had emerged. Their only weakness was their arrogance and neglect of the strong threat from the West.

As the army moved along past the legionnaires, one of the

troop stumbled over a pothole, hidden by the large crowds. Falling forward, dropping his helmet, the trooper was quick to pick it up when a whip lashed him heavily on the cheek.

"AARRGGHH!" the trooper put pressure on the cut to stop the bleeding.

"Move along you worthless grunt, or I'll keep on whipping you until you do," the legionnaire ordered.

"Maybe we would if your hands showed less haste with that whip. We have far to walk and such little time and your lashes are interrupting our steady march."

The legionnaire leaned forward over the edge of the small cliff, where they were positioned and questioned:

"What is your name, grunt?"

"My name is Koron," the trooper proudly replied.

"Ok, and what unit do you follow?" the legionnaire continued.

"I follow the fourth infantry ..."

"The fourth; that is a long way down the pecking order. Maybe you should question your motives before you approach a legionnaire with such disrespect."

"There is nothing wrong with my motives. Maybe you have forgotten yours. While our army marches as one unit, we are all individuals in this war. And as individuals, we should all be shown respect for our duties."

"My, aren't you a bright one for a fourth infantry trooper? But perhaps you have not been properly informed of your official position in this war. The primary infantry are individuals. They are our highest honoured troop. The backbone of our forces. Not the fourth. No, you are expendable."

"Where do you find honour in an expendable unit?"

Leaning back, winding his whip around his spiny, extended fingers, he turned to his fellow legionnaire.

"Looks like we have an outcast, Morgg."

"Outcasts don't belong in the army. Not until they have been cleansed of their foolish minds," Morgg added.

"What are you referring to?" the goblin asked.

"Every single trooper passing you here would die at any time, any place, if it meant vanquishing those disgusting vermin to the West. They don't need to answer any questions; their answers are clearly visible before them. But not to you it seems. Instead you stand here before me and you think that I should care about your actions on the field of battle. Your life means nothing to me nor does it to anyone higher than you. Remember that. Now pick up your helm and leave before my whip speaks my tongue."

Picking up his helm, and placing it back on his head, the trooper gave the legionnaire one final message of disapproval:

"Just think of this. How do you expect your army to act as one full unit when there is no equality; throwing in expendable troops into battle? Well, let me tell you this; the people to the West consider each and every soldier of importance to their cause. It doesn't matter how many times we outnumber them. Unless we bind together as a whole unit like them, we stand no chance in this war. We will crumble beneath their discipline and unity. Bear that in mind the next time you question the motives of one of your troop, regardless of where he stands on the field of battle," the trooper spoke before catching up with his unit.

Valor fumed at the Koron's comments and was lurching forward on his toes, ready to jump at the goblin when Morgg held him back, stating, "Don't worry about that senseless brute, Valor. He will not last long."

"Maybe you're right, nothing good ever comes to those who oppose their orders. But be sure, if I find him up to no good again, he'll wish he had never spoken back to us. Now come on, back to our work; less whining, more whipping."

Steadily riding down south to the village of Falstone, his resting village for his contest in Aldremayne, Mythrian felt more relaxed on his journey.

Exiting the kingdom capital region of Everlyn, he continued through the land of Cygnia's Roam.

Following the path down to Avalin, he could clearly remember the anxiety and excitement that filled him in the carriage on the way to his first contest. Standing on top of the hill, the village of Avalin before him, Mythrian stood for a moment to capture the redevelopments. A lot of work had gone into restoring the village. The majority of the tents had been replaced and stationed, but there were still giant depressions across the grounds, left from the troll's assault.

Travelling around the village, Mythrian stepped down from his horse to stand next to the troll. Still trapped within its vines, forever entwined with Mother Earth, Mythrian felt no negative thoughts about its attack.

From memory, the achievement was hard to swallow, for Mythrian knew how close he had come to losing it all. But standing up close to the beast, Mythrian came to realise what an extraordinary effort it had taken to defeat the beast. It gave Mythrian a much needed morale boost.

And it begged the question as to what greater things he could achieve.

Travelling on, further than he had ever travelled before, Mythrian made a short stop before the village of Tharamond. Regarded as the centre point of the kingdom of Aedorn, Tharamond is a quiet and relatively unknown village.

Most villages hold a building of particular importance. Tharamond has nothing in turn of particular value. Instead, the village is occupied by a large quantity of cottages, with many available for accommodation.

A great deal of the residents here are either retired or wanting to live away from any of the other hectic villages. Unless people are visiting the village to stay in accommodation; few enter, few leave.

Having bought himself some water and some food from one of the local stalls, Mythrian sat down on the smooth grass, relaxing in the calm, open wind.

Unlike his journey north, he had encountered no danger so far. Though he could never let his guard down, he felt no tension, no sudden threat.

The midlands have never had as many attacks as to the north and south. Because of this, many often travel to the midland villages as a retreat from the constant rumours and threats surrounding their own towns.

The most common area is the long flats of Llylandra, located to the south-west of Tharamond. Its low, golden pastures offer miles of open land, free to let the mind drift from important matters.

However, Mythrian was to head south-east in his journey to Falstone. There he would enter the region of the Plains of Tershia. Though duller than the areas around him, it still was a quaint region full of beauty.

With the clouds above moving swiftly on, Mythrian knew that time was of the essence. Finishing his food and mounting his horse, he continued the long journey down to Falstone.

The journey to Falstone was surprisingly longer than the distance of his last trip from Hamlynstone to Fayrmayden. However, the land here was straight, flat and accessible. It would not be long before the walls of Falstone were evident.

The peaceful midland region of Cygnia's Roam had long disappeared and as the sky darkened, the fifth sun fading, Mythrian decided to rest for the night.

Sitting against the bark of a tree, a sheet wrapped tightly around him, Mythrian looked up into the sky at the gloriously bold fifth moon. As it danced across the midnight sky, Mythrian's eyes slowly closed before he fell into a peaceful dream.

Upon wakening to the smell of morning blooms as the flowers opened to the new sun, Mythrian was quick and eager to restart his journey.

Midday approached and the giant frame of Falstone village came into view.

Falstone could be summed up in many words, yet Mythrian remained speechless. It looked very modern in its design; compared to the layout of other villages. Falstone was the centre of development.

Entering the village, Mythrian was confounded by the many paths and buildings before him. He had not expected the village to look so complicated.

He tried to ask several passers-by for directions:

"Excuse me, can you help? Excuse me ... where can I find accommodation for the contest in Aldremayne?"

But everybody ignored him. Everyone looked busy, for work was always on the go in this village.

Though he was lost, Mythrian noticed that a lot of the buildings around him were either work-related or were military barracks. This is probably where the settlement's trading and economical meetings take place. The village of Falstone itself must be located within the centre of this outer rim.

Perhaps they preferred to keep work and social life separate.

Mythrian hoped that it was more peaceful in the village itself. But he still needed directions to get through the large crowd.

Finding a local barracks, Mythrian asked the guard at the front door:

"Excuse me, can you help me ..."

He was quickly shunned by the guard:

"Pardon me young sir, but we are on guard. We are not supposed to talk to anyone until our shift is over and even then we prefer some peace and quiet."

"I'm sorry, I just wanted directions to the centre of Falstone. I'm here for accommodation," Mythrian apologetically replied.

Pointing to another local barrack, the guard answered the boy's question:

"See where those three guards are, walk up to them and then take the path to the right, it will take you to the inner walls. Tell the gate keeper who you are and he may let you into Falstone. Now please hurry along and let me continue with my work."

"Certainly, thank you," Mythrian answered before following the guard's directions. True to his words, Mythrian reached the village gates and stepped up to the gate keeper. To his surprise there were few wishing to enter the village.

Approaching the gate keeper, Mythrian stared at the bald man who was slumped on a stand. He looked very bored. His arm was holding the weight of his heavy head, while his mind appeared to be elsewhere.

Mythrian could have just sneaked past him into the village, but he thought it best to ask the daydreamer.

"Pardon me."

The old man came to life. "What? What do you want?"

"I am here for accommodation for the contest at Aldremayne," the boy returned.

"Alright, very good. In you go then."

But the man did nothing. The gates remained closed. Mythrian stood still, totally confused by the matter. Looking over towards the gate, which to him still appeared closed, Mythrian was expecting the man to pull a lever of some sort.

Unfortunately the man had fallen back into his daydream, still in his casual position. Mythrian was certainly not amused. He didn't know whether this was a joke or whether the man was blatantly rejecting him.

Clearly the people of Falstone had no sense of humour whatsoever, or manners for that matter.

"But how can I go in when the gates are locked?" Mythrian quizzed the keeper.

"The gates will open when you approach them. I'm just here to make sure nobody suspicious passes through. Do you expect me to walk all the way over there and open the gates for you?" the keeper replied with a sharp edge to his tone.

"Well, no offence, but your level of security worries me. What if I was a goblin in disguise, I could probably have walked straight through into the village and caused havoc."

"If you were a goblin, I would kindly welcome you into the village. This place needs something to wake it up," the old man quickly responded.

"Why do you think that?"

"I see the same thing every single day. Swarms of greedy people sticking their noses in their greedy shops. The people you see here are all very rich. Not sharing the slightest regard for us Gimlets."

"Gimlets?"

"Yeah, that's what they call us working class. Gimlets are short Halflings that live in tiny homes, usually made from a tree or buried in a hole under the ground. They call us Gimlets because, compared to their fancy houses, we live in nestled homes. The cheek of some people, hey? Where are you from anyway?" the man spoke.

"Hamlynstone."

"Hamlynstone. Unfortunately that doesn't ring a bell. Is it north?" the keeper responded.

"The furthest village in the north-west," Mythrian answered.

"I bet it's a model, working class village."

"It's a very small village, simple in its design."

"Yeah. You'll find the villagers inside Falstone are more open to conversation with us working class. But not out here," the keeper sneered at several rich citizens passing by.

Mythrian took a short moment to study the local folk, before turning to ask the keeper another question:

"If you are so fed up being a gate keeper, why do you still do it? If you are that uncomfortable in this area, surely you would try to get a new job?"

"Well, this job pays well and I'm not as young as I used to be. I'm too young to retire but too old to continue my old work as a craftsman."

"A craftsman. A true Gimlet then," Mythrian replied.

The old man was finally beginning to smile. It had been so long since he had spoken to someone from a similar, working class background:

"Yes, well, I was proud of my work until I was involved in a workplace accident and lost the use of my right hand. They gave me some compensation, but ... taking away a craftsman's tools is like taking away his heart and soul."

"I am sorry to hear that," Mythrian sympathised.

"Thank you for your empathy; it's more than I get from most of the people round here. But I'm holding you up. I'm sure you want to get into the village. You may go, just walk up to the gates and the guards will open them. I apologise for any inconvenience."

"Thank you, good day," Mythrian finished his conversation and headed for the village gate.

CHAPTER 18 ✝ THE
INTRODUCTION OF FINGAL

ENTERING THE VILLAGE, Mythrian felt much more at home with the surroundings. The streets were not as crowded; the buildings were older, smaller and to an extent, reminiscent of Hamlynstone. The overall aspect of the village was a lot brighter and spacious. Mythrian was keen to investigate the area.

Walking past several shops that were quieter and appeared more suitably priced, Mythrian followed the main street down to an impressive building; his curiosity got the better of him.

Entering the building, Mythrian passed through a couple of small entrances before he entered a hall. In front of him were several thrones on which three people sat. One looked of high importance, made evident by his very rich and extravagant clothing. To his side were two women who were also richly dressed. Perhaps his wife and daughter?

To his left and right along the walls, guards peered at the unexpected guest, who walked gingerly further into the hall.

Mythrian was thinking about turning around and heading back out, until one of the guards coughed, catching the attention of the man on the throne. Initially looking over to the guard, the lavishly dressed man instantly spotted Mythrian, feeling disconcerted in the centre of the hall.

"Greetings, young one, what business draws you here?" The man spoke warmly and proudly, luring the boy into the conversation.

"My name is Mythrian. I'm looking for accommodation. I am to take part in the contest at Aldremayne," the boy returned quietly, sensing the cold, hard, stern look on the faces of the guards, watching his every move.

"Mythrian. Of Avalin fame?" The man moved to the edge of his seat.

The boy was surprised to hear that his achievement had travelled so far and quickly.

"Yes, I am. You have heard of me?"

"Have I heard of you?" The man laughed loudly. "Mythrian, your achievement in Avalin is becoming a widespread tale. You're a hero and an inspiration to the young and gifted. Of course I've heard of you. I am greatly honoured by your presence."

"Thank you. May I ask who you are?" Mythrian asked.

"Certainly, my name is Henley, I am the Mayor of Falstone. I take it that you are new to this area?"

"This is the farthest I have ever travelled," the boy replied.

"You travel alone?"

"Yes. But the journey was calm. In fact I rather enjoyed it."

"Good, I am glad to hear that," the Mayor's broadening smile grew wider. "So you are here for accommodation? We hope you will enjoy your time with us. Have you seen much of our village yet?"

"No, not yet. I followed the road down to this very building. I must apologise for my unexpected entrance," the boy chuckled at his misunderstanding.

The Mayor continued to laugh at Mythrian's comments.

"How amusing. But you are entitled to visit any time you like."

The Mayor seemed very nice and welcoming but there was something about him that made Mythrian feel somewhat nervous. He seemed very fake in his laugh and body language, as though behind his smile he was more interested in the fact that the much spoken of Mythrian had visited his hall, rather than anybody else's.

But there was nothing to back these suspicions. Besides, Mythrian was pleased to have found the good side of the Mayor on his entrance. With the wide array of guards that he had, getting on the wrong side of him could have put Mythrian in a lot of unwanted trouble.

"Anyway, I'm sure you want to go to your accommodation. You'll feel more at home once you have settled into your room," Mayor Henley continued, before alerting one of the guards. "Please show this young man to a substantial room."

"Certainly Your Worship, this way young sir," the guard spoke.

"Thank you for your help. I'm sure I will enjoy my time here in Falstone," Mythrian finished.

"I'm sure you will. Falstone is a quiet, peaceful and ..."

"Sorry I am late Master." A young man, roughly Mythrian's age, stepped out from a door behind Henley. He was very colourfully dressed, perhaps having some sort of connection with the Mayor. His face was long and drawn. His body was skinny and frail and his skin was very pale.

Standing by his Mayor, leaning over with his hands on his knees breathing in large gulps of air, it seemed that he had run from a long distance away.

However his Master was not impressed with his entrance and leaned angrily over his throne, posing the question:

"Where have you been?"

"I am sorry, Master, there ... was an accident in the kitchen of the north tavern. One of the cooks had spilled a large pan of hot soup. Nobody else was around to help, so I volunteered to help her."

Henley raised a suspicious eyebrow. The young man had stuttered in his reply and the Mayor felt doubtful to his sincerity:

"Is that so?"

"Yes, Master. Just rushed back only seconds ago," the young man puffed his tired words out.

The Mayor was unsure and called one of the guards for guidance.

"Eron, if I may borrow a moment of your time? Have you not just come back from your duties?"

"About fifteen minutes ago sire."

"On your duties, did you happen to pass the northern tavern?" Henley continued.

"Indeed I did sir," the guard replied convincingly.

"And when you passed, did you happen to spot any incidents?"

"No sire. For the north tavern has been closed for refurbishment for nearly a week sire."

"Thank you, Eron."

The young man stood rooted to the spot, biting his foolish tongue. His eyes were flickering as his mind retraced his words. He had stopped his heavy breathing, but remained crouched, avoiding eye contact with his disgruntled Master.

"How long have you been listening?" Henley asked.

"Listening to what?"

"Don't try and fool me. I know you were listening behind the door," the Mayor argued.

The young man said nothing. He stared at his feet while he kicked at the stone floor, releasing small puffs of dust off the surface.

"Fingal, I grow tired of your lies. My trust in you is treading on thin ice. Don't push it any further," the Mayor firmly stated his authority.

"Sorry, Master."

"My dear Fingal. I fear you are going to be the death of me," Henley rubbed his aching head.

"My apologies, sire," Fingal spoke softly, almost down to a whisper.

The Mayor sighed as he noticed troublesome man had forgotten to bring with him.

"Fingal, where is my crown?"

"Your crown?" Fingal's eyes began flickering from side to side again. He nervously rubbed his hands together, trying to recall where he had left the item. But his Master was growing impatient.

"How many times do I have to tell you? I have a meeting later this afternoon at three hours past midday. I cannot be seen at this meeting without my crown."

"Don't worry sire, I will find it and bring it to you," Fingal stuttered.

"You'd better do, otherwise I will be forced to punish you. I can't afford to lose my crown," Henley responded sharply.

Mythrian was intrigued by the conversation, though he could not help but feel sorry for the young man. He asked the Mayor:

"Who is this young man you are questioning my lord?"

"This is Fingal, my helper," Henley replied.

"Helper?"

"Well, I do not wish to call him a servant. He helps me with tasks that a man of my position is not supposed to do. Like bringing me my crown!"

"Is there anything I can do to help? I would be willing to help Fingal retrieve it for you."

"No thankyou, Mythrian. I'm sure Fingal is capable of handling this himself," he spoke, turning and focusing on the young man, who in turn looked in the opposite direction.

"Besides, I'm sure you have your own important matters that you wish to attend to," Mayor Henley continued.

"Of course. Thank you," Mythrian gratefully replied.

"But thank you again for visiting. It was unexpected, but nonetheless, I am delighted to have met the widely spoken-of Mythrian. We will be watching your progress closely. I'm sure the tale of Mythrian has many more chapters yet."

Acknowledging Mayor Henley's words, Mythrian looked across to Fingal who stared back with anger in his eyes. Mythrian sensed that he was feeling jealous of the praise his Master was showing him.

However, Mythrian decided to ignore the young man and focused back on the Mayor.

"If you need help on any matter, just look for the eastern tavern. Take the east path around my hall and you will see it. There are guards in there who would be pleased to help you," the Mayor finished.

Bowing to the Mayor, Mythrian gave Fingal one more conspicuous glance, before exiting the hall.

Henley turned to his helper and ordered him to make a move himself:

"Why are you still standing there, go look for my crown! And don't return until you've got it."

"I'll find your crown sire," Fingal answered.

"I hope you were listening to what Mythrian had to say for himself. You could learn a lot from someone like him," the Mayor stated.

Heading back through the door behind his Master, Fingal muttered to himself, "Oh don't worry Sire, I'll be keeping a close eye on Mythrian."

A grin drew darkly over his concealed face.

CHAPTER 19 † UNDISCOVERED TERRITORY

A S EVENING BEGAN, with the moon pushing away the sixth sun, Mythrian found the eastern tavern.

The tavern was a very warm setting, with candles and aromas lighting up the newly constructed framework. Mythrian sat comfortably back in his cushioned chair, his beer sitting on a smoothly cut table. In his hands was a book which he had borrowed from the tavern's bookshelf. All were on the formation and growth of the southern lands.

The tavern itself was very quiet and subdued, which was good for Mythrian, as he wanted some time and room to settle down and relax for the night.

But having wandered around most of the village by now, Mythrian still could not understand why the village was so peaceful. There were not many in the tavern and those nearby talked very quietly in their conversations.

Perhaps most of the population were visitors and most of them preferred to stay close to their accommodations, using their time to rest and catch up on lost sleep travelling.

Momentarily putting his book down on the table to take a break, Mythrian sipped his beer, while looking through the southern window. Tomorrow he would be heading south for Aldremayne.

Though he still felt tired and homesick, he was gradually feeling excited about the time ahead.

However, Mythrian wanted to travel down to Aldremayne alone. He felt he could travel faster there and arrive earlier than being escorted down in one of the transport wagons. But he didn't know the way there, nor did he know much about the southern lands.

As one of the guards passed him, he asked for advice:

"Excuse me, could I trouble you for a few questions?"

"Certainly sir, how can I help you?" the guard poised himself.

"Do you have a map of the area?" Mythrian asked.

"Of Falstone or the southern lands?"

"The southern lands if possible," Mythrian answered.

Handing Mythrian the map, he placed it upon the table, using his mug to hold one of the sides down. Quickly scanning it, Mythrian asked:

"I've found Falstone, but where is Aldremayne?"

Pointing to the south east of Falstone, to a region that was marked as MG, there sat the settlement of Aldremayne. The guard spoke:

"If you head directly south from Falstone, you'll pass several woodlands before you enter a wide open region. This is Maison's Graze. Shortly in, you'll see a path heading to the east; follow it and it will take you to Aldremayne."

Analysing the map, Mythrian noticed there were other villages between his journey from Falstone to Aldremayne. It led him on to the question:

"Why have we been stationed here, when there are closer settlements to Aldremayne?"

"Well, the two nearest settlements of importance are Rhone and Gaidenhead. Gaidenhead is a trading village tucked within Emble forest. They export the largest amount of quality timber than anywhere else. Rhone is the military outpost for the southern lands. Neither have any houses up for accommodation. There is also Eyre, which is closer to here, but is of little importance, being more a simple, farming village."

Looking at the map on the table, Mythrian spotted another town, further to the west, though still close to Aldremayne. "What about this town, Bohdenbram?"

"Oh, they don't talk much down there." The guard drew a coy smile on his face. There was obviously something he knew about that village that he wasn't telling Mythrian.

Mythrian saw no further point in pursing this subject.

"Do you have any other questions you would like to ask?" the guard spoke.

Mythrian scanned the map quickly, knowing there were going to be others asking for the guard's help.

"What's this highlighted area below Aldremayne?"

"There is nothing below Aldremayne," the guard returned sharply.

"Then why is there a site marked on this map?" Mythrian questioned, wanting just a straightforward answer.

The guard refused to answer the boy's question.

"The land below Aldremayne is either uncharted or out of our kingdom limits. What goes on out there is of no concern to us. But if you're thinking about examining that site, I firmly suggest you don't. That is unless you're willing to face the creatures that swarm the unguarded land."

Mythrian had nothing more to ask the guard.

"If you don't mind, I've got others requesting my knowledge. Good day Sir."

Mythrian scratched his head irritably. "What could this marked site be? It can't be a village. But what?" he thought to himself.

Being the curious character that he is, he wanted to examine the site, but perhaps it was too dangerous for the moment.

Examining the map further, he noticed that close to the village of Falstone was the famous spiritual site of the Obelisks of Light.

The Obelisks were said to have been placed there by Ajia as a place of worship, where those who prayed would receive his kind help. The Obelisks are a ring of large stones, said to contain crystals of energy that can heal the worries and strains that weigh down on those in need.

People usually go there to worship during the day. Mythrian was too wide awake to sleep. So instead he thought about examining these Obelisks up close. After all, he was entitled to leave and return whenever he wished.

Finishing his drink, Mythrian headed off for the Obelisks of Light. He would not get there before nightfall but it did not matter, for nobody else would be around.

CHAPTER 20 † DARKNESS CRAWLS INTO HAGENHERDE

ELGRATOR HAD ASSEMBLED his high Generals and several councillors for discussion on an important topic in the Hagen council chamber. Standing over a large table with plans of action ready at their disposal, much was to be discussed in this meeting.

There was no real need for the councillors, for they said nothing at these meetings. They only backed their Majesty's comments; however, it was a sneaky ploy to put pressure on the other Generals, when they argued with his decisions.

The main debate in this meeting: Mythrian and the tablet.

"Let us begin this meeting. I have brought you all here on an air of concern and caution. A day ago, those who were in the hall at the time would have seen this young boy, who claimed to be the one; the finder of Ajia's tablet. With this, he claimed to be the holder of the tablet and its powers and stated that the East are planning a new campaign. Gethen has told me he has new information on this," Elgrator started the conversation before handing it over to his General in artillery.

"Thank you, Your Majesty. After yesterday's meeting in the Hagen hall, we have discovered a lot about our enemy to the East. As we first feared, it seems the enemy has learned much about the land as with the sea. Several boats containing belongings thought to be of their design were found this morning in Lingarde harbour. For this we have quarantined the area, as well as several spots along Gyda's Pass," Gethen spoke.

"How certain are you that these items you found with the boats, are from the East?" Galenor stepped in.

"On several of the tools found, there appeared to be a dark matter, as fine as dust, covering parts of the blades. With much searching, we have found no links to any matter found commonly in our kingdom. Our only guess is that they chiselled their tools on a certain type of stone, probably only found in the dark lands of the East; thus producing this fine dust. Of course, these could belong to Halfling groups, but with the series of attacks coming from the north, the links with Lingarde are all too close," Gethen elaborated.

"Ok, but what about the land? Surely all the attacks haven't been coming from the sea?" Galenor continued, wanting more guidance and knowledge on the East.

"At the moment it is too early to say how or when they have landed or entered our kingdom. What we do know is that their knowledge of our kingdom and of our landscape is surprisingly accurate. Had it not been so, we would have encountered these enemy forces long before they had come so close to Hagenherde's borders," Gethen stated.

A clever grin poured on to his smarmy face. He was very much like Elgrator in that he was very self-centred, believing everything always revolved around him.

Unfortunately this was the case, with many high officials and standing Generals. It is not an easy task to get to their position but the few who do can sometimes get very greedy. Far too much power and authority going to their head.

"What are you stating?" Galenor asked, wanting to quickly get to the point.

Galenor was far more open minded and much fairer than most of the other Generals. He did not like having useful knowledge kept away from him, though he often knew many of the Generals were holding information back from him.

He did not trust his allies for he was aware many could be deceiving him. Many of the high ranked Generals were craving his position as second in command to Elgrator. They always thought he was too kind. The Majesty of the kingdom should be more ruthless, like Elgrator.

Galenor always kept on eye open at all times and never trusted anyone, not even Elgrator himself.

"I am stating, Galenor, that there are spies in our lands. Human spies who are deceiving their own kind. Or closer to the point, Halfling spies. The enemy must be manipulating them, perhaps supplying them with gold and in turn, these spies are giving them information," Gethen replied.

"Gethen, we have had enemy spies in our lands since the last war. What makes you think these spies are human?" Galenor fired back.

"I'm not blaming anyone, Galenor ... as yet," the General instantly responded, "But don't you find it suspicious as to how in the recent attacks, the enemy has been slipping through our tight defensive system? After the barrage of attacks which began by Gyda's Pass, we have had the region of Arlyne's Drift quarantined. The only way the enemy could have passed our troops, is if someone was telling them our position. Then they would be able to find the narrow gaps to break through."

Galenor had his left arm resting on the table, holding his head in his hand. He refused to believe what Gethen was saying, even with the councillors sounding their calls of approval. Rubbing his finely trimmed beard, studying the plans on the table which he knew were not going to be used by the way this conversation was heading, he went straight to the point:

"So what do you propose?"

"We round up those we are suspicious of spying," Gethen concluded.

"Round them up? I'm sorry but I'm not following you. Are you saying we are going to start imprisoning people because they may or may not hold some sort of connection with these recent events?"

"Imprison is such a harsh word. All we want to do is make the kingdom a safer place. Unless we find these culprits, the bombardment will continue," the General explained.

"I'm sorry, but I am greatly opposed to this sort of thing. It could be damaging for our kingdom. People will be in fear of their own safety," the humble man tried to explain, but his words were having no effect on the siding of this argument.

"The people won't be in fear, Galenor. We won't be too intrusive. I'm sure our people will cooperate, because, like us, they will want this matter to be dealt with urgently."

"Gethen is right," His Majesty stepped in. "We have to act now otherwise we could be putting our kingdom under more risk."

"I'm sorry Your Majesty, but I totally disagree," Galenor spoke, rising up from the table.

"Do not overstep me, Galen. I understand your views, but as second in command you should show a little bit more respect to your Majesty's orders."

Galenor fell silent on His Majesty's comments. Nobody was siding with him in the hall. He had no choice but to listen to the plan.

"Here is the plan. Send scouts out to find Halfling bases. Have them round up the Halflings and search each one for information. Any items or artefacts found should be taken for analysis as well. It might give us some leads before we start searching our own people."

"Yes sire," Gethen replied.

"Speaking of artefacts, have you been keeping an eye on our young individual?" Elgrator asked.

"Mythrian?" Galenor swallowed hard. Surely they weren't going to imprison the young boy?

"He's heading for Aldremayne. Apparently he's taking part in the annual contest, held on New Year's Eve," Gethen replied.

"Excellent. Have a party sent down there. I want him arrested and brought back here on grounds of treason," Elgrator ordered.

"Treason? For doing what exactly?" Galenor stuttered. He didn't know what to say, only that he thought His Majesty and the other Generals had gone mad with power and fear.

"On the grounds of spying, placing false fear into the hearts of our people and of his insult to our God, Ajia, for claiming to be the holder of his powers," His Majesty explained.

Galenor stepped closer to his Lord, begging him to reconsider. "But Sire, you saw the tablet. Surely you do not think that it was staged? His words. His appearance. His markings ..."

"His markings. Do you honestly think that Ajia would allow

his powers to go to such a negligible mutant as Mythrian? He is a Halfling and a very dangerous one at that. I will not have you interrupting this meeting any more. My actions are final. Mythrian will be placed under arrest and tried for treason. Maybe then we will really see who is telling the truth ..."

As Elgrator was finishing his comment, Revan came tumbling through the door, nearly tripping over in the process. The door swung open sharply, just being stopped by its hinges before cracking hard against the stone wall. The crowd turned and looked suspiciously at Revan as he regained his composure, steadying his shaking legs.

Breathing heavily, Revan had been secretly listening behind the door. To save himself from a certain bombardment of questions, Revan quickly tried to make up an excuse:

"Sorry, Your Lordship ... An urgent message has just arrived ... for Galenor."

Elgrator sensed a cunning lie in Revan's words, but his speaker had never lied to him before.

After giving Revan a suspicious eye, he turned to his successor to allow him to leave. But as his High General walked past him, Elgrator stopped him, grabbing him by the arm:

"Do not think that your words in this meeting have cost you nothing. As second in command your orders are to follow mine. If you can't do that, then maybe you should be somewhere else. I'm watching you closely, Galenor."

Releasing his tight grasp, he allowed Galenor to leave the room with Revan. With his disruptive General out of the room, it gave Elgrator more freedom to openly discuss his plans with his loyal Generals and councillors.

Stepping out into the borders, Revan and Galenor stopped in front of one of the market stalls. The High General knew that Revan had been listening through the whole of the meeting, but it was the latter who began the conversation.

"What has become of this kingdom? Galenor, we cannot let them imprison Mythrian," Revan threw his arms open in disgust.

"I don't want this any more than you do, but did you hear them in there? I didn't even have a voice to be heard. I argued, but nobody would listen to me," the young man replied.

"But Galenor, that's not good enough. Can't you see what Elgrator is doing? He is blinding you ... and everyone. Have you never stared into Mythrian's eyes? Have you never looked into the eyes of those who are shamed for their appearance? I looked into Mythrian's eyes and I saw a light. I saw ambition and a spirit that would never die."

Stepping closer to his General he continued, "Every Halfling man, woman and child will be searched and maybe imprisoned; for what, because they are being accused of spying? Why would they spy on us? Why do they even care about us after all we have done to them?"

"Isn't that precisely the point, Revan? They hate us for degrading them. This is their response," Galenor replied.

"No, you see Galenor, that is what Elgrator wishes you to think. But why would a creature of good soul perform such an act of treachery? They do not want land. They do not seek revenge. All they want is redemption. To be accepted into our community. You see, this is how we have been blinded. We have been taught that the Halflings are a sub-breed who wish to match our superiority. They don't want to match anything. They have done nothing wrong. It is us that have done wrong and this is why I fear this search will destroy us and not them."

Galenor placed his hands on his hips and sighed. He could see the truth in Revan's words and he almost felt relieved hearing them, as though he had been lifted from the blindness cast over him by Elgrator.

"Your words are truthful, but it will take more than words to convince a kingdom that they are wrong," the General voiced his concern.

"I understand that. But I fear there is something deeper at work here. Something very dark is being hidden from us."

"Like what?"

"I do not wish to speak in such an evil tongue," Revan replied, "But my mind is consumed with the cries of thousands as they are stripped from their families, from their freedom. Their lives torn apart. They don't deserve this. I have never felt so much anger in my veins."

"Revan, words cannot explain how devastating the segregation of the Halflings will be, but we do not have the power to stand up to our authorities."

"Then what can we do? We can't let this happen. And if Mythrian is right about the East, then we are in great peril," Revan cried. His eyes were nearly in tears through the confusion and shock of Elgrator's orders.

"You're right. There is something odd about all of this. Even if Mythrian is wrong about the East, why would Elgrator be so worried about spies so close to home? And why would he wish to round up every single Halfling, rather than just a select few?"

"Galenor, we must be careful about what we say. Though you were right to argue in the meeting, I fear our involvement may have put our lives in danger."

"Do not worry, Revan, no harm will come to us. We are too important to be discarded," the High General added.

"I wouldn't be too sure of that, as yet. As sad as it will be, we must play along with His Majesty's orders. But we must be cautious of the situation around us. We cannot let this get out of hand," Revan spoke.

"I agree. But let us not speak of this any further for now. I will try to contact Mythrian but in the meantime, don't get too involved in this issue. The last thing I want is for one of us to get into trouble," Galenor replied.

There was a pause as they both took a heavy breath. They felt restricted as though they were both trapped in their own cell. There was certainly an icy chill in the wind, making them feel as though something was peering down on them, breathing its wicked breath on to their shoulders.

"Why don't you go and relax somewhere? You still have some time before Elgrator returns from his meeting," Galenor continued.

"I will. Thank you. Good day, Galenor," Revan rounded off, shaking the General's hand.

"Good day, Revan."

They both turned their separate ways, but they knew that they would be drawn together in the very near future.

Chapter 21 † A Long Awaited Message

"COME ON, FIGHT with all your might!"
Mythrian charged forward, throwing his sword
at his opponent with great force. As swords crossed,
shimmers of light danced across the blade against the full moon,
which sat low in the sky.

Both Mythrian and his opponent were short on breath, having
battled for a while but his counterpart was not finished.

"Evade the sword, Mythrian, you cannot hurt me, I'm already
a spirit. Evade, block and then strike!"

Mythrian attempted this but came to no avail. The spirit stood
two feet over his head and had he still been alive, he would have
crushed Mythrian in his grasp.

"Put some muscle into it! Your sword is the line between life
and death and at the moment you are swaying too close to the
latter."

Mythrian started to push the spirit back and finally began to
put some venom into his strikes. Suddenly, it was the spirit who
was on the defensive.

"That's it, Mythrian, you're getting the hang of it. Hold your
hands steady and release the power from your shoulders. Don't
think about taking a back step, that is a sign of tiredness and
weakness. Forward, forward!"

Mythrian began to shout as he lunged in with a flurry of strikes
at the spirit. Having been holding his sword with one hand, the
spirit was now having difficulty blocking the attacks with two
hands.

Mythrian was grasping the techniques of duelling and like

most subjects, he was learning quickly.

"Come on Mythrian, strike me down! Look for the opportunity and then take it!"

Mythrian then suddenly countered one of the spirit's strikes with such force that his opponent nearly let go of his sword. With an open target, the boy thrust his sword, cutting through the spirit's entity.

"Well done, Mythrian. You have accomplished your training in single handed combat. I hope it is of use to you in your quest," the spirit spoke.

"Thank you, Elrick. I am sure this lesson will not go unused," Mythrian replied.

"Good man. Now if you will excuse me, Mythrian I must go; my spirit form cannot stay here for long. Safe journey, Mythrian."

"Goodbye, Elrick."

As the spirit disappeared, Mythrian stood still in the centre of Falstone Obelisks. The power within the obelisks had granted him the power to connect with Elrick for some much needed training.

For a few moments he stood perfectly still, taking in the giant stones under the reflection of the full moon. Catching his breath, who could not admire the work and vision within the artefacts?

Gazing across at one of the stones that was sliced in half, most probably from natural causes, he noticed a note lying on top of its surface.

To his astonishment, it was for him:

"Greetings, Mythrian.

My name is Vispa. I hope your mother informed you of my position. There is much I need to tell you, however due to certain events I cannot speak with you as soon as I would hope to. But I know of a man who could offer more light on your quest. You will find him in the greens of Iriel. He lives by a river in a mushroom field, towards the east of the region. His name is Lindley Glonenbloom. Ask him your questions and he will answer them.

I will inform you soon as to when I can next speak with you. In the meantime, take care.

Vispa."

Though Mythrian was upbeat about the implications of the note, one thing was eluding him. How did Vispa know he was going to be at the Obelisks of light, even though it was a spontaneous idea?

Mythrian did not like the feeling that someone was watching him. He then took a moment to scan the area, making sure Vispa or somebody else wasn't nearby.

Tearing the note up so no one else would find it, Mythrian headed back to Falstone. He kept his eyes peeled for the rest of the journey.

† † †

Having got some sleep in his accommodation, morning broke and Mythrian was off to Aldremayne. Taking his horse rather than using the village transport, Mythrian hoped to get there by midday.

However, in the town outskirts where activity was busy, Mayor Henley was walking around in a frustrated mood. He was on a search. It seemed for someone in particular.

He approached one of the guards:

"Where has that little scoundrel gone to now?"

"Who do you speak of, sire?" the guard replied.

"Fingal, he's disappeared again. When I catch that wretched boy, I'll wring him until he turns purple-faced."

Taking a deep breath to calm his emotions, the Mayor explained, "He had just returned my crown for me, but now, when I need him to be with me at my royal meeting, he runs off. I really don't know what I am going to do with him. If you see him, send him to me won't you?"

"Of course, sire. I'll pass the word on to the other guards."

"Thank you. Have you heard of any rumours from the capital recently? I'm afraid taxes will be going up again next year?" the Mayor returned.

"I don't know but between you and me, a relation of mine works as a blacksmith on a small farm just outside of Hagenherde. He says that there is going to be a large scale emigration of Halflings. Apparently it is due to reports that some Halflings have been spying and then sending the information to the East."

"That's terrible, but why on such a large scale? Surely our top guards can extract the culprits, without the need to move or deport great numbers?" Henley replied.

"I'm not sure. Something is wrong in the capital and it won't be long before the guards will be down here, searching the village and the surrounding area."

"Then we will have to be ready for them when they come. Thank you for telling me," the Mayor replied.

"Yes sire. But that isn't entirely where my concerns lie. I noticed there was a young boy who stumbled into your household," the guard continued.

"Ah, you mean Mythrian. Yes, what about him?"

"Well, I fear he could get caught up in all of this. After all, did you see his markings? They are not normal for a human. They may take him for a Halfling. I do not wish to think about what they will do to him to obtain their answers," the guard explained.

"You're right. I will send word for him. Thank you. I'll see what I can do."

As the Mayor walked off with concern flooding his mind, the final transport wagons headed out of the main gate. The day was moving on rapidly.

CHAPTER 22 ✝ THE CIRCLE OF HEROES

HAVING REACHED ALDREMAYNE before the transport wagons, Mythrian was well ahead of schedule, with the seventh sun only just peaking over the distant hills. This gave him enough time to explore the village itself before his contest.

Just like Avalin, Mythrian was unsure of what to make of the village.

It was a welcoming village, with its villagers keen to meet its tourists and share the gossip in their travels.

From the entrance to the heart of the settlement where the famous arena stood, there was a colourful atmosphere that gently soaked into the boy.

The village itself was very old, having been established only a couple of years after the battle against Draigorn. Its sandy coloured walls and dusty floors gave it an almost exotic feel, enhanced by many hanging baskets filled with brimming colours.

To make the tourists feel more at home with the surroundings, the settlement had been built into sections. Each section had a particular use. The courtyard was for horses and transport, the market was for buying and trading, the training area for those waiting to get into the arena.

Mythrian happily visited all these places before making his way to the inner part of the settlement. There he registered.

"Hello, my name is Mythrian; I'm taking part in the arena."

"Yes sir, your name is here on my sheet. If you would just like to sign here so that we have knowledge of your arrival," one of the arena assistants spoke.

Signing his name, he asked the assistant for further details.

"When should I go into the arena?"

"About five minutes past the third hour, young sir. Just make your way through the double doors over there. It will take you into the arena circle. Address your name to one of the assistants in there and he will guide you in," the assistant replied.

"Thank you."

A third voice came from over the boy's shoulder:

"Ah, there you are. I've been looking all over for you. And now I have found you."

Mythrian could not recognise the tone. It was sharp, harsh and was aimed directly at him, as though he was in trouble.

Turning round, Mythrian was shocked to find the presence of Brennius. He was smiling at the stunned look on his pupil's face.

"Surprised to see me? I told you I would be here to see you in your contest. Did Salen not inform you of this in his letter?" his Master continued.

"He did. I was just caught off guard by that voice that sounded very unlike the Master Brennius I know," the boy replied.

The boy stepped closer to his guardian, who added, "I always did have to think of new ways to catch the attention of your wandering mind."

"How are you? I heard that you are currently residing in Alvocanen," the boy spoke.

"I'm just taking a much needed break," Master Brennius replied. His reply was short and quiet. He was not comfortable on the matter, knowing his pupil knew the reason behind his short term resignation.

Brennius did not want to appear weak in front of his pupil.

"But less of that for now; how was your journey? I expect you are tired," the old man continued.

"I don't think you would really want to know some of the full details of my journey, but what is important is that I'm here and in one piece," the boy explained.

"Oh," his Master laughed, "Well, hopefully after this tournament you will be given some time to rest. I wasn't sure how much you would have eaten over your journey, for I was not expecting it to be so long. So I brought you some more food, just in case."

"Thank you. To be honest, my journey has been so active I have hardly had the time to stop and think about food ... or sleep."

"Well, there you are. Anyway, I'm sure you want to head to your contest. I'll be watching you in the arena. I wish you all the very best."

Shaking the boy's hand, the old man placed his walking stick firmly in the ground before heading into the visitors' entrance of the arena.

For Mythrian, it was nice to have seen a recognisable face in what had felt like a long, endless journey already.

Near the entrance to the arena circle, Mythrian could hear the crowd as they grew louder, watching the performers within. He felt impatient to go in. But at least now he had registered; he just needed to be patient.

Entering the arena circle, he looked up in awe at the towering ring, its golden stone dazzling in the glorious sunshine.

Studying the arena, he noticed there were carved statues of previous heroes, embedded in its exterior wall. They were those who had outshone expectations or had achieved something momentous, something worth remembering.

How proud Mythrian would feel to have a statue of himself on the arena walls. Only time would tell.

In front of him, not far away from one of the arena entrances stood a crowd. A young man stood on a platform, addressing them. Mythrian joined the crowd to listen in.

"Today, I will not just put on a show like you have never witnessed before. I will battle a ferocious beast with nothing more than a spear to kill my prey. I have encountered many ferocious beasts from the deep and have gained much reputation from them. But let me tell you this ... if you thought you had seen evil before, you will dare not to look at the monstrosity that will charge through those doors. They say these creatures feed on punished goblins in caves in Siren's Gore. They feed only on the strongest and freshest of prey."

The young man was certainly in his prime, by his looks, not far into his twenties though his colourful stories made him seem a lot older. Long blond hair, straight faced and fairly muscularly built, members of the crowd grinned at the all too optimistic hero.

Some of them had seen the beast he was talking about during a trip round the holding cells. They knew that he couldn't fight the beast single-handedly. There was bound to be a restriction placed on the beast.

But the young man continued his gallant speech:

"Have any of you witnessed the beast? Its skin is like steel. Its limbs are columns of stone. Its back is as wide as five grown men standing shoulder to shoulder. To defeat this beast, you have to be cunning, cautious and precise. There are only a few small spots where the creature bears a weakness."

"What about its head? Is that as wide as five men as well?" one of the crowd members joked. His laughter was passed on quickly through the group.

"Its head is a gruesome thing. Its eyes are like black crystals, drawing in the light from its surroundings. Its skin is a violet-rose and is stretched tightly over its thick bones. Its mouth is nearly as wide as its giant bulk of a head, with teeth too large for its own mouth. If the fear doesn't break you, its unbreakable grasp will. Today, I will be your hero. Today, I will defeat this beast and prove that man will prevail against evil, no matter how large the obstacle is."

"Well, good luck," an onlooker replied sarcastically. The crowd moved away, laughing to themselves at the overly dramatic act. Unfortunately, the hero thought they were laughing with him, not at him.

"Be there, four hours past midday. I'll be ready for you. Will you be ready for me?" the young man finished, before setting off with a couple of friends into the arena.

Mythrian followed suit, realising there was little else to do outside the arena.

The large arena door closed heavily behind him. There would be no return to the outside world for him until he had fought in the arena.

CHAPTER 23 ✝ AN UNEXPECTED ARRIVAL

TWO HOURS HAD passed mid-day and the transport wagons from Falstone were finally making their way through the settlement doors.

However, one of the wagons was carrying an unexpected guest.

Having held on quietly to the underside of the transport wagon, Fingal released his grip, avoiding the wheels, before crawling behind an ornament to quickly hide.

Looking over the ornament, he noticed several guards by the entrance. None of them had spotted him. He had managed to get into the settlement without notice or clarification. Now he was in, he needed to find a way into the arena.

Wandering casually into the crowd, he marched his way into the inner area of the settlement. With the contest in the arena well underway, the settlement was filling up with crowds and participants.

Perfect for slipping in unnoticed.

But to progress with his deviant plan he needed to find some information concerning restricted areas of the arena. Only in there could he attempt his plans successfully, without anybody catching him.

It was in the training area where he spotted a couple of guards who were in conversation. Perhaps by listening into their conversation he could find some clues of how to get into the arena.

Crouching down behind a flower pot, pretending to be tying up his shoelaces, he listened in on the two guards on the other side of the pot:

"You off for your break in a moment?" one of the guards asked.

"Half past two, on the dot," the other replied. "You told Finchy yet?"

"No, why, can the poor old man still not tell the time? I'll go and speak to him. Where is he positioned again? They move him about frequently don't they?"

"Yeah. Have a wild guess where he is today?" the second guard replied.

"He's not guarding the holding cells is he?" the first guard laughed.

"Good ol' Finchy, guarding all the evil critters in the eastern courtyard. I walked past him earlier; I thought he was under hypnosis. He wasn't moving a muscle or a limb."

They both laughed loudly to themselves. Fingal had done with tying his shoelaces and was pressed up against the flower pot.

"He does his job well doesn't he?" the first guard continued to joke, "Are you ready to go to the canteen then?"

"I'll go and get Finchy and we'll meet you at the canteen. You have those plates warm and ready for us, ok?" the second guard spoke.

"Very good," the first guard acknowledged.

As they left, Fingal added another checklist to his plan.

"The eastern courtyard, hey?" he thought to himself. "Seems like I might have a bit of time before the guards leave their posts. Time to find out when our friend is competing in the ring. It wouldn't be much of a performance without me."

Picking himself up from the ground, he headed over towards the participation desk.

Inside the arena, Master Brennius was looking for somewhere to sit in amongst the crowd. Unfortunately for him, the seats were made of stone and had no comfort for a man of his age.

Wandering further round towards the centre of the semi-circled seating arrangements, a friend called him over:

"Master Brennius! Over here, my good man."

Standing up to greet the Master, Brennius greeted him likewise, "Brymley, it's been a long time. Too long as always. How are things?"

"The same as they were before Brennius. I work my socks off for the council and then after much discussion, they choose not to make me the Master of the Guild."

"So you still teach in Media?"

"Acasia now, regrettably. Media was getting too slumped down with too many problems. I moved to Acasia because it is a quiet and peaceful area. Well it was. But after I took up my position as a high teacher in the Guild, the council changed their evaluation on the students. Unfortunately I now find that as soon as the students are old enough to grasp the fundamentals, they are sent down to Heldergarde."

"Heldergarde?" Brennius returned, confused and disturbed. "I thought that place was abandoned after the war. The most southern military base now is Rhone."

"That's what they want you to think, but Heldergarde is active. There have been a number of reports indicating that enemy attacks are growing in the south."

"And they're sending your apprentices down there to help out?" Brennius concluded.

"I don't really want to think what they're doing with them. In my opinion, the council have lost their minds. But I don't really want to get involved in any of these matters, though I'm becoming seriously worried about where our futures our heading."

"You can always come up and stay with us at Hamlynstone," Brennius continued the conversation.

"Don't worry about me, Master; I'll plod on, like I always do. Besides, someone told me you're taking a little holiday," Brymley returned.

"Just for a little while. I have been working for sixty-three years straight you know."

"You're a good man, Brennius. It's a shame we don't have

more like you," Brymley added.

"Oh, I agree," the Master laughed with his former pupil.

"I hear one of your students is up next," Brymley spoke.

Brennius smiled with pride and anticipation.

"He is. How long have we to go?"

"About another fifteen minutes unfortunately. I'm surprised they don't keep us entertained with dancers or something. Just because the guards need a break doesn't mean everybody else needs one. I hate all this sitting around and waiting," Brymley replied.

"No worries, Brymley, I'm sure the time will fly."

CHAPTER 24 † FINGAL'S PLAN BEGINS

S TANDING BY THE east entrance to the holding cells, a guard stood alert. Or, rather, he was trying to be, but he failed to spot the shadowy figure of Fingal, ducking around the various features of the courtyard.

Behind the guard was a little enclosed area filled with various vases, many for ornamental value but as the sun had drifted over the wall, the area was enclosed in a dark shadow, perfect for hiding in.

Jumping into the area, Fingal pushed himself up against the wall. Seconds later, a guard came over to greet the standing guard.

"Alright Finchy, break time."

"It's about time. Boring my socks off standing here," the guard muttered, before eagerly heading off to the canteen.

With the guards gone, Fingal shuffled round to the door with a successful grin beaming on his drawn face. The door was padlocked but Fingal had no problems cracking it open.

He had brought with him a strong powder which, when poured on to the lock, dissolved and freed itself. Fingal quietly entered the holding cell, the last objective in his devious plan.

Closing the door and momentarily leaning on its frame, Fingal was captivated by the many cells and creatures from within. He closely inspected each one, the creatures groaning angrily from within.

"No. Too small, too weak. Come on, is there not a worthy creature among you?" Fingal shouted at the creatures.

He froze suddenly. The shock almost threw him back. His

heart missed a beat.

In front of him was a creature the likes of which he had never seen. Its hands were huge, capable of crushing a man's head with little effort. Fingal felt very weak, as he watched the creature moving its gigantic arms up and down as if it were pretending to be crushing a foe in its grasp.

Its head was enormous. Built like a battering ram, it seemed heavy on its shoulders, and with two giant eyes that swayed from side to side, waiting for the moment to strike.

Fingal gingerly crept up to its cage, keeping a safe distance from the bars.

"My, my, my. What do we have here? A Gorgoroth. I thought your lot weren't supposed to be let out of your darkened caverns."

The Gorgoroth seemed oblivious to Fingal, staring into the darkness as if he wasn't even there.

Fingal became impetuous.

"What's the matter, are you hungry? Hey, you want something to eat? Here you go," Fingal taunted the beast, throwing discarded bones at the creature.

Still it ignored him.

"I know you're hungry. You don't have to play dead with me. You want some food. I'll get you something to eat. Something young and fresh."

Fingal grinned as he noticed the creature moving its stygian eyes over to his direction.

"Now I have your attention."

In the combatants' chamber Mythrian was watching several of the other contestants training. There were several allocated posts where they were practising their attack or defensive skills. There was also a handful of instructors giving them guiding pointers or helping with any problems they had.

The idea of the arena is that the contestants do not know what they are to be thrown up against; how difficult the contest will be is dependent upon the person's age and experience.

Most of the contestants were keeping themselves to themselves, neither wanting help nor wanting to have discussions with fellow heroes.

A Chief walked up to the young conjuror and asked him, "Your name, young squire?"

"Mythrian, sir," the boy replied.

"Good. I'm Leger, the man in charge around here. I'm glad I've found you because you're up next. I tell you, this arena gets more crowded with contestants every year. The only reason I knew you were the one I was looking for is because they said you were young. Most of the young contestants are usually up first. They only hold some people back if they feel they bear something special. And you, my friend must have something special."

Pointing down to the arena door, Mythrian followed him as he continued in his speech.

"We have had a good day so far. The crowd is nicely warmed up and as far as the majority of the spectators are concerned, you are the main event."

"So they're expecting the very best from me," Mythrian returned.

"Indeed they are, but don't feel under pressure. Just do what you've got to do and I'm sure the people will love you for it."

Picking up a wooden sword he handed it to the boy, who stood confused, wondering why he had been given it.

"You want me to fight in the arena with a wooden sword?" Mythrian responded, puzzled.

"No, I want you to attack this hitting post. Show me what you've got," the Chief returned.

As Mythrian began hitting the post fiercely, Leger continued, "I don't know what area you specialise in, but it isn't going to help you in there."

The boy stopped and looked at the Chief. "I am a conjurer."

"Even so, the idea of the arena is to demonstrate the one thing heroes will use most of their time, their sword. It doesn't matter how powerful you are, every hero needs a sword and needs to know how to use one."

"How do I fare?" the boy asked.

"Very well. I understand you have had a little bit of training."

"Basic training, yes."

Picking up another sword, the Chief gave the boy several pointers.

"Always keep your sword close to you. Not too close obviously, but at a distance which feels comfortable for you. If you are right handed, which I presume you are, hold the sword so it aligns in a straight line with your right shoulder. Keep your feet shoulder widths apart and point your left shoulder slightly ahead of your right. This is the perfect defensive position. This is how you should stand in a one-on-one situation. The shoulders are the most important parts of your body, because it is from there that the power is delivered. When you strike, move your sword out to your side, to give yourself room and from your shoulders, push your arms forward, bringing forward that right shoulder. Do it correctly and it should do some damage."

Demonstrating his words to the boy, the Chief got into position, gave himself width, angled the sword and delivered a heavy blow against the post. So much so that his wooden sword split heavily.

Turning to the boy he continued lightly, "Obviously in the arena your sword won't break like mine. But follow this, keep your eye on your opponent's actions and watch your timing. You should have no problem."

"One more question," Mythrian added, "What exactly am I going to be facing in the arena?"

"That is not for me to tell you. When you're out in the wild nobody will tell you what stands around the corner. Nor should you try to judge it. You just have to be prepared and ready for it when it comes."

"Ok. I see your point," the boy replied.

"Good. Now you've still got a few minutes left. Keep practising until I give you the word," Leger finished.

As the Chief walked away, Mythrian got into the defensive stance and began attacking the post. It would only be a few more minutes.

CHAPTER 25 † THE ENTRANCE
OF MYTHRIAN

I N THE ARENA, Master Brennius and Brymley were sitting in the audience, waiting patiently for Mythrian's entrance. Over their shoulders came the sound of conversation. Neither of them were nosy enough to listen, but the voices were too loud to ignore.

"Have you ever faced a Gorgoroth before?" one of them asked.

"No. But I have faced enough creatures before to know plenty on how to defeat such a deadly beast as the Gorgoroth. You see, it's all about weaknesses. Every creature has one or two. What makes a hero great is how fast he can calculate these weaknesses and then strike them there. I have perfected this art and I intend to show you the quintessential approach of tackling this," the young man responded.

He was drawing a large crowd for his battle with the Gorgoroth. Most of them had just come to laugh at him. They knew he wouldn't tackle a Gorgoroth single-handed. Behind their questions there were hidden chuckles.

To his side, his ever loyal followers were watching questioners carefully, almost like bodyguards.

Brymley certainly wasn't interested in his words.

"Doesn't he go on and on?"

Master Brennius grinned while he nodded his head.

Near the young man a spectator sat down, with a devious grin on his face:

"Hey, Lucian, I heard you're fighting a Gorgoroth. Big things they are. I heard they like to eat their own body weight in food.

That would probably make you the appetiser."

The man and two of his friends laughed at the young man. Lucian said nothing.

"I'm sorry Luci, I meant no offence. We're all rooting for you. That is unless you get beaten and then we will be rooting for the Gorgoroth."

"You may laugh all you want. But it takes a brave man to stand up to a Gorgoroth. And since I am the only one here willing to do so, I suggest you owe me a little more respect."

"You've got it," the man finished, rubbing his hands together confidently.

Soon after their conversation, a man rushed into the arena circle through a door, under the audience.

Brymley turned to the people sitting behind and ordered, "Quiet. The contests are beginning again."

Now in the centre of the ring, the speaker addressed the crowd:

"Thank you for your time. The contests will proceed. Please welcome our next challenger, Mythrian, Champion of Summoner's at Avalin."

As the crowd cheered for the arrival of the next combatant, Mythrian stood underneath the entrance doors, calming his nerves.

Leger stood by his side. "Are you ready my boy?"

Mythrian nodded as he shook his arms and legs, pumping up his blood and energy.

Holding out a iron sword, Leger handed it to the boy. "Good luck."

Grasping the sword, Mythrian walked out of the darkness into the arena. As he walked out into the light, his eyes were momentarily blinded by the sharp light from above.

The seventh sun was stationed right above the arena and burned so brightly, the sand beneath Mythrian's feet was smouldering from the heat.

As he looked back towards the door from which he had come out, the audience loomed over him. Their faces were hard to make out in the intense sunlight but their hands in applause were visible.

As the cheers roared louder and louder, Mythrian was burning with high adrenaline. He turned and faced the opposing double doors where his counterparts were to exit.

The holding cell doors were overshadowed by a giant square building. Visually it was impressive but Mythrian concentrated on what was to come out of the door.

Steadying himself into his defensive position, he stood patiently still.

Waiting.

Returning back to their posts, one of the guards returned to his shift at the holding cells' door. When he arrived, he noticed the padlock missing.

Turning the handle, he pushed on the door but it refused to budge. He stared in confusion to where the padlock once was. Someone must have got inside and locked it from within.

Banging repeatedly on the door, he ordered, "Come out. Come out whoever is in there. That is an order."

Putting his ear near to the door, he heard nothing. No footsteps or any other sounds.

Inside the holding cell, Fingal heard the guard's call but refused to open up. He was staring secretly out of one of the thin windows, watching Mythrian from afar.

Turning back to the cells, he walked past the cell of the Gorgoroth.

"Oops," he spoke sarcastically, unlocking the padlock from the cage. The chains fell loosely on to the ground.

He stepped away from the cage, laughing sinisterly. With the creature free, all he needed to do now was to find a place to hide.

To the corner of the room was a small cupboard filled with equipment and linen; there were adequate resources for him to hide amongst. There was also a window looking on to the arena, where he could watch his plan unfold.

Closing the cupboard door behind him, he heard the Gorgoroth begin to move. Reaching out with its long arms, it grabbed the chains around its limbs and ripped them off with devastating might.

As the cage door was rattled open, the Gorgoroth pushed itself out. Free and unrestrained, it headed for the arena.

At the holding cells, several guards had taken notice of their fellow worker, banging frustratedly on the door.

"What's up, Finchy?" one of the guards asked.

"It's the door. Someone has got in and has locked it from within," Finch replied.

"Alright Finch, you stay here and make sure nobody comes out. We'll get a ram and batter the door down."

"Better get a few more guards and all. Whoever is in there might have unlocked some of the cages as well," Finch returned.

"Good idea. Come on," the guard called to his co-workers as they rushed to get a ram to batter the door down.

CHAPTER 26 ✝ BATTLE OF THE GORGOROTH

IN THE ARENA there was silence. An uncomfortable silence swept both competitor and crowd. None of them knew why there was such a long pause to begin.

Mythrian stood still but as the seconds passed, his sword lowered slowly. His fingers were tingling, as if they were sensing something; a bad vibe nearby.

The sound was drawing ever closer.

A shudder ran through the boy. Tremors grew from beneath his feet. In front, the holding cell doors were shaking.

The shaking grew and grew until even the audience could feel the stands beneath them shaking. Then everything stopped.

BANG!

The holding cell doors ripped open. There, standing in the giant gateway nearly filling its size, was the mighty Gorgoroth.

The crowd jumped up on to their feet. Mythrian stood a gasped.

This was not part of the show. This was a trap.

From the crowd, people shrieked at the sight of the giant beast compared to the frail image of the boy. It was a mismatch that swords could not overcome.

"Mythrian!" Brennius screamed, jumping up from the stand as if he was a young man. "Someone get him out of there!"

The onlooker behind Lucian questioned, "What is that horrible abomination?"

Lucian returned, "That is the Gorgoroth that was supposed to be released during my turn in the arena."

While guards in the combatants' chamber were quickly trying

to get out into the arena, one of the watchers in the crowd had a crystal with him. He threw the crystal into the air and as it dispersed, a blue beam of light shot forward towards the beast.

Unfortunately, a shield had been cast over the top of the arena ring to stop members of the crowd becoming involved with the performance. The beam hit the shield and evaporated on impact.

Trudging into the arena, the beast looked up at the blazing light. It stood in awe of the light, enchanted by it.

Living in the dark caverns of Siren's Gore's deepest pits, Gorgoroths never see the light of day. It was an overwhelming sight and the beast appeared motionless, distracted by its beauty.

Spears landed on the Gorgoroth but barely scratched the surface. Pulling out the spears, it looked towards Mythrian. Behind him, guards were running out with nets to contain the Gorgoroth.

As they surrounded the beast, Leger called to Mythrian, "Get out of there!"

Mythrian was about to turn around when the beast released a powerful scream. It sent the guards flying back.

Grabbing some of the nets, it swung the guards who were clinging on and threw them back into the combatants' chamber.

Leger was knocked unconscious by two of the guards who flew straight at him.

Lots of guards were entering the arena, trying to trap the Gorgoroth, but all were failing and being thrown wildly backwards.

With only several guards remaining in the arena, Mythrian closed the chamber door to stop any more from coming through. The beast was like nothing he had ever witnessed before, but it was not invincible.

If he could have beaten the Troll at Avalin, then he was more than capable of tackling this ferocious beast.

While the remaining guards were being pummelled against the walls, guards at the holding cells were battering down the door. After several unsuccessful attempts, the door finally gave way before being kicked open by the hasty guards.

Running through the holding cell, the guards spotted from a distance the open arena doors. Reaching the doors, they momentarily paused at the sight of the Gorgoroth.

"How on Ajia did that get out?" one of the guards cried.

The Gorgoroth heard him. It turned and walked towards the door.

They rushed forward to tackle the beast, but it got to the door first and closed it. The seven guards put together could not push back the one Gorgoroth.

But to stop them from getting through, it punched through the stone above, bringing down a large amount of boulders that held the door shut.

With both doors closed, Mythrian and the Gorgoroth were free to do battle.

Everyone looked on in surprise and shock as the boy stood up to the giant beast. He was calm and relatively focused, yet the beast did not appear slightly threatened by the boy's brave appeal.

The Gorgoroth released a gargantuan scream that threw Mythrian back.

Crouching down to lower his centre of gravity, Mythrian held firm before regaining his composure and walking back towards the beast.

The Gorgoroth began to clamp its teeth, grinding them as if telling the young boy to jump into its mouth.

Picking up a spear, Mythrian pointed it at the creature to try to ward it away. It was closing in on him in small, heavy steps.

It appeared slow and sluggish but Mythrian wasn't going to be fooled if it wasn't the case.

"Go for its ankles," several members of the crowd cried out.

On that note, Mythrian threw the spear high at the beast's shoulders. As the beast jerked back focusing its attention on pulling the spear out of its collar bone, Mythrian sprinted through the gap under its legs, slicing at the creature's ankles in the process.

The creature yelled but it did not fall.

Mythrian took some steps backwards to avoid any backlashes. The beast turned its head, bearing a face that fuelled anger and aggression.

Its huge chest inhaled huge gusts of air. Its breaths quickened.

It grunted loudly, building itself up into a ferocious rage.

Suddenly, without any warning, the creature sprang and ran predatorily at the small target. Ducking its shoulders down, it smacked the boy hard in the chest, sending him hurtling through the air.

As his back smacked into the wall, Mythrian could hardly breathe with how vigorous the hit was. He didn't have long to react to the next blow.

Throwing his limp body out of the way, he narrowly missed the Gorgoroth as it crashed through the walls.

Fingal was in hysterics, amused by the powerful beast as it tried to release itself from the wall. However, it did give some time for Mythrian to catch his breath, as he crawled across the sand, coughing and choking.

Using his sword to drag himself up to his feet, Mythrian stood his ground as the creature drove forward at him again. By his feet was another spear. He held it closely in his hand, waiting for the beast to come into range.

But just as the creature was about to hit him, Mythrian swivelled to its side, stabbing the spear as he went. It landed in the Gorgoroth's hip joint, slowing it to a standstill.

Some of the crowd cheered as the beast slowed down. Some were still too afraid to watch.

The beast felt that blow heavily and it appeared to hobble on its leg, injured from the attack. It had even more trouble trying to pull the spear out. It remained wedged and until it came out, the beast was immobile.

"Come on, you worthless beast. Don't just stand there, kill him!" Fingal shouted from the cupboard. He had to watch his tone with the guards in the next room, but he was solely focused on the event in front.

Sensing an opportunity to bring the guards in to catch the beast, Mythrian headed for the Combatants' chamber door but just as he reached the door, a spear landed in his leg, bringing him to the ground.

The Gorgoroth made a lucky attempt with a throw. Though it remained still, its clumsy grasp had managed to throw a spear that momentarily paralysed the boy.

Mythrian was in some agony. He couldn't reach or lift himself up to the door and the spear was in too deep to touch or pull out. He crawled away as far as he could from the beast as it slowly hobbled over.

The crowd was roaring Mythrian on, but it was the Gorgoroth again who was in control. It moved into the centre of the arena.

With the spear still in its joint, the creature broke off as much as it could. It would not be able to run at a great speed, but its mind was focused on the boy, not the pain. The pain was injected into its anger, its anger infused into its adrenaline.

The Gorgoroth brushed its foot across the ground, just as a wild creature does when it faces a confrontation.

Mythrian noticed this and looked up into the crowd. There, looking down on him with mournful eyes was his Master, Brennius. The old man did not move a muscle and yet the boy could tell that he wanted the boy to stand up, to fight the beast to the end.

Mythrian drew all the strength he could gather. Inside, the heart was willing, but the body was too drained to continue. But this did not stop him. He knew he had power within. All he needed to do was to transfer that power; reinvigorate himself.

Painfully pulling out the spear in his leg, Mythrian stood wearily on his legs, throwing his sword away and any heavy items he carried, including the tablet which he removed from under his shirt.

Then he composed himself, building up the energy within. His markings began to illuminate in response.

"Attack him!" Fingal muttered urgently. But the Gorgoroth stood still.

Mythrian began to shake on the spot. The energy was flowing quicker and quicker through him. The power grew so much that he was lifted off the ground, hovering in the air.

The crowd stood in amazement. Brennius could not believe his eyes. No one had ever witnessed power on this level.

The markings on Mythrian's body were lambent and enlightening that he appeared like a beacon, reflecting on the wide blue ocean.

Azure light cascaded around the arena.

Fingal was growing deeply infuriated with the beast's failure to attack the boy.

"What are you waiting for? Get him now. Finish him quickly!"

But the Gorgoroth was mesmerised by the light, just as it had been from the crystal when it dispersed upon the shield. Like the crowd it was amazed by the power flowing from the boy.

Mythrian's body was empowered. He could no longer feel the pain from the attacks. It was time to finish it once and for all.

Raising his hands up in the air, a huge wind filled the arena, pushing the Gorgoroth back. It tried to fight it, but even its gigantic frame could not withstand the powerful gale.

With the beast on the back foot, Mythrian threw his arms forward. A white spirit flew out of the boy, as though his very soul was leaping out of him and it soared through the air, tackling the beast.

The beast was picked up like a leaf in the wind and the spirit drove it back, straight through the Holding Cell wall.

As rubble fell on top of the Gorgoroth, it remained trapped and crushed. Its visible hand fell limp on top of the rubble.

But more importantly, the Gorgoroth had brought down the wall around the cupboard area. Fingal stood in shock and fear for his life as the crowd pointed to the culprit.

"There he is, the one responsible for this," a crowd member shouted.

"Get him!" another ordered.

Fingal shrieked and ran for his life as the crowd raced out of the arena to catch the culprit. Unfortunately for Fingal, there was nowhere to run and he was quickly found and stopped.

Outside the arena, the pleading Fingal was crawling across the ground, begging the crowds as they shouted and jeered. Through the crowds, pushing his way to the front was Master Brennius.

"What on earth possessed you to try to kill Mythrian? I'm going to turn you into goblin stew by the time I'm finished with you," Brennius shouted at the small man.

"Please, it was a terrible mistake. I am sorry for what I have done. I've learnt my lesson. Please let me go?" Fingal begged.

"Let you go, after all you've done? Not until you have been punished for your treachery," Brennius continued in a very harsh tone.

"Please, forgive me?" Fingal cried.

"Let him go," a voice shouted above the crowd.

As they stepped aside, Mythrian stepped up to his Master and the culprit on the floor.

"Stand up. Go back to Falstone and tell your Mayor everything you have done. He will deal with you," Mythrian ordered.

"But Mythrian, he tried to kill you. He deserves strict punishment here for his crime," Brennius argued with his pupil.

"No. I do not blame him. He has his reasons and I'm sure that if he explained them, it would shed a different light on this event. But let us not argue. I gained a momentous victory in the arena and I wish to share it with you. To Falstone Obelisks for celebrations! Let us feast through the night and celebrate the New Year. I'm sure it will be a prosperous year for many of us."

Looking down to the young man still cowering on the ground, Mythrian offered him his hand and continued, "Come Fingal, let us erase the past. A new year brings new chances, a new friendship."

"I'll agree with that, Mythrian. Thank you."

Mythrian called to the crowds, "To the Obelisks of Light."

The crowd cheered enthusiastically behind as they gathered food and drinks and headed for the Falstone Obelisks, to welcome the New Year.

CHAPTER 27 ✝ RESURRECTION

S IREN'S GORE WAS erupting. Inside its cauldron of red rock, the heart of the volcano was active and was raging with great activity. The surrounding lands were being shaken by the phenomenal force of the mountain.

Mordryd was running around the main chamber, preparing his disciple's reincarnation. He was impatient, keeping a watchful eye on the moon as it moved over the mountain top.

Dark clouds were building over the volcano, with the heavy sound of thunder rumbling through the thick darkness.

"The time is nearly upon us. A new dawn, a new destiny," Mordryd cried to the skies above.

Kobar approached him. "Master, the apparatus is set. We are ready to begin."

Mordryd was extremely excited. So much that he appeared in a state of trance, carried away with the impending moment. There was so much power in the heart of the fires.

He could sense it. He could feel it. He couldn't wait a second longer to see it.

Pointing to the sky, Mordryd bellowed, "The moon is nearly set. Begin the procedure!"

Trudging over to the centre of the activity, Kobar called out to his minions, "Lower the chains!"

Releasing their grip on the chains, they fell into the fires but they did not burn or melt, for the lava in the main chamber is not like any other pool of fire. It has a heart, its own organism. It is a chamber for souls of darkness and tyranny.

As the chains were dipped into the fire, several minions carried the tablet out in its chest towards the pool. Taking it out of the chest, it was placed into a metal casket on a pulley.

As it was lowered into the heart of Siren's Gore it violently reacted with the lava. The tablet's markings cut sharp, jagged lines across the pool, bleeding in its fiery gorge of orange and yellow.

Thin streaks of lightning sparked across the pool, emitting powerful flickers of light after the outburst. Several of the streaks spontaneously latched on to some of the minions, drawing them into the pool.

It bubbled out of control as it ate away at the bodies of the minions. The others close to the pool moved to a safe distance. The markings now covered the pool and were thickening, the power within expanding and devouring.

Kobar looked over to his Master. He was not nervous, but he had never before witnessed such power as his Master had. His Master was unmoved, hypnotised by the markings across the magma.

"He is awakening?" Mordryd spoke, gazing at the pool. He quickly rushed on to a high ridge built into the chamber. From there he watched the moon move across the sky.

All the minions and Kobar watched their Master closely, waiting for him to give the signal. It was a long wait, an uncomfortable wait as they watched the pool of fire bubbling out of control.

As the seventh moon moved over the mountain, it covered the peak of the volcano. Light funnelled into the many chambers, cornering every shade of darkness.

For them, their time had come.

"The moon is in place. The creation can begin. Raise him from the fires, quickly," Mordryd ordered.

As the minions grabbed on to the chains and began to pull with all their might, they felt a heavy weight pulling them down.

"Pull you beasts. PULL!" Kobar shouted.

They heaved and pulled under the heavy strain. The weight from within the magma was rising.

As the lava began to boil on the surface, a shape emerged from under its skin. Though its head was shaped similarly to a human's, its flesh was as black as coal.

"Rise, RISE!" Mordryd cried with delight at the process.

More of its body emerged. Its hands were bound in the chains and it hung limp within them. As it rose further out of the fires, its chest was revealed. Its heart was visible and it shone in a bright yellow, just like the markings on the magma.

As its body fully appeared it was lifted high above the fires. There it hung, as segments of molten rock broke off its charred skin.

It suddenly awoke.

Its head rolled from side to side, as it took in its first breaths of air. Its fingers twitched as a new lease of life ran through them. Its eyes opened and closed, adjusting to the bright lights coming from the lava below.

Mordryd bowed in his presence:

"My Lord, you have returned."

The creature moved its head limply over towards his Master. It did not speak, it just stared with those inflamed eyes, burning with anger and hatred.

Mordryd smiled deviously as he once again looked up at the sky.

"The clouds are building, ready the mirrors!"

Above Siren's Gore the activity within the clouds was out of control, as wave after wave of lightning slashed across the night-time sky. Bolts clashed against the volcano, bringing giant boulders crashing down the slopes.

Inside, Mordryd was waiting patiently for a bolt to shoot into the main chamber. The power of the tablet was drawing it closer.

Behind him, several minions brought in a giant ball cast of silver; the perfect conductor. Around the pool were minions, holding in front of them mirrors, all aligned in a perfect circle.

Patiently they waited as flashes of lightning lit up the chamber. They didn't have to wait for too long.

As the clouds covered the moon above, a bolt of lightning lashed through into the chamber, connecting with the silver ball. The ball absorbed the lightning and within an instant, shot it back out towards the pool.

Lifting the mirrors so they caught the outburst, the bolt bounced off the mirrors before threading into the creature above the pool.

Screaming in agony, the creature shook wildly, trying to free itself from the chains. But the power was too strong and it gave in to the power.

As it did so, the power within its heart began to spread across its body, dyeing it in markings of fiery amber. The markings were sharp, sudden and defined.

As the markings crawled on to his face, he let out a giant scream as he released bolts of lightning around the chamber. The power was indescribable. Even the minions, who were brought up to feel no fear, cowered away from the creature.

The resurrection was a complete success.

Watching his disciple harnessing the power of the tablet, Mordryd smiled upon him: "Of all creations, I present you the ultimate. Arise Lore!"

As it bellowed into the sky, the dark clouds travelled quickly over to the West, bringing with them chaos and destruction to rain down upon their peaceful land.

CHAPTER 28 ✝ THE BEGINNING
OF THE END

A T THE OBELISKS of Light near the village of Falstone, celebrations were aplenty with the New Year approaching. The seventh moon was dancing across the sky, bringing a new dawn and a new year with it.

Underneath the silky moonshine, the villagers below were eagerly awaiting the countdown:

"Ten ... nine ... eight ... seven ... six ..." they counted down in unison. All around the country everybody was doing the same from their cottages and Guilds.

"... five ... four ... three ... two ... one ... Happy New Year!" the villagers rejoiced, downing their drinks as they toasted a new beginning.

Leaning against a boulder, in his hand a nearly finished mug of fine wine, Mythrian enjoyed the calm and lifting sight of the people dancing through the night.

Approaching him with a large jug of wine, the young man asked, "More wine, sir?"

"Thank you, Fingal," Mythrian held his mug out as the young man poured the jug.

"Anything else?" Fingal added.

"No thank you, this will do. Good job."

"Pleasant night for it, isn't it?" the young man continued. His face was calm and appeared to have some colour to it, less pale than it had been.

Mythrian nodded in return, "It certainly is, Fingal. It certainly is."

Deep down, something was troubling him. He sensed

something was wrong. But it seemed too distant as though its call was from far away, coming to him only in whispers.

As the crowd merrily danced around the Obelisks, dark clouds carrying loud clashes of thunder and lightning drew across the sky. The light changed fast and a cold, bitter wind swept through the open area.

Some of the villagers stopped and noticed the skies moving across. They were moving and increasing at an unnaturally fast rate, covering square miles within seconds.

As the placid violet skies were plunged into a gorge of dark matter, the crowd below quickly grabbed blankets or clothing to make themselves warmer.

Mythrian's senses were picking up very disturbing signals; that strange, empty feeling, as light falls into darkness, and everything stands still and quiet.

Inside he felt a sudden readiness to fight back. An instant reaction, as though his mind was warning him of a close and growing danger.

But it wasn't just his mind that was reacting to the disturbing changes in the surroundings.

Watching the progression of the clouds moving over, Fingal turned to look at Mythrian. His jaw dropped; confounded by what he saw.

"Mythrian, your markings, they are … changing!"

As the crowd overheard the young man, they turned and focused on the boy.

His markings were changing. The spiral curls were uncoiling and were sharpening. All over his body, this was happening. It was as though he was transforming, shifting his form.

Mythrian moved his head down from the skies and looked to where the crowds were pointing. Just as Fingal had said, his markings had changed and they had taken a new form.

His facial expressions were the same and yet the sharp, blade effect of his markings made him look fierce; full of rage and fury. It was a very different Mythrian to the one they knew.

"What has happened to you?" Fingal questioned.
Mythrian sensed the beginning of the end.
"It has begun ..."

MAP 1 ✝ THE WESTERN KINGDOM
PROVINCES AND PLACES OF INTEREST

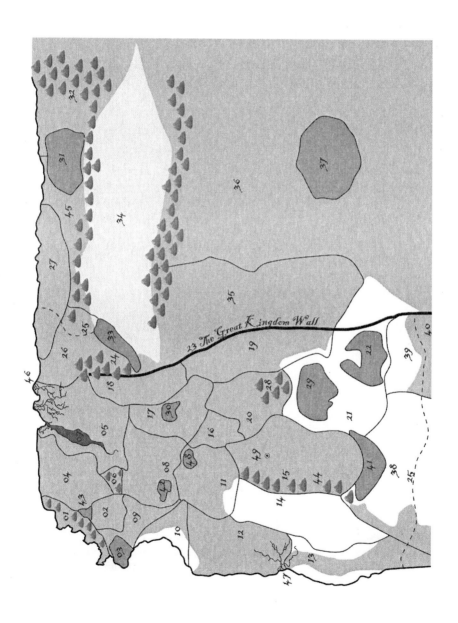

1. <u>Cronian Valley</u> – the most north-western of all provinces in the kingdom. Covered by a valley that sweeps the region. The habitat on the eastern side next to the town of Hamlynstone is flat, green grassland, whereas the western side near the sea is muddy and boggy.

2. <u>Lochrian Plain</u> – One of the smallest regions in the kingdom, it holds the villages of Hamlynstone and Anthelstone on its western border. It is mainly covered in well cut, green grassland all over.

3. <u>Wild Woods of Anthelstone</u> – Stretching out from the western coast are the woods of Anthelstone which have been known to hold witches within.

4. <u>Yeden's Stryding</u> – Lowland that is often flooded by the seas in the colder months. It holds two settlements; Hierheldon a huge fort controlling all northern activity and Armyn; where many of the kingdom's weapons and armour and other forms of equipment's are stored. When the area is flooded by the seas, the settlements are cut off on small islands .

5. <u>Arlyne's Drift</u> – Broken up by the large lake, known as Gyda's pass; the land to the west is boggy and marshy, whereas the large area of land to the east is covered in fertile and lush grassland. In the grassland area, there are three settlements, Fayrmayden, to the north–west of that is Arlandyne and the third, located by the coast, is the settlement of Lingarde, which ships in food from the sea.

6. <u>Hills of Twyndall</u> – The Hills of Twyndall hold within their mountains, caverns full of crystals, which have been used by apprentices and soldiers as they hold magical content. Mythrian finds himself trapped within them on his adventure. Near the mountains is the settlement of Mignmedia.

7. <u>Gyda's Pass</u> – A large lake that has drifted in from the Northern Ocean. It separates Arlyne's Drift between a boggy side to the west and open grassland to the east.

8. <u>Everlyn</u> – The heart of the Kingdom which holds Hagenherde, the capital of the Kingdom. It holds grass roots like the Lochrian plain and Arlyne's Drift; the grass is well preserved and kept under good condition.

9. <u>Pacian's Roam</u> - Holding the settlement of Helianthe, the region comprises both arable and rich grassland. It carries on north to the Cronian valley and separates the Lochrian plain from the woods of Anthelstone. As the apprentices find on their journey to Helianthe, it holds many apple orchards which follow south into Cygnia.

10. <u>Earian's Path</u> – Earian is covered much by arable plains which join onto Pacian's Roam to the north and Cygnia to the east. Its west coast is covered in sandy beaches as the land drops heavily to the coast. It holds Earyth which is a quiet village where most of the villagers are farmers.

11. <u>Cygnia</u> – Considered the central region in the western kingdom, it has both arable and grassland regions, with the latter joining onto the roots of Everlyn to the north as well as the dry grassland south to the flats of Llylandra. It holds three settlements: Avalin, where Mythrian has his tournament; Tharamond, a quiet secluded settlement used as a retreat from life back at home and Calderon, which all the western settlements use as a town to buy and sell all their trade and goods. Calderon also has a Guild for Apprentices.

12. <u>Lythfield Pastures</u> – Another mostly arable region. It holds three settlements, one, Oysthian, which is a southern fishing village, the southern equivalent of Lingarde to the north. There is also Amynthian which borders on the wetland region and Shyreham, which is a farming village like Earyth.

13. <u>Ludlynn's Fields</u> – Just holding the one settlement of Thyme, another farming village. Like Earian's Path it is arable but slopes down to the Ocean where there is a long beach. Some of the dry grassland from the flats of Llylandra crawls in from the east.

14. <u>Flats of Llylandra</u> – A long stretch of low ground used primarily for crops, which goes from the border of Cygnia to the southern border of the Kingdom. Looking across the land, the many crop fields give it an amber glow. It is separated by the grassland areas east by the Median Border. They often trade their crop foods for fruits from the farming villages further west. The five settlements are from north to south; Alchander, Aspia, Media, Emeryn and to the west of the former settlement, Kyne. Aspia and Emeryn both hold Guilds for apprentices.

15. <u>Plains of Terchia</u> – Terchia is quite overgrown and in some areas, quite desolate. The region used to hold quite a few old settlements and much of the land where the settlements used to be, is broken and has stuttered in its re-growth. It is mainly around the borders of the region where the land is more open and clear. The main settlement is Falstone which has had a lot of work on it and the area around it to make it stand out as one of the most attractive and wealthiest settlements in the kingdom. Rhone to the south of the region is a settlement which acts as a mini fort to protect the south.

16. <u>The Old Kingdom Capital of Aemenia</u> – Once the pride of the old Kingdom in Aedorn's time. Nobody visits the old site, leaving the past to the past and as such, through its destruction, the region is cold and empty. A small area of the region to the west is covered in grassland, but much of it has been burned and has stunted its re-growth. Many of the ruins of its old Capital, Aemenia, still stand.

17. <u>Calerian Domain</u> – Covered in Grassland like most of the eastern regions. It has richer, lush grassland to the north-east which continues into Accorian's stretch and Arlyne's Drift. South-west, it is darker and more overgrown, where it leads into Aprinia. It has one settlement, which bears the same name as the region, Calerian, and is situated next to a forest, being primarily, like Gaidenhead and Thyreian, a settlement full of woodsmen using the nearby forest for work.

18. <u>Accorian's Stretch</u> – Running alongside the Atlian Mountains, this region is covered in fresh, open grassland from north to south. Near the south, the Great Kingdom Wall separates it form the Valley of Kendral, whose mountains touch just short of the Kingdom walls. There are two settlements; Dymanthia to the north and Diademah to the south.

19. <u>Protea</u> – Known as the entrance to the Kingdom of Aedorn, Protea is a mixture of grasslands, similar to that in the Calerian Domain. Its only settlement is Ledathorn, which is similar to Hamlynstone in being a quiet, peaceful region with little activity.

20. <u>Aprinia</u> – This region is covered mainly in rough grasslands, except to the south where some of the light green fields of Iriel cross over the region boundary. The only settlement in Aprinia is Alvocanen, the fort of magic and enlightenment. It borders next to the peaks of Dwyer's Rise.

21. <u>The Land of Iriel</u> – Iriel is covered in unnaturally light, pale green grassland which carries on through to Maison's Graze to the south-west. It also holds the two biggest forests in the Kingdom, Emble Forest and The Greens of Iriel, though the latter is more broken up with many short greens as the title suggests. The two settlements are Eyre, which sits next to the Green of Iriel, which is mainly a farming village, the other being Gaidenhead, which sits by Emble Forest and is used by woodsmen.

22. <u>The Greens of Iriel</u> – Bordered by small forests, the greens of Iriel is one of the most secluded places in the entire Kingdom.

23. <u>The Great Kingdom Wall</u> – A giant wall, running from the Atlian Mountains to the north to Ynyr's Range, deep to the south. It is thirty-five feet high and fifteen feet dense.

24. <u>The Atlian Mountains</u> – A pinnacle mountain range dwarfing many of the other ranges and mountains in the Kingdom. The Fort of Altarmein sits on top of it. It has few people residing in it, acting more as a lookout for enemy sightings; however it is capable of holding a big army.

25. <u>Kingdom Border</u> – Cutting across Lyllian's Gaze to the north; and Lyndale and Maison's Graze to the south, the border is a boundary given to the people, to show where the protection of their land ends.

26. <u>Lyllian's Gaze</u> – A big area of Grassland, only used by the nearby settlement of Altarmein, it goes from the Atlian Mountains to the Kingdom border.

27. <u>Amblynn Down's</u> – A land that stretches quite far away from the border, though the two settlements, Cathelcairn and Thyreian, are inside the boundary: the land is predominately grassland, but its forests have an unusual red, autumn colour to their leaves and the fruits are of a reddish orange colour as well.

28. <u>Dwyer's Rise</u> – Situated in the region of Aprinia, Dwyer's rise forms around the south-east of the fort of Alvocanen. It is quite a tightly packed series of mountains, with flat tops, almost like a valley. It has grass on top of its flat areas.

29. <u>Emble Forest</u> – The largest forest in the Western Kingdom; it is often in use by the nearby settlement and its woodsmen. It is quite a dark forest despite being in the light green lands of Iriel. It holds the strongest wood in the kingdom, which makes it the most valuable forest in the land.

30. <u>Forests Of Calerian</u> – Like Emble Forest, a forest used by the nearby settlement of Calerian for timber. Its trees are thinner, good for making bows for archers.

31. <u>Hollman's Hollow</u> – A big forest, bigger than any in the western kingdom, Hollman's Hollow has been taken up by bandits. Greedy men, who after Ajia's disappearance formed a band to live outside the kingdom under their own rule. Criminals or people who had committed bad deeds often go there to join, being in large, safe numbers and out of reach of the western kingdom. Before anyone knew bandits occupied the forest, woodsmen had travelled to the forest to start work on it, but they were all killed and as such, nobody enters the forest, other than those who call themselves bandit.

32. <u>Eidoros Mountains</u> – A pinnacle mountain range, north of the enchantment and the Valley Of Kendral, Eidoros is the range which separates the land of Dremenon and within it, Siren's Gore from the western Kingdom. Its mountains light up in a violet-indigo colour scheme when caught by the light.

33. <u>Forests of Beldorn</u> – A large forest which breaks up the northern mountains of the Valley of Kendral and touches the border of the Atlian Mountains and the Great Kingdom Wall. Though the valley of Kendral has forests around the borders of its mountains, Beldorn is bigger, more compact and higher up than the other forests.

34. <u>Valley Of Kendral</u> (Known to hold Halfling encampment) – A long stretch of land, said to hold many Halfling encampments, it is dwarfed by the long stretch of mountains that run straight from the border of the western Kingdom to the Eastern world. There are trees all around the border of the mountains forming an oval area of patchy grassland in the centre. The Land has never been charted as no human has ever dared enter it.

35. <u>Outer Borders</u> (Known to hold Halfling encampment) - Always under watch by the guards on the Great Kingdom wall, the outer borders might look like an area of beautiful open grazing, but they hold a Halfling encampment and many hidden caverns, thought to be from where the evil forces rose when Draigorn raided the west.

36. <u>Land of the Enchanters</u> – Sacred land, strictly forbidden for anyone of the western kingdom to cross. It holds the Enchantment, the forest in which the Gods watch over the land they created. It is clear, beautiful grassland all over.

37. <u>The Enchantment</u> – The home of the gods. A mystical forest where the spirits of the gods lie within each tree, but are run themselves by Ajia; the main god who lives in the biggest tree in the Enchantment.

38. <u>Maison's Graze</u> – A large area of land, situated to the south of the Western Kingdom. Most of the region takes after the Land of Iriel with its light green, lime coloured grass, but to the west, it has arable lands which wrap around the two settlements of Acasia and Bohdenbram. Acasia has a Guild for Apprentices. The other settlement in the region is Aldremayne, home to the arena fort, where heroes battle inside its ring for the entertainment of the crowd who travel great distances to witness the spectacle. The Kingdom border cuts through the region.

39. <u>(The Lowland) Greens of Lyndale</u> – The land around Lyndale dips surprisingly low for unknown reasons. Because of this the greens from Iriel and Maison's Graze grow darker the further they stretch into the region.

40. <u>Misty Moors Of Myrondone</u> – A dark, misty region of land as the name suggests, it is out of the kingdom's borders, but still Guards go into it, as there is said to be a secret settlement somewhere within it. It sits beside Ynyr's Range.

41. <u>South Shields Forest</u> – Separating the Plains of Terchia from Maison's Graze, the woodland is very compact and very dark. As such, few do not delve too far into this woodland.

42. <u>Gwynan's Gorse</u> – A small woodland, close to the village of Avalin which holds competitions for apprentices every year; the forest is quite open, but is never used much by the nearby settlement, or woodsmen on a whole. The witch who follows Mythrian re-casts the giant rock Troll in the forest of Gwynan's Gorse.

43. <u>Unnamed Woodland</u> (Where Mythrian is found) – An unnamed woodland to the north of Hamlynstone, sitting at the border of the Cronian Valley, is where Mythrian, the main character, is found by a scout and taken back to Hamlynstone to grow up in the Guild for Apprentices.

44. <u>The Median Border</u> – A long series of mountains that divide the crop and arable lands of the south-western plains and the grassland roots to the south-east of the Kingdom.

45. <u>Plateau of Meredyth</u> – Out of the Kingdom boundary, it is a long region which runs from Lyllian's Gaze all the way to the Eidoros Mountains. To the west, it is mostly grassland, however towards the east, where it wraps around the forest of Hollman's Hollow, it is muddy and the grassland is broken and poor.

46. <u>The Rivers of Lynia</u> – A series of lakes which cut through the northern segment of Arlyne's Drift. The area around is entirely wetland, though there is a long constructed path, leading to the fishing village of Lingarde, which is located near the northern ocean coast.

47. <u>The Rivers of Estia</u> – Larger than the rivers of to the north, Estia is a series of wetlands which completely dominates, the southern area of Lythfield Pastures. It is a valuable source of water for all the farming settlements in the west.

48. <u>Emory Forest</u> – A dense forest, situated close to the eastern border of Avalin. Though it is officially under the rights and protection of Avalin, little has been done to preserve its woods and the Forest has been deemed to unsafe for anyone to enter. Mythrian however enters here, to look for the Mayors crown which was last seen in the woods.

49. <u>The Obelisks of Falstone</u> – A megalithic monument, of great power. The Obelisks were said to have been placed there by Ajia as a place of worship. Those who pray, receive help from and guidance him. The Megaliths themselves also contain crystal, capable of harnessing great power within the site.

MAP 2 ✝ THE WESTERN KINGDOM
TOWNS AND SETTLEMENTS

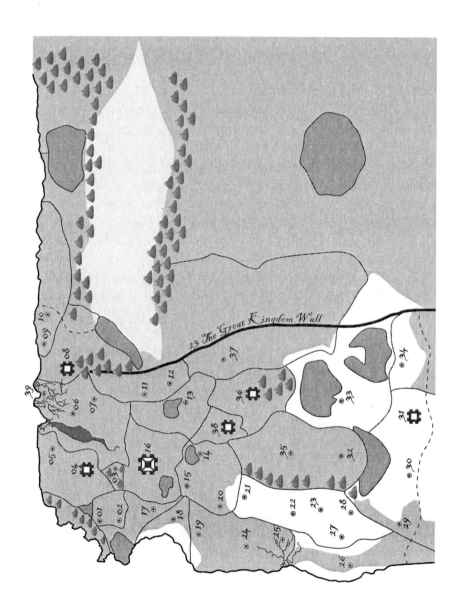

1: Hamlynstone; (Ham-Lin-Stone)
2: Anthelstone; (An-Tell-Stone)
3: Mignmedia; (Mine-Med-ia)
4: Hierheldon; (High-er-Hell-Don)
5: Armyn; (Ar-Min)
6: Arlandyne; (Ar-Lan-Dine)
7: Fayrmaiden; (Fair-May-Den)
8: Altarmein; (Ol-Ter-Mine)
9: Cathalcairn; (Cay-Ful-Care-N)
10: Thyreian; (The-Re-An)
11: Dymanthia; (De-Man-The-Uh)
12: Diademah; (Die-A-De-Ma)
13: Calerian; (Ca-Leh-Re-an)
14: Tharamond: (Far-Ra-Mond)
15: Avalin; (A-Va-Lin)
16: Hagenherde; (Hay-Gun-Herd)
17: Helianthe; (Hell-I-An-The)
18: Earyth: (Eh-Rith)
19: Shyreham: (Shy-Er-Ham)
20: Calderon; (Cal-Der-On)
21: Alchander; (Al-Shan-Der)
22: Aspia; (As-Spy-Er) (Birth place of Aedorn)
23: Media; (Med-E-A)
24: Amynthian; (A-Min-The-an)
25: Osythian; (Oh-See-hun)
26: Thyme; (Time)
27: Kyne; (Ki-N)
28: Emeryn; (Em-Er-In)
29: Acasia; (A-Kay-C-A)
30: Bohdenbram; (Bow-Den-Brahm)
31: Aldremayne; (Al-Dre-May-N)
32: Rhone; (Row-n)
33: Gaidenhead; (Gay-Den-Head)
34: Eyre; (Air)
35: Falstone; (Fal-Stone)
36: Alvocanen; (Al-Vo-Cay-Nen)
37: Ledathorn; (Lay-Da-Thorn)
38. Aemenia; (A-Men-Ya)
39. Lingarde (Lin-Gar-D)